Justine Elyot's kinky take on erotica has been widely anthologised in *Black Lace*'s themed collections and in the most popular online sites.

She lives by the sea.

Praise for Justine Elyot

'If you are looking for strings-free erotica, and not for deep romance, *On Demand* is just the book . . . Indulgent and titillating, *On Demand* is like a tonic for your imagination. The writing is witty, the personal and sexual quirks of the characters entertaining'
Lara Kairos

'Did I mention that every chapter is highly charged with eroticism, BDSM, D/s, and almost every fantasy you can imagine? If you don't get turned on by at least one of these fantasies, there is no hope for you'
Manic Readers

'. . . a rip-roaring, rollercoaster ride of sexual indulgence; eloquently written, at times shocking, and always entertaining'
Ms Love's Books

Also by Justine Elyot:

On Demand
Seven Scarlet Tales

Fallen

Justine Elyot

BLACK
LACE

1 3 5 7 9 10 8 6 4 2

First published in 2014 by Black Lace, an imprint of Ebury Publishing
A Random House Group Company

Copyright © Justine Elyot, 2014

The Random House Group Limited Reg. No. 954009

Addresses for companies within the Random House Group can be found at:
www.randomhouse.co.uk

A CIP catalogue record for this book is available from the British Library

The Random House Group Limited supports The Forest Stewardship
Council® (FSC®), the leading international forest-certification organisation.
Our books carrying the FSC label are printed on FSC® -certified paper.
FSC is the only forest-certification scheme supported by the
leading environmental organisations, including Greenpeace.
Our paper procurement policy can be found at:
www.randomhouse.co.uk/environment

Printed in Great Britain by Clays Ltd, St Ives plc

ISBN 9780352347664

To buy books by your favourite authors and register for offers visit:
www.blacklace.co.uk

To all the erotic writers, before or since

Chapter One

A small crowd was gathered outside the premises of Thos. Stratton, Antiquarian and Dealer in Rare Books, of Holywell Street, Strand. Largely composed of legal clerks taking their lunch hour, it jostled and catcalled beneath the Elizabethan gables from which one still expected to hear a cry of 'gardy loo' before slops were emptied onto the cobbles.

Some would argue that the shop itself was little better than those aforementioned slops, an abyss of moral putrefaction and decay. Despite the passing of the Obscene Publications Act some ten years previously, many windows still displayed explicit postcards and graphic line drawings. The object of the crowd's interest today was a tintype image of a young woman. She was naked and sprawled in an armchair, luxuriant flesh hand-tinted to look warm and inviting. One of her legs dangled over a chair arm, revealing split pinkened lips beneath a dark bush of hair. Her nipples had been touched up, too – in a figurative sense – improbably roseate against alabaster skin. Most shocking was the positioning of her hands, one of which cupped a breast while the other delved inside that displayed furrow. If she had derived any pleasure from her explorations, it did not show on her face, which was blank and stony. But nobody was looking at her face.

A woman, smartly but not showily dressed all in black, cut a path through the grinning throng. The young men fell back naturally, tipping hats and begging her pardon. A less formidable-looking woman might have found herself joshed or even groped, but nobody would have dreamt of doing any such thing to this lady.

She paused to evaluate what had been creating the sensation and the men around her looked away or to their boots, suddenly sheepish.

'For shame,' she said, then she put her hand to the door of the shop and entered to the dull jink of rusty bells.

A pasty young man whom nobody had cautioned against the excessive use of pomade double-took at the sight of her.

No woman had ever crossed the threshold of the shop before.

Panicking, he came out from the behind the counter.

'I think you may have the wrong address, madam,' he said, placing himself between her and a display of inflammatory postcards from which a portly woman wielding a whip glared out.

'I wish to speak with Mr Stratton.'

'Oh.' The youth found himself at a loss, his eyes darting wildly around the room at all the potentially feminine-sensibility-violating material on display. 'He is out.'

'When do you expect him back? I am able to wait if he will not be too long.'

Two of the clerks entered, throwing the shop boy into worse throes of confusion.

'Oh dear, customers. Perhaps you might wait in the back room? But it is not comfortable and . . . oh, it is not a place for a lady. Pray, put that down, please, gentlemen, it is not for common perusal.'

He spoke the word 'perusal' with absurd emphasis, as if bringing out a rare jewel from the duller stones of his workaday vocabulary.

'What, is it too dirty for the likes of us?' said one, sniggering.

'Please bear in mind that there is a lady present,' begged the shop boy.

The lady in question simply swept onwards into the back room.

Oh, if the clerks could have come in here, then they would see how tame, how positively innocent the self-loving young lady in the window display was.

The woman in black sat by the grimy back window and cast her eye over a box of postcards. Far from averting her gaze, she picked one out and examined it. A woman in a form of leather harness knelt behind another, younger, girl. This one smiled sweetly and broadly towards the camera whilst on her hands and knees. And behind her, the other woman pivoted her hips forward, ready to drive a thick wooden phallus directly into the rounded bottom of her playmate.

The visitor's lips curved upwards.

'Lovely,' she breathed.

The rooms above the shop had been used, over the years, for various purposes. They had been stock cupboards, brothels and family dwellings but never, until that late spring day in 1865, had they been used as a schoolroom.

On that afternoon, however, James Stratton had tidied away all the ink-stained papers from his well-worn desk and replaced them with a slate and chalk and an alphabet primer, with which he was doing his utmost to teach the buxom young woman beside him to read.

'I do know me letters, though, Jem,' she said, declining to place her finger beside his underneath the *A*. 'I can tell that much. It's just putting 'em together I 'as trouble with.'

'So if I wrote a simple three letter word, such as this . . .' He paused to write the word *cat* in as perfect a copperplate hand as the sliding chalk would allow. 'You could tell me what it said?'

She leant closer to him, very close, so that he could smell that cheap musky perfume all the fallen girls wore, mixed in with sweat and last night's gin and last night's men and, way beneath it all, a faint whiff of soap. He knew why she was doing it. She wanted to distract him with her breasts, and very fine breasts they were too, but today he was fixed in his purpose and he intended to achieve it.

'Why, that curly one's a *c*, I think, and the middle is definitely an *a*. Yes, definitely. The one at the end, I don't know, it might be an *f* or a . . . but *caf* don't make sense, so it must be a *t*. *Cat*!' She spoke the word triumphantly, beaming up at him with teeth that were still good, lips that were still soft and plump.

'Very good, Annie. I'll make a scholar of you yet.'

'That you won't. Who wants a whore what's read the classics anyway?'

'You'd be surprised,' he said, his lips twitching into a smile. Annie always had this uniquely cheering effect upon him for some reason, though what kind of a man this made him he didn't dare explore. She'd made her living on her back since she was fifteen and now, at twenty-two, she was quite an old hand at the game, yet somehow she refreshed him.

'Would you think better of me if I could quote yards of Latin while I rode your cock horse?'

'Hush, Annie,' he tutted, regarding his slate with resigned despair. It was clear she was not in the mood for concentration.

'Besides, I've usually got my mouth full when you're around,' she continued cheerfully.

'Now, I won't hear this,' he said sternly, jabbing a finger at the primer. 'Eyes down, Annie, or I shall have to take measures.'

'Ooh, "take measures"? Like in them stories you write? I'd far rather you read me one of those. Go on, Jem. It's too hot for this, and I didn't get much in the way of sleep last night and me head's all stuffed with rags. Tell me one of your stories.'

He ran a hand through luxuriant dark hair, exasperated at how easy it was for her to tempt him off his virtuous path. Truly, the road to hell was paved with good intentions, and he drew ever closer to the fiery void. But she was right. It was too hot and the buzzing of a fly against the grimy window played his nerves like a fiddle.

Besides, he needed a final read through of that latest story before he dispatched it. Annie made a splendid captive audience, always hanging on his every word. Perhaps she could be captive in more than one sense, if he bound her wrists to the bedstead . . . but no. Much as she pestered him for his latest chapters, she had never shown the slightest sign of sharing his darker proclivities. She was a girl of simple tastes, at heart.

'Oh, all right,' he said, closing up the ranks of upper and lower case letters with a thump. 'But tomorrow we must study in earnest, Annie, and I will accept no excuses. Do you mind me?'

'Of course, sir,' she said, the sweet little word of deference stirring him more than he cared to admit.

'Good. Well, then. Go and sit on the bed and I shall bring it to you.'

She scampered up, her gaudy skirts swishing, and climbed up on to the high bed that took up the greater part of the room, plumping up pillows behind her.

James opened a desk drawer and took out a sheaf of papers, all covered in his tightly packed script, tied with a scarlet ribbon.

'Is it the one about the dairymaid who went to the bad?' asked Annie, unlacing her much-patched boots and throwing them off the end of the bed. 'That's my favourite. Poor girl, though.'

'My clients pay a premium for exquisite distress,' said James, taking his place beside her. 'This unfortunate dairymaid has kept me in shirt linen and port wine for upwards of a year now. Speaking of port wine, would you care for a drop?'

'Oh . . . maybe afterwards. Come, I want to know what will happen to her. Had she not just been tied to a fence post and whipped by four swells on a spree in the country?'

'Indeed she had.' James released the papers from their ribbon and held them before his face.

Annie laid her head on his shoulder, settling into his chest with a comfortable sigh. He had to put one arm around her so as to have the freedom of its movement.

He cleared his throat and began to read.

'*A high-set sun illuminated the meadows and hedgerows, its rays roving over the breathing and the inanimate alike. It bathed cow and sheep, parsley and nettle in its golden warmth, but today, could it but know it, there was a fascinating addition to the bucolic serenity—*'

'Never mind that, what about Emma?' said Annie.

'Don't interrupt, or you may find that you share her fate.'

She wriggled delightedly against him and James wondered, not for the first time, why his idle threats excited her so.

'*How pitiless that post-noon heat felt to Emma as she tried in vain to extinguish the fire that raged at her rear. Those fellows, all four of whom still stood about her, leering and laughing at her fate, had plied the whip with a most diabolical will and her poor little round bum was all welted and throbbing, as if stung by a swarm of bees.*'

'Poor creature,' murmured Annie, but James chose to ignore her this time.

'*As if it were not enough that the quartet's insolent eyes roamed at will over her naked body, Emma feared that any moment a cart from one of the neighbouring farms would pass by, its wheels throwing up a cloud of dust, while the men on the box would see her bare, whipped bottom and, should they choose to alter the angle of view, her breasts squashed against the post to boot. Worst of all, the ringleader of that devilish coterie had made her spread her thighs apart, so that he could flick the tip of his whip lazily over the soft flesh located within, thus opening her tender little cunny to the gaze of whomever chose to feast upon the sight. And such a passer-by would see the swollen lips and the fat red bud that nestled inside, all downed with Emma's pale, sparse hairs. They would also see that little portal, once so tightly guarded, now the happy resting place of many an eager cockstand while Emma lay on her back or her belly, welcoming all to her glistening quim.*'

'Heavens, Jem, how does it all come to you? It's too rich for me. I never thought my ears was delicate, but you make me blush.'

'Should I stop reading?'

'Oh no, go on, do.'

'*No matter how she strained against her thick rope bonds, she could not alter her shameful position, nor could her hands, tied high above her head, reach down to shield or soothe the agonies of her posterior.*

"Sirs," she begged, "I have paid the price for my wanton behaviour at the inn last night, and heavy toll you have exacted from my poor sore bottom. Won't you please release me now and I will thank each of you on my knees, with my mouth."

"Why, that's a fine offer, naughty maid," spoke the chief of the swells. "But we have another means of showing your gratitude in mind. For when a man helps a maid understand how she has erred by applying merited chastisement, he has surely earned the right to take such payment from her as he desires."'

'What client is this?' asked Annie. 'Who reads this story?'

'I have no idea,' said James truthfully. 'My uncle makes all the arrangements, by correspondence. It could be anybody.'

'You don't know their names?'

'I know nothing about them. I picture a lonely, wealthy old gentleman alone at a bureau, for some reason, but it could be anybody. I write what I myself would care to read and, by some stroke of fortune, it appeals to people I shall never know nor meet.'

'But it ain't made you rich, or you wouldn't be living here.'

'No,' he said, with a tight smile. 'It will never make me rich. But it pays my bills while I am writing my other material.'

'Oh yes. Your novel. You'll remember me when you're as famous as Mr Dickens, won't you?'

'Is that sarcasm I detect?'

'No, indeed! I believe you will be famous one day. But I hope you won't put me in none of your books.'

'I might put you in this one. Then perhaps I will have the means to whip you into silence.'

Her mouth formed an 'O' and she sucked in a breath, her cheeks flaring red.

'Carry on, I'm sure,' she said.

'"*Oh, Sir, I wonder what you can mean,*" *the fearful dairy girl said. For never before had her offer to bathe a manhood in the luxurious warmth of her mouth and tongue been rejected. Many dozens of pricks had she sucked in her dissolute life, and many gallons of their creamy issue had she swallowed, licking her lips with satisfaction of a task well completed.*'

'Stop there.' Annie's voice was a whisper.

'Is it not to your taste?'

'It's dreadful hot in here. Help me loosen these stays.'

'Annie . . .'

James knew what his neighbour was about when she knelt before him, thrusting out that plump white bosom of hers, but he tugged at the thinning lace all the same with a world-weary air.

'I reckon that Emma doesn't have the lips for it,' said Annie, holding James' gaze with bold intent. 'Those black-guards would've been queuing up to get in my mouth. Don't you reckon?'

She puckered her generous lips and James, having pulled the sides of her bodice apart to free some of that tight-bound flesh, patted her cheek.

'Really, Annie, I don't expect payment for teaching you. There is no need.'

'It wouldn't be payment, Jem. It'd be for friendship. For comfort.'

'Comfort,' echoed James, looking down at the delicious slopes of her cleavage.

'You know I've always liked you.'

'And I you, Annie, very much, but don't you tire of it?'

'Tire of . . . well, in the ordinary way. But this ain't the ordinary way, not when it's you and me.'

She dared a little dart up and a peck on the lips.

He grabbed her by the elbow and held her face close to his.

'You're too good to me, Annie,' he said. Their mouths brushed, tasting closeness, a salt-sweet flavour.

'I want to be good to you, lovey,' she whispered. 'I want you.'

Surely, thought James, it would take a man of stone to resist a pretty girl's offer to slide her pink, wet lips down the length of his shaft and suck it to completion. And he was no man of stone.

He made no move to stop her when her fingers began tugging his chemise from his waistband, nor when she unbuttoned his braces.

'That Emma should come to me,' she said under her breath. 'I could show her how to keep her lips always soft with beeswax.'

'Beeswax?' said James, tickling her behind her ear with his forefinger.

Annie had his trousers and undergarments around his knees now.

All he had to do was lie back and . . .

'Feel the softness,' she breathed.

He did. He felt the softness, as she kissed him from tip to root and then with her saucy tongue bathed his heavy sacs.

'Oh, you're too good,' he muttered when the wet ring of her lips sealed itself around his girth.

He shut his eyes, slowly feeding every inch of his erection into her, imagining it as something medicinal that would benefit her health. It was what she needed, a good mouthful, a swallow of cream to keep her warm for the rest of the day.

He opened one eye and watched her head of brassy ringlets bob up and down. The curls were falling loose after the exertions of the night before and needed re-twisting into papers before she put on her working clothes again. James liked the effect, though; the metaphor of it. He was like one of those ringlets, once so coiled and taut, now snaking down into perfect laxity. Where would it end? Where would his life go, now that it was all in a day's work to write obscene literature and get himself sucked off by his best friend, the whore next door?

He put his hands to her head, positioning her so that he could watch her hard at work, see that scandalously painted mouth staining his cock red with whatever bizarre compound of beetroot juice and berry she had put on her lips before coming to his room.

Lord, but she was a good little cocksucker, getting his blood up to just the exquisite degree he liked before he plunged into that final rush. And here was his crisis, high up above him, way down beneath him, meeting in the middle and roaring out of him.

He took a fistful of ringlets and emptied himself into her, feeling his strength drain out of him in short bursts until he was fatally sapped, wasted by pleasure again.

Spent, he watched her take his cock from her mouth and swallow ostentatiously. Then she lay down on her back, stretching like a cat, and looked up at him, licking her lips.

'Yum yum,' she said.

She reached up and grazed his whiskers with her knuckles.

'Was that good?'

He bent to kiss the mouth that tasted of him.

'You know it, minx,' he said.

He felt for the hem of her skirts, all mud-spattered and stained from the street, and began to raise them, knowing in advance that she would not be wearing drawers underneath.

'What you got in mind, my bad boy?' she asked, eyes like mischievous saucers.

'Less of the boy, if you please. I'm five years your senior.'

'Old enough to know better then.'

'Old enough to know.'

He placed his fingers on her exposed thigh. How soft the flesh, giving the illusion of spotlessness, a virginal air that would deceive the worst of roués. He bent his head and kissed the marble-like skin, his lips drifting up and further up.

'Oh, Jem,' she whispered, leaning back, throwing her arms above her head.

Last night's men.

A loud rapping on the door broke and swept away the vague disgust that had made its unwelcome presence felt via his nostrils.

'Christ,' he hissed, kneeling up and shaking his head at a crestfallen Annie. 'Who is there?' he called.

'It's me, James.'

His uncle – his employer, landlord and instigator of his Faustian pact.

'What do you want?'

'I have a visitor for you.'

'Oh?'

James tugged down Annie's skirts and hauled her off the bed, sending her back to the desk with a pat on her rump.

Standing by the door, fastening his clothes back into a state of decency, he said, 'I don't expect anybody.'

'I dare say, but please let us in.'

James opened the door halfway and peered out on to the gloomy landing. He almost didn't see his uncle's companion, so perfectly did her black attire blend with the lightless surroundings.

'A lady,' he said, nonplussed. 'Please come in.'

'I see you already have company,' sniffed his uncle.

'Annie, you may leave now. Put the book away until next time.' He smiled weakly at his guests. 'I am teaching her,' he said.

'No doubt,' said his uncle.

James' eyes fell, rather injudiciously, to his crotch, just at the very moment his uncle's did. The younger man coloured and looked away, watching Annie skip from the room with a wink.

'Does she have much to learn?'

The question, phrased in a low, ironic voice, diverted James' attention immediately to his female guest.

'Please, take a seat,' he invited, pulling the spindle-backed chairs away from the desk and offering them to the woman and his uncle. He sat himself on the edge of his bed, the only other available place.

'Thank you.' She was perfectly economical in her movements, he noticed, as she tucked her black skirts neatly behind her and lowered herself into the chair. Her spine was straight, her shoulders set a little back, her chin raised to display a slender neck.

The face, with its heart shape and quiet grey eyes, possessed an ageless quality – a stillness. James felt he could look into it endlessly and not tire, like looking out to the silver expanse of a calm sea. He supposed himself to be ten years her junior, or more, but she could be anything from twenty-five to forty-five.

'Excuse me,' he said, standing again and holding out his hand. 'I don't believe we have met. James Stratton.'

'Yes,' she said, failing to reciprocate his gesture. 'Your uncle told me your name.'

'And might I ask . . .'

'You might ask, but I'm afraid I cannot tell you my name. If you wish, you may address me as "Madame".'

He looked at his uncle for any clue as to what the purpose of this meeting might be.

'Let me explain,' said Madame. 'Please, sit back down, Mr Stratton.'

He subsided back on to the bed, watching her keenly.

'I am here on behalf of my mistress. She is a wealthy single lady, a client of yours.'

'A client?' For a moment, James could not imagine what she might mean. 'You cannot intend to tell me that . . . a lady . . . commissions my work?'

'I intend to tell you precisely that, Mr Stratton. Furthermore, this lady has formed a desire to make your acquaintance.'

'To make . . . my . . . acquaintance?'

James looked between his uncle and Madame, increasingly bewildered.

'Before I extend any invitation, I must impress upon you the requirement for absolute discretion. Nobody should ever be told of this visit. You must sign a document swearing secrecy. Do you agree to these terms?'

'I, er, well, yes. Yes, I think I do.'

'You must do more than think,' she said severely.

James, by now thoroughly itching with curiosity, simply held out a hand again.

'Give me the document. I will sign it.'

She took from her reticule a small folded paper and gave it over to James, who read it at the desk.

It was clear and simple enough. He, James Stratton, would never speak of what occurred tonight, the 27th inst., to a living soul, the details to include the location of the meeting, the persons met and everything that should transpire.

With a pleasant sense of embarkation on adventure, he signed with a flourish and presented the paper to Madame for her approval.

'Thank you,' she said. 'You will present yourself on the corner of this street and the Strand at eight o'clock this evening, where My Lady's carriage will be waiting to convey you to her place of residence. Do not be late. And dress properly.' She frowned at his shirtsleeves and loosened neckcloth.

'Oh . . . of course,' he said, tightening his collar straight away.

The lady wasted no more time in pleasantry but excused herself, Uncle Thomas Stratton bowing and scraping all the way like a human comic aside.

Chapter Two

St Clement Danes struck eight.

Oranges and lemons, thought James, the childish rhyme serving to displace his nervousness.

He hoped the propriety of his dress would pass muster in tonight's company. He had spent at least twice as long as was his habit at his toilet. He had even gone to his favourite Fleet Street barber for a wet shave, something he only treated himself to when especially flush. His collar was starched into submission, his best paisley-patterned silk necktie wound and knotted around it. His waistcoat was crimson with a gold thread detail and he'd polished his watch and chain. Many a time he'd pondered pawning or even selling the keepsake, but now he was glad of its respectable weight in his pocket.

Annie had lent him her clothes brush and he had removed every speck of lint and trace of the streets from his trousers and coat. His shirt was impeccable, his boots shone like dark mirrors and he'd dabbed on a few spots of the latest cologne from Floris behind his ears.

Whoever he was to meet that night, she couldn't possibly take exception to the figure he cut.

The whores certainly didn't, milling around him in little clusters, calling out blandishments as they passed, giggling and pouting when he waved them onwards.

'You look like a fine gent. Want to show a girl what's what?'

'Come home with me, lover, I'll make you comfortable.'

'Sweetheart stood you up? I can kiss you better if you like.'

He watched them move on from the corner of his eye, hearing a little of their conversation before the smoke and shouts of a Strand evening swallowed it up.

'Always nice to land a looker, ain't it? I don't get enough of his type. Shame.'

Her deep sigh made her shoulders sag. He saw her take a little tin flask from her boot and swig at it before offering it to her cronies.

The clop of horses approaching the corner tore his eyes from the working girls. The carriage they pulled was a handsome one, a brougham, painted dark green with a coat of arms on the door.

'Mr Stratton?' The coachman looked down, his face neither welcoming nor otherwise.

'I am.'

'Good. You can get in then.'

He was tempted for a moment to try to engage the man in conversation, make some enquiries as to the identity of his mysterious hostess, but he sensed this would be a fruitless task, so he simply climbed up and sat himself on the leather seat inside. The carriage wheeled round in the widest part of the Strand and set off westwards. At Charing Cross, it made a turn for Haymarket, the streets now thick with painted women and men in loud waistcoats, then escaped into less bawdy Pall Mall.

The route they took appeared circuitous, involving a great deal of doubling back and looping around. The brougham stopped altogether near Green Park and the coachman appeared at the door.

'You're to put this on,' he said abruptly, proffering a silk square folded into a rectangle.

'What? A blindfold?'

'That's it. The mistress won't have you seeing the address or the streets round about. She's most insistent on that score.'

'I say, but you can't ask a man to blindfold himself. It's the most irregular thing I ever heard of.'

'It's blindfolded or not at all. Now, would you care to kneel on the carriage with your back to me so's I can secure it? Or I can take you back down to the Strand. It's no trouble, either way.'

James hesitated for a moment, then dropped down on to the clean-swept floor of the carriage, kneeling as directed.

The man placed the cool silk over his eyes and tied it tightly at the back of his head, so that sly peeks under the fabric would not be possible. He experienced the blacking out of his vision as a pressure, a heaviness weighting his eyelids. Strange phantasmic specks and curls danced in the velvet dark.

'There, that's done,' said the gruff coachman. 'Can you find your way up? That's the boy. Now. Keep it tight, or you'll be out on the pavement on your backside and that'd ruin a very smart suit, wouldn't it, sir?'

Stratton, confused by the coachman's strange mixture of deference and insolence, merely nodded, feeling the blindfold tighten when his head moved.

The door slammed shut and he heard the crack of a whip

followed by the slow clop of hooves. He tried to keep a record in his mind of left and right turns, loops and swerves, but he was hopelessly entangled within five minutes. They could be in Euston or they could be in Southwark for all he knew.

The blindfold heightened every bump and pothole in the road, but it also made him feel rather erotically charged. He pulled off one of his gloves and let the leather drift over his bare palm, enjoying the tingle of it.

He began to preview the night's activities, wild imaginings filling the void left by his sight. She would greet him, naked but for some ropes of pearls, and she would let him touch her all over before suffering him to remove the blindfold. His hands would rove over full breasts and engorged nipples, following her curvaceous form down to her rounded buttocks and her smooth, soft thighs and thence, between them.

Breathing more heavily, he put his glove to his mouth and breathed in its intoxicating scent. He might keep his gloves on while he touched her. He might put his kidskin-sheathed fingers up inside her deep, warm well and fill it.

The coach stopped with a jolt and James realised, somewhat to his horror, that he was sporting rather an unmistakable cockstand.

He could not imagine the elegant woman who had called on him viewing such an affliction favourably and he did his best to cool his blood while he waited for the coachman to leave his box and open the door.

He was assisted in this by the coachman's rough, rather peremptory hold of his elbow, and the large amount of horse dung on the road before him, which required the performance of a complicated dance with his escort if it were to be kept off his shiny boots.

But he succeeded, with sheen intact and erection suitably deflated.

The house had wide steps, he noticed on his assisted ascent, and could have been in any one of those fashionable London squares that had sprung up, west of his own district, for the containment of the idle rich during the Season. He pictured a wedding cake of a house with stucco aplenty and a handsome portico protecting the fiercely whitewashed porch.

Belgrave? Eaton? Grosvenor? He tried to run through all the potential addresses, but wasn't well acquainted enough with the area to tell which one it might be.

The door was opened, before any bell rung, and once they were safely inside, the coachman removed James' blindfold. He found himself blinking at a black-skirted maidservant, her head bent to show off the frilly cap she wore atop it.

'Mr Stratton?' she whispered, so low that he almost didn't catch it.

'Yes,' he said.

'May I take your hat? Come this way, sir.'

There was something about the smell of a fine house, James thought, which inspired confidence. One could almost believe that here, in this beeswax and lemon scent, no disease or sickness could ever penetrate. Its spaciousness and spotlessness were alien to James, who had lived in a succession of shabby city boltholes since his inauspicious birth.

Good health, it seemed, was a privilege for which one must pay.

His radical beliefs threatened to surface, disquieting his mood, but before he could ponder the thought more deeply he had been shown into a gracious drawing room.

It wasn't what one might call fashionable; its wealth

of mahogany and dark red hangings gave it a ponderous splendour but owed much to the taste of preceding decades. It was a decidedly masculine form of décor, as well – surprising in a house he understood to be occupied by a single woman.

'I'll go and tell Her Ladyship you're here, sir.'

Her Ladyship?

A genuine aristo, as if the surroundings and the carriage hadn't already confirmed it. There were portraits hanging on the wall, of stiff old fellows with military bearing and girls in giant hats petting small dogs. Was she one of those giant-hatted girls?

He thought about sitting down on one of the chaise longues scattered about the room, but judged it futile, as no doubt his hostess would arrive with all dispatch, and he would have to stand again.

Footsteps and low voices emerged from the oppressive silence, gaining in volume until two women stood in the doorway and he offered the reflexive bow of the head.

He recognised the woman on the right, still in black silks, but of a more magnificent cut than those she had worn for her visit.

About her companion there were several things to note.

Like the drawing room, she seemed about twenty years behind the fashion. She did not wear the ubiquitous crinoline but was clad instead in a narrower-skirted gown of 1840s cut and design. The neckline was low, allowing a fine set of diamonds to draw attention to the lady's décolletage, which glittered brilliantly. The lady was fair-haired and the gown a flattering shade of blue watered silk.

The most singular thing about her, however – the thing that James could not look away from – was the fact she was wearing a Venetian carnival mask.

He could see nothing of her face except her full lips and her pretty chin. Yes, she was pretty – very, he supposed, even without the benefit of a full view of her eyes. Her figure was trim and neat. Apart from the diamonds she was startlingly free of fuss, frill and adornment.

She clearly did not want to be recognised. She must be from the very cream of high society. The thought stimulated him and the evening's possibilities grew even more lurid in his imagination.

'He is here,' she said in a clear, rather breathy voice.

James, thrown into mild confusion by her failure to address him directly, found that his words of greeting died in his throat.

'Yes, Mr Stratton is here. Shall I take you to him?'

'Please.'

'Good evening, Mr Stratton.' The older lady spoke, conveying her mistress towards him with a hand on her elbow. 'I trust your journey here was pleasant.'

'Rather circuitous, but certainly comfortable,' he said, frowning slightly at the advancing pair. Did the mask cover her eyes? It didn't seem to.

'Allow me to present your hostess. I have described her to you as my mistress, but I shall not do so here, under this roof. And I'm afraid I may not tell you her name. You are to call her Miss Quim.'

James started, shocked beyond measure by the bluntness of the woman's words.

'I beg your pardon?'

'Please bear with us. Things will become clearer in due course. Now then, Miss Quim. Kneel for our charming guest, my dear, who has been good enough to come all the way from the Strand to tell you his tales.'

The young beauty fell at his feet without a murmur, bowing her head so that he looked down upon flaxen plaits held in place with jewelled combs.

'I'm, ah, delighted to make your acquaintance, young lady,' he said. He couldn't bring himself to use the epithet her companion had suggested, not yet.

More discomfiting still, she put her pretty full lips on the toe of his boot and kissed it, breathing in the scents of leather and street dust with apparent delight. She repeated this procedure with his other foot after a moment or two.

'Miss Quim accepts your authority over her,' said Madame with a flicker of a smile. 'You have already made an excellent impression, it seems.'

'I'm gratified,' he said.

He saw her little white hand reach back to tug at Madame's skirts.

'Yes, dear, you may speak,' said Madame.

'Please describe him to me, ma'am.'

The sensation of being in over his head deepened. Her Ladyship, it appeared, could not see him. And furthermore, she addressed her servant in deferential terms. Much as he longed to see equality among men, he had never expected to witness an inversion of rank as flagrant and startling at this.

'I described him to you earlier, Quim. He is much as before, but better dressed.'

'He is still tall and handsome?'

'If one is so inclined, then yes.' Madame's tone was dismissive. 'Now quieten down, Quim. You are skittish this evening. Let me seat you.'

She helped the lady to a chaise longue then turned back to James.

'I haven't offered you a drink,' she said.

'Ah. No.' James had not taken his eyes from the blind beauty sitting with her hands folded in her lap and her pretty neck bowed, just a yard away from him. 'Brandy. I think. Would be congenial. Or wine. I . . .' He looked at Madame, whose expression was of resigned scorn.

'Yes, she is lovely, isn't she? Brandy, you said. Please do take a seat, Mr Stratton.'

James didn't want to sit down. He had the impulse to pace, to keep his head clear by maintaining some form of bodily activity. He felt that, if he sat, he would place himself beneath the mysterious older woman and fall into some kind of thrall – whatever it was that bound her mistress to her must be strong indeed if it meant she accepted being called that . . . curious . . . name.

But he could not remain standing without looking unmannerly, so he took his place as close to Miss Quim as he dared and waited for Madame to bring him his drink.

'I say, this is excellent cognac,' he exclaimed, taking his first sip from the heavy crystal balloon.

'The best,' said Madame with a smile. She sat opposite him, a queen in her court. 'Miss Quim has exquisite taste in the finer things of life, Mr Stratton, as perhaps you will find out for yourself.'

'Yes.' He turned his head to Miss Quim, who still affected an extraordinary interest in her lap. 'Why am I here? If I might be so bold as to ask.'

'I thought I had explained the purpose of your visit.'

'You said she – your mistress – enjoyed my stories.'

'You look as if you don't believe me.'

'She . . . I hardly know what to say. I always thought my client was a man.'

'I sense that you are shocked, Mr Stratton. Like so many

men, you are content to fantasise about women who enjoy the sensual pleasures, but horrified when confronted with them.'

'No. That is not at all the case,' he protested, but her words gave him pause. Was he like that? Was this why he felt so unsettled? No, surely it was the unfamiliarity of the situation and its bizarre build-up – blindfolds, for Heaven's sake, and obscene names given to fragrant young women. Nobody could take that in their stride.

'Then why can you not accept that Miss Quim is a very ardent admirer of your work?'

'I do accept it. You have told me so, and I am here. However, I know that most of my stories are purchased by men. All of them, in fact, apart from these. You must excuse my natural presumption.'

Miss Quim raised her hand, in its elegant white glove.

'Speak,' said Madame.

'His voice. It is just as you said it was. Oh, ma'am, I think I can have no objection.'

'Objection to what?' asked James directly of his hostess, noting how Madame's lips stretched in a thin smile.

'Quim speaks too soon,' said Madame coldly. 'She must take her time with this decision. It is not to be lightly made.'

'If I am to play some part in the lady's existence . . .'

'Yes, sir, you will play your part. But first you will kindly do as you were asked and read to us. Have you brought some material?'

James hesitated, taking refuge in the brandy.

'I have, of course.'

'Then we would be obliged if you would do us the honour . . . Quim. Prepare yourself.'

James watched with a blend of horror, fascination and

arousal as his faceless young hostess stood and lifted her skirts and petticoats to her waist, revealing delicate cambric drawers and silk stockings. She sat back down, a bunch of silks and linens and cottons around her middle, while her legs were splayed open, bent at the knee.

Stratton had seen enough shapely calves and well-turned ankles in his time, but something about this scenario was so furiously stimulating that he doubted his ability to read for a moment or two. What on earth was going to happen?

He unrolled his sheaf of papers and cast a glance at Madame, who was gazing right between Miss Quim's thighs with a dreamy expression on her face.

'Should I begin?' he asked.

She waved her hand at him. 'When you are ready,' she said.

James cleared his throat and spoke.

'*Agnes could not deny that she harboured some anxieties about this new course of treatment, but her husband and Dr Rodd had reassured her at length and now here she stood in the physician's private Jermyn Street rooms, awaiting the administering of this unusual prescription.*

She walked to the comfortable leather bed, noticing suddenly that it was furnished with straps at both ends, not to mention a central band to pass over the patient's waist. She surrendered to momentary fear and hastened to the door, but she was too late. Her husband and the physician arrested her progress, each taking hold of an arm and escorting her to the bed, upon which she was placed in a face-down position.'

James' eyes slid irresistibly towards Miss Quim. Her dainty fingers fluttered about her raised skirts, sometimes brushing her thighs. She stared towards him, unseeing, breathing quickly.

'*The straps fell, cold and heavy, over her wrists and then, once her skirts and petticoats were raised, her ankles.*'

'No crinoline for that young lady,' commented Madame.

'No, indeed, I try to consider the practicalities.'

'I have forbidden Miss Quim from wearing a crinoline, have I not, Miss?'

'Yes, ma'am, you have,' said Miss Quim.

'Foolish fashion, and one which lends itself to impropriety and uncleanliness.'

There was a pause while James wondered what exactly Madame considered improper, if this was not.

'May I request the gentleman to continue, Madame?'

Miss Quim's voice was delightfully tremulous. James felt a rush of blood and the sheaf shook in his hands.

'Pray do,' said Madame.

'*Agnes cried out in alarm as the doctor's capable hands lifted her skirts above her bottom. Now only the thin linen of her drawers stood between modesty and exposure. Her husband took her captive hands and pressed at them with enough firmness to convince her that no protest on her part could sway his resolve. While thus engaged, Dr Rodd passed the central tether over her middle, ensuring when he buckled it tight that her skirts were now held fast in position. Until she was freed of her restraints, Agnes must have no other course than to show her legs in their stockings, and her spread thighs, and rounded bottom to all who cared to look upon them.*'

Miss Quim's fingers were inside her drawers.

The little start of shock this gave James caused his voice to waver and tail off.

'Continue,' snapped Madame.

James took a deep, steadying breath.

'*Dr Rodd spoke over Agnes' little cries, stilling them.*

"*Now, consider, Mrs Ticklish, that you are fortunate I perform this necessary physic with only your husband in attendance. If I have any more misbehaviour from you, I shall ensure that your next course of treatment takes place in view of my students. They would benefit greatly from seeing your condition tended, I am sure."*

Agnes stiffened and silenced straight away, picturing herself under the hot, avid eyes of a dozen young men who would sketch her and take notes.

"Now, here is my advice to you, Ticklish. I will demonstrate the treatment in the first instance, which you may then administer yourself with no lesser frequency than thrice weekly."

He paused to pull down Agnes' drawers, swiftly, to the knees.

She tried so hard to kick and evade her doctor's efficient hands, but it was no use. Her perfectly pert little bum lay bare to the men's gazes, not to mention the sweetly parted lips in their downy thatch of gold.'

Throughout this recitation, James had done his level best not to look at Miss Quim and her wandering fingers, but temptation mastered him at last when a tiny gasp reached his ears.

He saw her hand working furiously inside those finely laundered drawers, her outlined fingers flexing and spreading against the cambric. Her cheeks were stained with a guilty flush and short, panting breaths streamed from her lips.

He wanted to kiss those lips. He badly wanted to kiss them, now, to stride over there and stop them up and take out her hand from her drawers and replace it with his own.

'Why have you stopped?' demanded Madame.

His ears burned and he wished his trousers might not be quite so tight.

'These conditions,' he muttered. 'They hinder my . . . my . . . performance.'

'One more sentence,' said Madame. 'One or two at the most. She is close.'

He cleared his throat again and found a scrap of sense with which to carry on.

'The Doctor smacked her thigh hard, stilling her, then laid his hand between her dewy nether lips.

"They are just as wet as you feared, Ticklish," he said in sombre tone. "She is most desperately in need of our treatment. She is swollen with wanton gluttony down here. Small wonder you have been unable to satisfy such unnatural desires. Pray hand me my birching rod."

And now James had to stop in earnest, for Miss Quim's little breaths had turned to a low, consistent wail, her body doubled over, head between knees.

'Thank you,' said Madame.

James was unable to acknowledge her words, too transfixed by his client's throes. It wasn't a dream. This beautiful woman had just masturbated herself to orgasm while he read to her.

He waited until her tensed shoulders dropped and she subsided into a rag-doll pose, sighing out the last of her raptures, then he turned to Madame with a questioning look.

Madame responded to it by ringing a small bell on one of the marble and gilt occasional tables.

'Let us allow our treasure some time to revive,' she said briskly.

When a maid appeared in the doorway, she ordered tea.

'How long have you been writing, Mr Stratton?' asked Madame, making urbane conversation while they waited, Miss Quim still incapacitated with her hands in her underwear.

'Ever since I quit my last place,' he said. 'I was, for some time, a master at a national school, but it did not suit.'

'A teacher?'

'A poor one. I resigned half a dozen years ago, since which time I have scraped a living from writing these stories, together with articles for various magazines.'

'You are a journalist?'

'Of sorts.'

'Oh dear.'

'Oh, please be reassured, no part of anything that happens here tonight will ever be reported. I have signed the contract and I take it seriously.'

Madame glared at him for a moment or two before nodding.

'I will accept you at your word. But I shall also take every magazine at the newsstands and scan them for possible allusions to my mistress. Be warned.'

'I understand.'

Miss Quim had withdrawn her fingers from the seat of pleasure and held them in front of her, as if unsure where to place them next.

'Go to your new master, Miss Quim, and present to him your disgraced fingers,' instructed Madame.

New master? At what point had this been arranged? James felt he ought to question it, but he was loth to break the decadent spell that lay upon the room and besides, the writer within him wanted the story to unfold without interruption.

Miss Quim, skirts rearranged into their original decorum, dropped to her knees and began, slowly and steadily to crawl in his direction.

'Say something, Mr Stratton, that she might more easily find her way to you.'

Here, kitty, kitty.

'Oh. I await your arrival,' he said, still not quite able to use the epithet 'Miss Quim'. 'You realise that I have witnessed your shameful behaviour, do you not? I have never seen the like, even from the lowest of whores.'

'Oh, well done,' enthused Madame. 'Well spoken.'

Miss Quim adjusted her path, aiming accurately for James' shiny boots, the ones she had kissed.

She knelt up and raised her blank eyes to his.

He felt a tremor pass along his spine, and then another as she raised her fingers.

He smelled the evidence of her wanton behaviour, faint and delicate at first, until he seized her wrist and drew the aroma close. He inhaled it deeply.

'Oh . . . you . . . bad . . . creature,' he sighed.

He looked sideways at Madame, as if for permission. She nodded.

Was this real? Did he truly have *carte blanche* to treat this aristocratic young lady according to his dark and oft-suppressed desires?

He took Miss Quim's fingers into his mouth and sucked at them while she trembled fit to swoon.

'My words did this,' he said in wonder, pressing her wet fingertips to his cheek.

The maid arrived with the tea tray and he dropped Miss Quim's hand as if it were afire.

'*Tch*, do not mind the maid,' scolded Madame. 'It is plain you were not brought up with staff.'

'I was not,' he admitted, rather gracelessly. 'Does it make me unworthy of your attention?'

'Not at all, young man, and I hope you are not going to lecture us on radical politics, not now that Miss Quim has taken such a shine to you.'

Madame stood and took hold of Miss Quim by the shoulders, raising her to her feet.

'Now,' she said briskly, guiding her charge to the sofa. 'Let us be on a more equal footing.' She snapped her fingers and Miss Quim's entire demeanour transformed from meek to poised in that single instant.

'Kindly pour the tea, Mrs Shaw,' said Miss Quim, her voice now confident. 'And I must introduce myself to our guest. My name is Augusta, Mr Stratton. I won't be called "My Lady" even though I am entitled to be so. Even when I am in society, which is rarely indeed, I don't like to be deferred to.'

'Then you must call me "James".'

'No, I do not think I shall. It pleases me to be respectful of all people. I even address the parlourmaids as "Miss Such-and-Such". They do find it terribly novel to begin with, but they grow used to it.'

'Should you like sugar?' interrupted Madame, or Mrs Shaw, as James now knew her to be named.

'A little milk only,' he said, still transfixed by the altered state of Lady Augusta.

'And now I must explain to you a little more of my reasons for inviting you,' said Augusta. 'Except I am so terribly nervous I hardly know how to begin.'

'You have no need to be nervous of me,' said James.

After all, you were not too nervous to rub your clit before my very eyes.

'Oh, but I want to be nervous of you,' she exclaimed, her face so bright and vivid, her eyes shining behind the mask so that one could be forgiven for presuming that they possessed sight. 'I want to tremble at your every word.'

'Do you?' asked James mildly, accepting the most delicate Sèvres porcelain cup and saucer he had ever seen in his life from Mrs Shaw. 'I would very much like to know why.'

'When I first read your work, I had a presentiment that you were somebody I should meet,' she said. 'Did I not, Mrs Shaw?'

'Oh, indeed, I have been party to endless speculation as to your face and form and manner and . . . let us simply say that your writing has exerted a certain fascination over Augusta.'

'But how have you come to know it?' James asked, leaning forward. 'Perhaps my imagination fails me, unluckily for a man in my line of work, but I cannot fathom how it has come about that you have . . . that . . . we are here tonight.'

Augusta shook her head and stirred her tea with the daintiest of silver spoons.

'Mrs Shaw has been my companion since my mother died,' she said. 'It was seven years ago, and I was sixteen. She introduced me to a new world of reading pleasure, far from the stuffy old volumes that made up our family library. At first, it was sensation novels, you know, Mrs Oliphant and Mr Wilkie Collins and so forth. My life here is necessarily quiet, which has perhaps skewed my tastes towards the overly dramatic. But then, one day last year, she was reading to me from a periodical and I suppose it must have been an exceptionally slow night, for I made her read the advertisements and . . . well, sometimes the advertisements are the most interesting part of the whole thing, don't you agree?'

James made a short laugh of recognition. 'Do you recall all those ciphers and riddles in *The Times*? They enjoyed a sort of vogue, although one rarely sees them now. All the heavily encrypted messages between doomed lovers. I made quite a pastime of trying to decipher them.'

'I couldn't read them, of course,' Augusta resumed, 'but I recall my parents remarking upon them over breakfast. But to continue – whichever periodical it was, and I don't recall – perhaps it was *All The Year Round* – it carried an advertisement for your bespoke story services. Mrs Shaw and I talked of it all night long. Oh, how we talked of it. For we knew exactly what kind of stories you must mean. The kind one can't ever find in libraries.'

James tried to recall the wording of the advertisement but, since it had been placed by his uncle, the particulars eluded him.

'You and Mrs Shaw have a very confiding kind of relationship,' said James, wishing he could block out the image of the two women indulging a myriad of perverse desires from his mind.

'Yes, Mr Stratton,' said Mrs Shaw sharply. 'We do. We are what you might call kindred spirits, and in our intimacy no subject is deemed unfit for discussion.'

'Which is as it should be, in my view,' James chimed in eagerly. 'But my view is not the common one, I fear.'

'Indeed not. You observe the need for discretion.'

'There is much material for scandal,' said James with a nod. 'Do continue, Lady Augusta.'

She put aside her cup and saucer and reached for her fan, perhaps needing its broad span to hide her blushes.

'I had become consumed with the need to know what passes between a man and a woman behind the closed doors of the marital chamber. In my condition, I am unlikely ever to marry, yet I have all the passions of a woman. Oh, but perhaps you are shocked to find that real women do have passions. After all, we are widely considered to have no such feelings.'

'I do not subscribe to that view,' said James hastily. 'It is a ridiculous notion. I have met enough women to know . . .'

'Oh, so you are a man of experience?' Lady Augusta flickered her fan archly.

'I should say so, judging by the young woman who fled from his lodgings when I visited,' said Mrs Shaw.

'I am not some chaste paragon,' muttered James.

'No, and so much the better.' Augusta beamed from ear to ear. 'I was *so* afraid that, regardless of your highly coloured writings, you might prove to be a milksop schoolmaster of fifty who had never seen a woman unclothed.'

'This would have disappointed you?'

'Oh, indeed. I had set my heart on youth and virility and finally I have found my mark.'

'Finally?'

'Oh. Perhaps I should not mention it.'

Both Augusta and Mrs Shaw shifted uncomfortably against the cushions.

'Mr Stratton, are you acquainted with any other practitioners of your . . . art?' asked Mrs Shaw awkwardly.

'There are a few who call into my uncle's shop from time to time. I wouldn't say I knew any of them *well*. I take it I am not the first gentleman to be tried?'

'I have visited several others,' confided Mrs Shaw. 'Urban Satyr, for instance, oh dear me, he wouldn't do at all. The man is eighty if he's a day. As for A Concupiscent Fellow, he looks as if the slightest incidence of concupiscence might cause his heart to fail. And Fanny Tickler is riddled with the pox.'

'I see.'

'But I knew from the moment I read your work that you were the one,' said Augusta, with an appeasing note, as if she had been caught out in an infidelity. 'You spoke to my heart.'

'Your heart? I'm not sure that's the anatomical area I aim

for,' said James with a self-conscious laugh, causing Augusta to snap her fan closed and jab it in his direction.

'Oh, you beast, you're teasing me. I love to be teased.'

'And you have brought me here to voice your appreciation of my writing?' James still felt he was a long way from the crux of the matter.

'That is the first and simplest of my designs,' said Augusta. 'But I have others. You see, once I became swept away in your delicious, dangerous prose, its spell was upon me. Mere reading could only satisfy for so long.'

A heavy silence pressed upon the room. James experienced it as a tightness of the trousers, especially about the crotch. 'Mere reading' was not enough.

Surely she did not intend to propose . . .

'I want a lover, Mr Stratton,' she whispered into the thick of the air. 'I want a lover who is also my master.'

James tried to think of objections. It was a mad scheme, it would end in scandal, she or he would fall in love and then what? At bottom, however, the prospect of being this elegant young woman's dominant lover was a temptation he was ill equipped to resist. It was more than her beauty, more than the intoxicating thought of her submission. It was her social position that allured him more than anything. He, the boy from nowhere, grubbing a living in a Holywell Street crib, mastering *her*, a lady. The upside-downness of it was all too exquisite.

'To clarify.' Mrs Shaw's efficient enunciation broke into his growing elation. 'Her Ladyship proposes an arrangement whereby you visit her here twice weekly for assignations of a personal nature. She wishes to leave the nature and content of those assignations entirely in your hands, but she trusts that you will be guided by her desire to experience some of those acts you so eloquently describe in your fictions. She is not inclined to pay you for your time, but any expenses incurred in the way of clothing or accessories will be met by her on production of your invoice.'

'Oh, for heaven's sake, I am not for sale!' he exclaimed. 'Naturally I do not ask for her money – what kind of man should that make me?'

Mrs Shaw nodded. 'Your sentiment does you credit, Mr Stratton, but you must recognise that there are many less scrupulous men in the world.'

'Regrettably so.'

James bowed his head. A beat or two of silence followed, broken by Lady Augusta's delicate cough.

'Your answer, Mr Stratton?'

'I . . . I am inclined to accept. Must I sign any agreement?'

'None other than the secrecy agreement to which you are already bound. I mean to give you a free hand over me, Mr Stratton.'

Her voice quivered over these words, luxuriously.

She was dying for it.

James half-closed his eyes, his cock stiffening anew.

'I shall endeavour to use it wisely,' he said.

'Well, then, that's settled,' said a brisk Mrs Shaw, rising to her feet. 'Shall we make an appointment for Wednesday next? At the same time? I shall arrange a little supper *à deux* for you, to allow you to become better acquainted. Come now, Augusta, we have kept Mr Stratton long enough. I shall have Paulette call for the carriage to be brought back round.'

She rang and gave the necessary order before picking the black satin blindfold back up.

'If you don't object, Mr Stratton,' she said softly, though it was clear that objections would be given short shrift.

'Oh. Of course.'

He stood before Mrs Shaw and allowed her to re-tie the silken rectangle before his eyes.

'How should you like me to dress, Mr Stratton?' asked Lady Augusta, once his vision was black and his eyes pressed shut.

For a moment of disorientation, he wondered why it should matter what Lady Augusta wore if he could not see her. Then he realised that she referred to their next meeting.

He could ask her to wear anything, or nothing. She would agree to it.

'Oh, dress as you would for dinner,' he said, shaking his head.

'As you wish, sir,' she said faintly. 'Good evening.'

'Good evening, Miss . . . Augusta.'

'Come now, I shall show you to the door.' Mrs Shaw propelled him from the room, speaking gently into his ear as they processed through the hallway.

'If you should be tempted to break our bond, Mr Stratton, you may be quite sure that my vengeance will follow you from this life to the next. You're a fine-looking fellow and our Augusta is taken with you, but do not think that a replacement couldn't be found as easily as blinking. Not that she blinks often. But you take my point.'

'Indeed I do, ma'am.'

'Good. I'll bid you a good evening, then.'

A gust of night air greeted him with the opening of the front door, and then the carriage driver had his elbow, helping him down the stairs and away from this most peculiar of households.

As the streets of London rattled by, James tried to make sense of the evening, but now he was out of the house, it had more the semblance of a dream than anything real. That beautiful creature wanted to kneel before him, open herself up to him, give him everything he demanded of her.

It was like something out of his own fictions.

He'd never done much more than smack the rump of a few of the local girls around Holywell Street during a romp. He knew they saw more than their fair share of genuine violence and abuse and he didn't want to remind them of anything unpleasant. No, affectionate slap and tickle in jest was as far as he had ever gone. Heavens, he hadn't even been able to cane the boys he taught. Not that he'd needed to; they seemed to accept his authority without a struggle, thank the Lord.

He'd suppressed this part of his nature ever since he first became cognisant of it, at the age of around twelve or thirteen. Indeed, he had come to believe that no real woman ever desired to submit to the indignities he pictured himself visiting upon them. These acts belonged in the well-thumbed pages of the books that were passed under the counters in his uncle's shop, intended to titillate male lusts and appetites with no reference to feminine desires.

And yet she was female . . . and she wanted him to . . .

The carriage stopped and the coachman came in to take off the blindfold. Through the blur, James noted that he was near Green Park, as before. The short journey to the Strand had a strangely magical air that evening, whether because of his recovering vision or the balmy spring night he could not really say. Fate had thrown him a rope. He had taken it. Was he right? He couldn't say.

Holywell Street soon wiped the stardust from the air, as narrow and fetid as it ever was. A group of girls, many of them familiar to him, leant against the stage door of the

Olympic Theatre, waiting for it to disburse its crowds of likely punters.

'You're quite the toff tonight, darlin'.'

It was Annie, linking her arm with his, cheerful in her best bonnet, despite the tiredness around her eyes.

'Do you like my neckcloth? I may sell it to Abraham across the street if my luck doesn't turn soon.'

'I thought your luck was turning now,' she said slyly. 'Ladies visiting. You was seen getting into a fine carriage earlier. Where've you been, Jem?'

'What is it you say to me when I ask you? Curiosity killed the cat.'

He tweaked her nose and she squealed.

'If you're mixing with the quality you won't have time for your Annie no more,' she lamented.

'Oh, that's nonsense.'

They stopped at the rickety side door that led to the rooms above the shop.

'Come up and have a glass of wine with me, Annie. If you can spare the time.'

'Don't they feed you, these grand swells?'

'Actually, no.' James realised that he had eaten not a morsel since the middle of the afternoon. Perhaps that was the missing element conferring this enchantment upon him. Prosaic, but more likely that than the work of fairies. 'Their hospitality is somewhat lacking.'

'Will you tell me about it?'

'No, for I am sworn to secrecy. But I should like some company.'

'Then company you shall have.'

Chapter Three

The sensation of being blindfolded was becoming familiar to James. He wanted to tell the coachman not to trouble himself – he had taken a turn around London's most exclusive neighbourhoods during the course of the week and had convinced himself that Lady Augusta lived on Eaton Square or its environs. The number of steps, the extension of the portico, the singular width of the front door, the size of the windows all fitted with his experience. But he supposed he ought to go along with the charade nonetheless. He didn't want to be sacked from this particular position.

He stretched out his limbs and tried to anticipate each jolt and creaking twist of the carriage, testing his theory by his knowledge of the London street map.

His thighs ached and he regretted anew allowing Annie to distract him from her alphabet so that he ended up pushing her against the wall and having his way with the wayward wench, her legs wrapped around his waist while he bore her weight.

He must stop being beguiled by her, or she would never get past three-letter words. Not that she needed to learn too many of the four-letter variety.

Oh, what a lovely cock, Jem. Stick it in, nice and hard. I love a good fuck.

He tried not to let his memory linger over the lascivious events. If his indiscipline had had any good effect, it had been in taking the edge off his excitement this evening. He must try to sustain a clear head and a calm manner. Lady Augusta did not want some over-eager overgrown schoolboy tonight.

She wanted a master.

He sat up poker-straight and thrust out his chin, practising his manner, as he had done each night for the past week.

'Miss Quim,' he said aloud. He had to learn to say it with authority, without coyness or a tremor of incipient laughter. He lowered his voice, trying for menace. 'Miss Quimmmm. Assume your position, madam.'

He grabbed at the silver-topped cane he'd bought for threepence off Old Abraham. It looked new, especially after he'd rubbed over the tip with a mixture of bicarbonate of soda and water. It was in the shape of some mythical bird's head or other, maybe a roc, and it looked fierce. It was far too heavy for flogging anybody with though. Perhaps he'd have to go back to his former place of employ and beg one of the old rattans.

He jabbed with the cane at the wall of the carriage, imagining it to be the slender stomach of Lady Augusta.

'On your knees, girl,' he said.

Good God, he sounded like a bad parody of a melodrama villain. He should grow a moustache to twirl while he spoke.

This was going to be an embarrassing disaster, it was clear.

'Be natural, Stratton,' he commanded himself. 'Be your own self. This is what has brought you to her.'

The carriage lurched to a halt. Yes, surely Eaton Square. The rights and lefts all tallied.

At the top of the steps, the coachman retired, leaving James to his fate.

Did he wonder what was the purpose of the young man's blindfolded visits? Did his position as household retainer mean that he was party to it all? There must be gossip among the maids, surely . . .

The maid herself answered the door, the same one as last time, judging by her voice.

'Come in, sir, and let me take your hat and cane.'

'Oh, I may keep the cane if you don't mind. But please remove this blindfold; the coachman has tied it very tight this evening.'

He griped about it as if it were a pair of boots or a cravat. It was a blindfold.

If the maid found anything outlandish in this, she did not show it, bowing her head politely to James and leading him further into the house.

A different room this time, not that gracious, spacious drawing room in which he had taken tea with his new . . . associates.

This room was perhaps a breakfast room, with a glass roof and views to a somewhat overgrown but beautiful garden beyond. It was lit by candles alone, and many of them, a forest of gold and silver candelabras covering every available surface. The amber light was alluring and magical, throwing its enchantment down on to a small round table, set for two.

'Take a seat, sir, and I'll tell Miss Augusta you are here.'

James went to sit down, immediately regretting that he had not left the cane in the cloakroom, for what was he to do with it? He could hardly lay it on the table. In the end he propped it between his knees, an awkward third leg protruding out to the stone-tiled floor.

Where was Mrs Shaw tonight? Was she not to dine with them?

His question was answered when Lady Augusta entered the room on Mrs Shaw's arm.

He rose to his feet immediately, intending to shake their hands or kiss them or whatever they expected him to do, but Mrs Shaw motioned him back down.

'Pray, stay seated, Mr Stratton. You are not expected to stand on ceremony.'

Lady Augusta had been striking enough at the first meeting, but now she robbed him of his breath. Her hair had been curled in a somewhat old-fashioned but still attractive style, exposing her soft white neck, which curved down to an eye-catching décolletage.

Her gown, still un-crinolined, was of dark silk brocade, embroidered with golden fleurs-de-lys. The short sleeves exposed pale, delicate arms, braceleted with diamonds. More diamonds glittered about her throat in a garland design, fascinating the eye.

James, for all the effort he had made, could not but feel rather shabby.

Her blindness offset his disadvantage, though, and he soon forgot his embarrassment when Mrs Shaw helped Lady Augusta to her seat and then left the room without further comment.

'You look quite beautiful,' he remarked. 'I am honoured.'

'Oh, don't be honoured, sir,' she said.

She called him sir, as if it were the most natural thing in the world. He, a lowly wretch, and she a woman of independent wealth.

'Why should I not be?'

'Take it as your right, sir, as no more than you deserve.'

A maid appeared, an unfamiliar girl, carrying a silver tureen. The one who had answered the door followed with a dish of bread rolls.

James mulled over Augusta's words while the soup – mock turtle – was dished out. The familiar maid stayed to pour the wine and stand by the door.

'Are you . . . is it all right to speak freely in front of the maid?' asked James in a stage whisper.

'Oh yes. Paulette is party to all our secrets. The kitchen staff might only know a little, but she is my personal maid and she dresses me for . . . for . . . well, we have plenty of time to discuss such things. Do you like mock turtle soup?'

'I have never eaten it.' James tried a spoonful. 'I find it perfectly pleasant, thank you.'

'I don't eat it much myself, but Mrs Shaw thought it the kind of thing a man would like.'

'You must thank her for me.'

'We rarely have to consider the needs of men in this house. Do you mind having *service à la Russe*?'

'I . . . hardly know.'

'Mrs Shaw tells me it's becoming very fashionable now. Prevents all the courses getting cold, all laid out together they way they used to be.'

'I see. But do you never entertain, then? In a house of this size and grandeur, I would imagine supper parties and balls to be a frequent diversion.'

'Oh, no, I am quite a recluse. I'm afraid polite society shuns me, for the most part.'

'But why?' A drop of soup fell from James' spoon as it stopped just before his mouth. 'Why would you be shunned?'

'It is because of my blindness. Oh, not as a thing in itself – people are not so cruel and stupid as that. But I have a cousin, a set of them, in fact, and they have conspired since my father's death to transfer my inheritance to them. Their case is that I am not legally capable of managing my own affairs. They have done everything in their power to discredit Mrs Shaw and try to prove that she manipulates poor little weak-minded me. They have tried to have me removed to an asylum. But I can speak up for myself and any lawyer can see that my intellect is far from feeble.'

'Indeed. That is shocking. They seek to rob you, and to use your impairment of sight against you?'

'That's right. But as well as being stupid and cruel, they are rich and influential, so good society sides with them. I must confess, I rather helped their case by emptying a decanter of wine over Bertie's head at my coming-out ball. It was my last invitation.'

'I had no idea you possessed such spirit,' laughed James.

'Oh, but of course. I have to, in order to survive, you see. But the constant exercise of vigilance against my enemies, and the sustenance of spirit, as you call it, fatigues me sometimes. And at those times, I wish for nothing more than to be meek and obedient and submissive to a man who has nothing to gain from me.'

'And that man—'

'Is you. I hope. If you wish it.'

'It is such an extraordinary proposition. You must excuse me if I seem hesitant to accept it as fact. I appreciate your explanation of your circumstances, though. A little context makes a great deal of difference to one's perceptions.'

'Which were?'

Augusta paused, holding a piece of bread coquettishly close to her lips.

'I had no idea what to think. No idea why a wealthy and

attractive young woman could possibly require such a . . . service.'

'And do you understand a little better now?'

'A little. You have no desire to marry at all?'

'I cannot trust any suitor to be genuine, Mr Stratton. Fortune hunters or decoys sent by my cousins – these are all a woman with my defect can expect.'

'I'm sure that cannot be true . . .'

'Have you ever been blind?'

Her voice, so sweet and mellifluous before, had hardened almost beyond recognition.

'Of course . . . not.'

'Kindly restrict your observations to subjects you understand.'

James let his spoon clatter into the empty bowl.

'I am sorry.' Augusta's capitulation was swift and imme-diate, her voice back to its earlier timbre. 'Please forgive me. I spoke out of turn. You must not allow me to speak to you so.'

James understood that she was asking him to be stern, but he felt his sympathies prevented it. But no. He was here to satisfy her deviant desires. He must endeavour to do this to the best of his ability.

'Indeed I shall not, Augusta,' he said in a low voice. 'Any more such disrespect and I shall be forced to contemplate disciplinary measures.'

'Oh.' It was a tiny exhalation, but her face was rapt and flushed at his words.

Paulette came forward to remove the empty soup dishes and the tureen.

'Shall I bring up the veal, Miss Augusta?'

'Please do.'

James, who had been overtaken by a momentary giddiness at the chance to play out a role he had often rehearsed in his bed at night, returned to Earth.

'Veal?'

'Cutlets. Breaded. With green vegetables and I think some scalloped potatoes. I didn't want to serve you anything too heavy. Does it suit?'

'Very well, thank you. Please – tell me about Mrs Shaw.'

'Mrs Shaw is my mistress,' said Augusta.

'I do not quite understand how that can be. Please humour me with an explanation.'

'It was not always so. When she first came to me, for many years, she was my companion and my assistant. But when we started reading the books . . . oh, those books . . . we found we had a natural inclination towards a good deal of what was described. And, quite fascinatingly, Mrs Shaw's inclination was opposite to mine. So if she read me a scene in which a young lady was being birched, she enjoyed the fantasy of being the one who wielded the rod, whilst *I* . . . oh, but you know about me.'

'Not half as much as I want to know,' said James, feeling some discomfort at the crotch now that birchings had been mentioned, with a titillating hint that the two women of the house may well have indulged themselves in the pleasure. 'So you . . . experimented?' he prompted over her blushes.

'At first, it was only play,' Augusta whispered. 'I was curious to experience new sensations.'

'How did it begin?' James was avid for juicy morsels of detail.

'I wondered aloud how painful it would be to be struck with a riding crop, in the manner of some or other heroine of a story – one of yours, I believe. Mrs Shaw did not seem to take the suggestion seriously, but later on that day she went to town and purchased just such an article. I don't ride, you see, at least, I haven't done since . . .'

James stowed the last few words away for later consideration, eager to stay on the subject of Augusta's first foray into flagellation.

'So Mrs Shaw returned with a riding crop? And what then?'

'She reminded me of my earlier curiosity and asked if I truly wished to experience such unusual delights. Within a few minutes, she had me upended over a footstool, striking me over my skirts with the whip.'

'Not heavily, I trust.'

Augusta laughed. 'Heavily enough. But I was a wicked creature, and that first taste had awakened a predilection.'

'Did you think it would?'

'Yes, I always thought it would, because of the way your stories affected me. Mrs Shaw and I feigned extravagant horror and amazement that such things should be at first, but I think, at heart, we always understood each other. It was a question of finding our footing. So at first, I would hear your stories and then think of them at night in my chamber, alone. But once the crop was bought and tested . . . well . . . certain licences were permitted.'

'Between mistress and servant?'

'Oh, you know the paradox of it, Mr Stratton, sir. I pay her wages, but she commands me.'

'And now you are . . . intimate?'

'We share a bed, Mr Stratton. Does that shock you?'

He was too giddy to think of touching the veal. Was that shock? It seemed like something much richer and more delicious than that.

'Women sharing a bed is commonplace enough in the circles I inhabit,' he said, coughing over the shake in his voice.

'I keep forgetting. You are not high-born.'

'Not in the least. Rather the opposite.'

'And yet so well-spoken and so . . . eloquent in your descriptive prose.'

'You are most kind.' He paused. 'Am I to understand, then, that you are a Sapphist?'

'Mr Stratton, clearly I am not, or you would not be here. No, I do not crave a female touch. But I do crave *a* touch, and Mrs Shaw's is more than adequately skilled. And she is wonderfully adept with the rod. Are you? I imagine you to be a true master of the art.'

James paused for a moment, tempted to overstate his severely limited experience.

'Well, that is for you to judge, Augusta,' he said. 'At your leisure. I hope you will have plenty of opportunities to do so.'

'Oh, so do I,' she exclaimed, putting her hand over her bosom. 'Very much so. So you are a willing participant in my little scheme? I have so longed for this, Mr Stratton, so much. You cannot begin to imagine.'

'Do not challenge my imagination, Augusta.'

She sat back with a happy sigh.

Gratifying as this was, James could not ignore a persistent little nag of anxiety that he might not meet Mrs Shaw's standards. From what Augusta said, the pair of them had been playing at mistress and slave for some while now.

However, as his straining trousers reminded him, he had something she didn't. He hoped the novelty of a male playmate might make up for his lack of expertise, at least to start with.

'Mrs Shaw is a wonderful woman,' said Augusta, 'but she cannot compare with what you have to offer me. Your lovely voice alone sends shivers of pleasurable vibration through my body.'

'Won't she be jealous?'

Augusta was silent for a moment, then her tinkling laugh broke out over the plate, seeming to set off its silver glint. 'What an extraordinary suggestion,' she said.

She pushed her plate away.

'I think I've eaten enough. How about you, sir?'

'Is there to be no sweet course?'

'I am conscious of the passage of time, sir, and impatient to . . . to . . .' She laughed again, a forced, nervous thing.

'Augusta, I will need your forbearance to begin with. I do not know you well and I fear I might act in a manner that will surprise or alarm you. If I do, will you tell me?'

'Of course. Mrs Shaw says I am to tell you that if you require her assistance at any time, she is on hand to give it.'

'Thank you, that may well be useful.'

He put his napkin to his lips, slowly. Now that the moment had come, he almost wanted to put it off.

Paulette came forward for the plates and bore them off downstairs.

'She is gone,' whispered Augusta, once the doors were shut. 'And we are alone.'

'Yes, we are alone. Stand up, Augusta.'

She fluttered her hands a little, then pushed back the chair and stood, proud little chin up, eyes levelled at him as if she saw him quite clearly.

'I fear I cannot refer to you by that sobriquet Mrs Shaw prefers. Forgive me. May we decide upon an alternative?'

'As you wish, sir.'

'A term at once of endearment and ownership . . . what might suit? My own? No, too bland.' His mind catalogued all the popular affectionate tags. *My life, my soul, beloved, adored one*. They were all far too romantic for the purpose. 'My pet,' he wondered aloud. 'Ah, now that might suit. What do you think?'

'Your "pet"? I should love to be your pet, sir.'

'And as my pet, you shall undergo obedience training. Why, yes, I think that serves perfectly.'

Pleased with himself, James sat back and crossed his legs, looking Augusta up and down, imagining that diamond-adorned neck in a stiff dog's collar.

'Did Mrs Shaw pick out your gown tonight?' he asked.

'Do you like it, sir?'

'Answer a question promptly when put to you, pet,' said James with a touch of severity.

'Of course, sir. Sorry, sir. No, I chose it myself.'

'How?'

'By touch, sir. I reach into my wardrobes and run my hands over the frocks until I find the one I want.'

'Why did you choose this one?'

'Because of the cut. The neck is low and the waist very small.'

'You think it shows your figure to your best advantage?'

'I suppose I do, sir.'

James rose from his chair and moved slowly but deliberately towards Augusta, circling her, taking her in from all angles.

'Well, and I shouldn't deny it,' he said softly. He was close to her, so close that she almost flinched when he brushed past her, his breath falling on her soft white neck. A sense of his power over her surged into him, intoxicating him with its potential. 'You have a very fine figure, pet. But how much of it is due to the gown? I think we should investigate further.'

He stopped, just behind her shoulder, and spoke into her ear, watching the flush rise from her throat upwards with each murmured word.

'I don't suppose you can take it off by yourself, can you?'

She shook her head, inclining it towards him as if asking to be touched.

He ran the tip of one forefinger along the neckline, finding the top button concealed behind a frill.

'Does Mrs Shaw dress you?' he wondered aloud.

'No, Paulette does, sir.'

'Your little maid dressed you for tonight. Did she know what she was dressing you for?'

'I think she may have had an inkling, sir.'

'An inkling?' He bent and kissed her downy nape, glorying in the shiver he felt pass through her. 'That her mistress was dressing up solely to be undressed again. By a man.'

'Do you mean to undress me, sir?'

'I rather think I do. Keep perfectly still now.'

He hoped he would not prove himself hopelessly inexperienced in the art of disrobing a lady. The Strand girls rarely bothered to do more than lift their petticoats, revealing very little beneath. Sometimes they might loosen a stay or two, releasing breasts to be squeezed. The business of dressing and undressing was too laborious to bear much repetition in the busy lives of Annie and her sisters.

The satin-covered buttons proved easy enough to manipulate from their loops and James was emboldened to drop a kiss in each newly opened space, like little staging posts en route to the grand destination. Her chemise and her corset soon announced themselves to his eye. He grimaced slightly at the unforgiving tightness of the laces. How did these girls breathe? No wonder the doctors were all so set against these contraptions. Nonetheless, it was an attractive garment, of a rich red silk with golden swirls embroidered all over it and his heart beat faster in anticipation of what she would look like once the dress was gone.

Just below Augusta's tailbone, the buttons ended and James pushed her sleeves down her arms to help her out. A woman's clothes were like shackles, he thought, pinning her down and confining her in her place. The quantity of petticoats beneath must weigh as much a small child. He loosened each with assiduous care until they lay in waves about her feet, ready to be stepped out of.

And now he could see her lower legs and the swell of her calves, clad in white silk stockings. He took a position in front of her and clasped her around her waist. His hands almost spanned it. How deliciously her snowy bosom rose and fell, ready to burst from its whalebone confines.

'Has any man seen you thus before, pet?' he whispered.

'No, sir, no man,' she said unsteadily. 'You are the first.'

He put a finger to her lips.

'And has any man kissed this mouth?'

'None, sir.' Her breath tickled his finger and, in an impetuous motion, she held it against her lips and kissed it.

'But you have imagined how it would feel?'

'Very often, sir.'

'How does it feel when Mrs Shaw kisses you?'

'She never kisses me, sir. She does a great many things to me, but she has never kissed my lips.'

'Why not?'

'Because I want my first kiss to be from the man I love. Oh, I know it sounds ridiculous, given my wickedness, but I must hold something back to belong only to that man. What else can I give him that has not already been given elsewhere?'

'You intend to marry, then?' asked James in some surprise.

'I think not. Men are fortune hunters who charm the ring on to a woman's finger and lead her a wretched life ever after. But I do intend to love. Really love, regardless of propriety.'

'You are quite remarkable,' said James, letting his finger drift from her lips to a spot behind her ear, which he stroked, to her obvious pleasure. 'And I won't deny that I want to kiss you very much. But I shall forbear. May I kiss your neck instead?'

'Oh, don't ask permission,' she begged. 'Please, take anything you want of me, but just allow me my one foolish fancy. Everything else is yours, sir, everything.'

He slipped his hand around the back of her head and lowered his lips to her soft flesh, trying to avoid the scratchy diamonds. She exuded an irresistible fragrance of warmed jasmine and musk that made him want to eat her. But he managed to restrain himself to gentle, whispery kisses that covered every inch of available flesh between her jawline and the necklace.

His free hand made its way to her waist, tracing in wonder the astonishing curve from her bosom inwards and then the flare out to her hips.

'Don't you long to be free of this constriction?' he asked, pressing into the stern whalebone with both thumbs.

'When I was a girl, oh yes, I did. But I have learned to embrace it.'

'How?'

'Mrs Shaw made me think of it differently. Instead of a cage, I was to think of it as a strict lover who kept me confined and bent to his will.'

James shut his eyes for a moment. Oh, Mrs Shaw. The more he heard of her, the more he thought he ought to fear her.

'How fascinating,' he said. 'But tonight you have your true strict lover, and he commands that you be released.' James looped a finger into one of the ribbons, and gave a teasing little tug, not quite hard enough to effect unlacing.

'Release me into your keeping,' she whispered.

And then the laces were undone and the two halves of the corset pulled apart. Augusta did not fall to the floor, her body unable to function without its whalebone support, and neither did a mountain of flesh spill forth, the way James sometimes imagined it must do. But her breasts were freed and her silhouette assumed a generosity the severe clutches of the corset had not permitted.

On the whole, he thought he preferred it.

He put the corset with the gown and went to stand behind Augusta, pulling her back into him and wrapping one arm around her stomach. With his other hand, he pulled her hair free of its pins and clips and feasted again on the back of her neck. He enjoyed the way her thighs, in their thin cambric drawers, trembled against his. She felt hot, almost feverish, in his hands.

'You wanted a man,' he said into her ear. 'Do you like what you have?'

'I like it,' she said. 'The reality of you lends power, force to my imaginings. I see how weak they were now. I feel so defenceless . . . exactly as I dreamed of feeling, yet more so. There are a thousand little details my fantasies had missed. I am trying to fix each one in my memory.'

'Oh?'

'For instance, the way your whiskers feel. I had forgotten that men had such things. It is so long since I saw one.'

'You were not born blind?'

'No. But please . . .' She rubbed her cheek against his,

seeking contact with the aforementioned whiskers. 'Touch . . . taste . . . take what you want.'

James pulled himself together. It should not be left to Augusta to dictate the course of events. He needed to be more decisive, firmer.

With this in mind, he let his hand slip lower and cupped a breast. It was less full than one of Annie's but with a delightfully stiff peak at the nipple, almost pointed, making a triangular dint in the silk of her camisole.

With the pad of his thumb he circled this devilish little nub, all the while caressing the underside of her breast and sucking at the side of her neck. She laid her head back against his shoulder with a moan of abandonment.

'Hot-blood,' he whispered. 'I knew it. You will need a great deal of attention, pet.'

'I know it, sir.' She rubbed herself against him, sinuous as a cat, her bottom pushing his crotch.

Inflamed, he gave her soft skin a warning nip before reaching down to remove the camisole entirely. Now he could see the enticing red of that nipple, set atop its pale conical mound. Its neighbour looked starved of attention, so he provided some more to both, flicking and fingering the exposed flesh until she reached a peak of arousal that was almost discomfort.

'Please . . .'

'Pet?'

'I cannot say the words. But I beg you . . .'

He pinched each nipple and she yelped, then sighed with pleasure.

'They are yours,' she said.

'Do not tell me what is mine. I am perfectly well aware of it. These –' He pinched the nipples again '– shall be at my disposal whenever I wish it. I require you to keep them in this condition.'

He put his hand to her waist and spun her around.

'How shall I do that, sir?'

'However you can.'

He bent his head and took one nipple into his mouth, breathing over it before closing his lips and sucking. When he put his tongue against the hard round surface, he flicked its tip, hoping it would tickle.

'Oh, oh, oh,' exclaimed Augusta, hopping from foot to foot, as if having her nipples sucked provoked a kind of St Vitus's Dance.

'You writhe like a basket of puppies,' he complained, coming up for air. 'Next time I do this, I shall have you tied.'

Augusta's long contented sigh made him smile and pat her bottom.

'Not such a cruel suggestion as I thought, hmm?'

His hand wandered over those cotton-covered curves until he found the split that he knew these drawers always had. Augusta gasped and clutched at his lapels.

'Shameless, aren't you?' he said. His hand was inside the slit now, feeling her warm rounded cheeks against his palm. 'Shameless little pet begging to be used and had by me. Mmm.' What he could do to that arse. What he *could* do. He could do as he liked with it.

'Let's have these off, shall we? Drawers, stockings, the lot. I need a good look at you.'

Augusta made no protest as he pulled off the remainder of her clothing. She held on to his shoulders obediently, lifting each foot as he tugged down her stockings and slid the drawers over her heels and toes. When, finally, she stood naked, he took a few steps back.

'Stand up straight,' he said. 'Lift your arms. Yes. Point your fingers to the ceiling, like that.'

How that pose showed off her breasts, high and firm. Breasts he had already fondled and tongued. Breasts that were already his.

The dark triangle of her pubis drew his eye rapidly downwards. Her haunches were slim and her belly, now the corset was gone, was no longer flat but soft and gently convex.

'Up on your tiptoes,' he said, 'and turn around for me. Slowly.'

She strained to maintain the grace of a ballet girl, keeping her arms arched over her head as she made the one-hundred-and-eighty-degree rotation. James had once written a lurid short story about a ballerina and her sadistic teacher, and he was put lasciviously in mind of it, especially when Augusta's full, firm buttocks revealed a small cluster of healing bruises near the curve of one cheek.

'What are those?' he asked.

'What, sir?'

He strode quickly up to her and cupped the buttock with one hand, pressing his thumb into one of the bruises.

'Here, pet. How did you come by these marks?'

He saw her shut her eyes, in a rapture, presumably the effect of having a man's hand on her bare bottom. Now that he was close, he could smell her, feel the heat of her.

'Mrs Shaw, sir. She beat me.'

'Why? Had you misbehaved?'

'Yes, sir, I had. She said I needed to be punished.'

'What did you do amiss?'

'I . . . I lusted after you, sir. I told her I was eager for your visit and she said I should be whipped for my wanton nature.

She said, as you were not there to punish me, she had best do it herself.'

'She was wise.' James swallowed. His cock was engorged beyond belief, but he must pace himself, he must not relinquish his self-control. 'She may act as my proxy in that respect. And so . . .?'

'And so she made me bend over a stool in the drawing room, sir, and she lifted my petticoats and parted my drawers and whipped me with a wooden yard rule.'

'A yard rule?'

'Yes, she keeps it especially for the purpose.'

'Is it very painful?'

'Very, sir. I do not like to be whipped with it, for it always leaves bruises.'

'Is it the worst of her arsenal?'

'Oh no, it is not the worst.'

James patted her bottom with his open palm, causing her to shudder and sigh.

'Which instrument of chastisement holds that particular distinction?'

Augusta pushed her rear against James' hand, appearing to beg for more, harder, but he held back, waiting.

'I cannot quite decide, sir,' she said in a low, indistinct voice. 'Sometimes I think the cane, and then at others, the birch rod.'

'Both fine implements,' he said. 'But of course, you will behave impeccably at all times, so I will not need to use them.'

'I will try my best, sir.'

He moved his hand around her hip and took her sex in a firm grip, pushing his fingers between her lips. She was very wet and warm there; no Strand girl had ever promised more.

'Mrs Shaw was right to say you have a wanton nature,' he

murmured into her ear, kissing the lobe and the tender skin behind. 'Was she not?'

'Yes, sir, she says I should have been a whore, not a lady.'

'I can see why.' His fingers moved, up and down, skimming the folds, rubbing against the protuberant hood of her clitoris. 'Spread those legs wider, pet.'

She obeyed immediately, pushing back against him and breathing hard and fast.

'This is all mine now,' he said. 'It all belongs to me. I can touch it, taste it, have it whenever I like. Do you have any objection to that, pet?'

'No, sir.'

'Good.'

He pulled his fingers out and patted her quim.

She gasped with disappointment.

He took advantage of her open mouth to pop his fingers, slick with her own juices, into her mouth.

'I licked this off you last week,' he said. 'Now it's your turn.'

As she dutifully sucked, he tried to pull his thoughts into order. He ought to have a plan, a carefully structured step-by-step seduction map. Instead, he was careering all over the place, wherever his senses took him. If he kept this up, he'd overexcite himself and the evening would end too soon.

Her pleasure was the focus, not his. He must keep that in mind.

'Now I'm going to take you over to your chair,' he told her, leading her by the arm across the floor, 'and you are going to show me how you pleasure yourself.'

'Oh.' It was an expression of involuntary dismay.

He sat her down in an armless, velvet-upholstered chair and stepped back.

'No? What was that, pet? Were you considering dis-obeying me?'

'No, sir.'

'Good. How does that velvet feel against your bare skin?'

'Slightly prickly, sir, but otherwise comfortable.'

'Have you forgotten that I watched you pleasure yourself only a week ago in this very house?'

'No, sir, but . . .'

'But?'

She bowed her head.

'I find it difficult, sir, unless somebody is reading to me.'

He was taken aback, but fascinated by this confession.

'Truly?'

'Yes, sir, truly.'

'And why do you think that is?'

'Because . . . the story takes me out of myself. I am too self-conscious otherwise, and certain fears take hold of me. Certain horrible thoughts.'

'Horrible thoughts?'

'Principally the thought that my blindness is God's judgement on me for having a nature such as mine.'

'Oh, that hoary old tale about the sin of Onan affecting one's eyesight? You know that is untrue, surely.'

'I know nothing, sir, and even if I did, the act of self-pleasure places one in a peculiarly vulnerable frame of mind which makes rationality a difficult thing to achieve.'

'Yes. Yes, I see that.'

'You see. I cannot. I prefer to think along different lines when I am . . .'

'I understand. And if I did it for you, would you still need to be read to?'

'No. Not if you were doing it. In that case, I should wish

to be fully conscious of what is being done to me.'

'Then perhaps that is what I shall do. Open your legs, pet. Show yourself to me.'

The naked female form was something James was still unused to, for all his years of living alongside prostitutes. All the tissue and flim-flam of modern ladies' dress was like a shell, as distant from its contents as that of a turtle. Why did they conceal some attributes and accentuate others? Why were breasts more acceptable than legs? Why show off a trim waist but hide a shapely posterior? To see it all in its pale vulnerability was always a novelty at first, and nothing more so than what Augusta showed him now.

She sat with her hands gripping the sides of the chair and slowly spread her thighs.

James knelt, the better to see the parting of the slit and the lustrous pink-red folds within. As always, he thought of ripe fruit, of a split nutmeg or a Turkish fig, soft and juicy inside its skin. He bent closer and breathed in.

She did not smell like Annie. Annie was a kind of potent olfactory stew, but Augusta's scent held only a single note, a pure distillation of feminine desire. Its strength lay in its delicacy. He wanted to taste it, but he held back, instinctively feeling that Augusta needed to be taken slowly, a step at a time.

'I am looking at your sex,' he said, feeling a little ridiculous, for surely she must be aware of this.

'Oh, I shall die,' she said faintly. 'I am a shameful creature.'

'Or are you shame*less*?' He took a light hold of her thighs and enjoyed the squirm that ensued. 'Tell me it is mine, pet.'

'All that you see is yours, sir.'

'What is it that I see? I wish to hear you name it.'

'Oh, must I?'

'Yes, you must.'

'My, my quim, sir.'

James smiled at the way her lips formed the word, so unwillingly. Looking up he saw her blush an even fiercer red.

'It is more difficult for you to say it than it is to show it to me?'

Augusta nodded.

'And yet Mrs Shaw refers to you as Miss Quim. You are not unfamiliar with the term.'

'She calls me that because she knows how it embarrasses me. She could not have chosen a more humiliating title.'

'She is an admirable mistress,' remarked James. 'I hope I can match her as a master.'

He put his thumbs on her lips and pulled them apart, revealing more glossy redness around her peeking clit. She ground her bottom against the velvet but he held her firm and waited for her to be still.

'I see every part of you,' said James. 'I see your clit, swollen and begging to be touched. You want me to touch it, don't you?'

'Oh,' whimpered Augusta, and she turned her head away from him.

'Don't you?' he repeated. 'I shall call for Mrs Shaw if you do not answer me.'

'Yes, sir, yes.'

'And beneath it, this little untouched hole. You are a virgin, I take it?'

'Yes, sir.'

'But you wish for me to deflower you?'

She was silent.

'Augusta, you understand that I must be clear on what you expect from me. I know you have said that all is mine but I must know that you understand everything that my possession of you will entail. You want me to breach your maidenhead? Yes or no?'

She faced him once more and nodded fiercely.

'But can you be careful?' she whispered.

'Yes, I can be careful,' he said, knowing exactly what she meant. 'And besides, it shall not happen today.'

'Shall it not?' She sounded a little dismayed.

'I do not know if you have earned it yet, my pet.'

She breathed in raptly, excited by this thought.

'How must I earn your favour, sir?'

'Why, by being a very good and obedient pet and doing as your master bids you. Spread your legs wider. I want you to feel that you have stretched to your limit, yes. That looks a little uncomfortable.'

'It is, sir.'

'Hold that position.'

James felt he was falling into his stride now. He liked his tone of softly-spoken authority and sensed that it pleased Augusta too. Really, it was not much different from writing one of his filthy fictions.

He rose to his feet again and braced one hand on the back of the chair, standing over Augusta. He wondered if she had any sense of his shadow over her, or whether her awareness of his presence relied on the sound of him shifting position, the scent of the macassar oil in his hair, the warmth radiating from his skin.

He kept his other hand at Augusta's crotch and let his fingers cover her clit before beginning an infinitely slow massage of that engorged bud.

'You are very wet down here,' he said softly. 'Very slippery. Are you always as wet as this?'

'Mrs Shaw says it is a shame to be so. She says it is nature's proof of my wickedness.'

'Mrs Shaw is a very wise woman. You are a wickedly wanton thing. Perhaps I will have to punish you for it.'

He watched her tilt her head back and bite her lip. She was gripping her knees, working at keeping herself as wide open as possible.

'Yes,' continued James, keeping his voice even and low like a stage hypnotist he had seen at the Old Mo some months before, while his fingers continued to ply Augusta's clitoris with unhurried strokes. 'Such a willing little whore as I have before me here must be whipped into goodness. And I don't think that will be the work of a day. No, it will take a great deal to put this little trollop on the path of virtue, won't it? A great many tears and stripes and sore bottoms are in prospect, a great many indeed.'

He noted how her chest rose and fell with increasing rapidity, her face now a permanent stormy crimson.

It was almost enough to make him take pity on her. Almost.

'You are wetter than ever,' he whispered. 'I think this thought excites you. I think you will kiss the rod. Won't you?'

'Oh.' She could do no more than groan. She bucked on James' hand, straining every sinew in her effort to find that elusive burst of rapture.

He sped up his rhythm, rubbing firmly but not too hard, enjoying the uncontrollable tremor of her hips and thighs.

She must be close, he thought, judging by the increasing fury of her squirming.

'If you take your pleasure from my hand, sweet pet, you must expect punishment to follow,' he whispered into her ear, and that threw her into a climax of sobbing intensity.

He stroked her through it, kissing her succulent neck until she subsided, limp and spent, head lolling on her shoulder.

'Next time,' he whispered before straightening up, 'you will beg my permission first.'

He put his hand to his crotch, since she couldn't see him. It was painfully hard. How long could he hold out before the exquisite torment turned to plain agony? Five minutes, he thought, perhaps ten.

He surveyed her near-lifeless form, seeing how her expressionless eyes had rolled far back in her head.

'Can I get you anything?' he asked. 'Some water?'

She nodded, still panting.

He poured a glass from the jug on the table and held it to her lips. She sipped gratefully, the high colour fading from her cheeks, until she was fully revived.

James felt a new tension between them, as if they had now crossed a line that could not be uncrossed. He had brought her to that most intimate of states and his fingers were drenched in her spendings. It was hardly surprising that she could find nothing to say. Should he initiate some kind of conversation that would pinpoint her reaction to all of this? Was she all right? Or did she regret her actions? Had she perhaps found him lacking in some way? Or had he performed satisfactorily.

Self-doubt consumed him and he looked anxiously at the crystal carriage clock on the mantel, wondering if he should simply leave.

Did she expect him to carry on being the dominant lover? Or could he speak more naturally now?

She finished the water and he replaced the glass.

'Speak to me,' he said before he could stop himself.

'I'm sorry,' she said quickly.

'No, do not be sorry. Unless you truly are. Are you sorry for what has happened?'

'I do not know what to say to you,' she said, a slight quiver in her voice. 'I have never . . .'

'I know. I only ask from concern for your welfare. Are you . . . all right?'

'I felt so perfectly at peace with myself while you touched me,' she said softly. 'And now you are all the way over there, and I fear I have disgusted or offended you.'

'Oh no, indeed.' He darted forward and knelt at her feet, noticing with some gratification that she had not yet thought to close her legs. Perhaps she awaited his order? 'No such thing! You are speaking nonsense, pet.' He bent and kissed each inner thigh. 'It is natural that you should feel a little strange. I feel somewhat so myself.'

'But is it a good kind of strange?' she asked, half-laughing, tearful with relief.

'A very good kind of strange. This is new to you but you will soon settle. You are safe with me, Augusta. I will take good care of you.'

'That is part of what I felt. Safe. Cared for. And yet you spoke so cruelly. It is such a paradox I can scarcely collect my thoughts.'

'Our sensual natures are complicated, pet,' said James. 'Both yours and mine. We can only surrender to their peculiar commands.'

He put his fingers to her lips.

'Do you remember how you licked your essence from my fingertips before?' he said. 'I think the time has come again.'

She smiled and parted her lips, sucking at James' fragrant fingers with diligent enthusiasm. He could not help but imagine how her mouth would feel transferred a little lower down his body. Perhaps he would find out soon enough.

She laid her cheek against his palm, nuzzling it affectionately.

He had performed well enough. She was not disappointed.

Now he had to work out what should happen next.

He withdrew his fingers from her mouth and patted her cheek.

'Dearest pet,' he said, 'here is my hand. You have met it in the form of pleasure-giver and you will soon be very familiar with its little tricks and treats. Kiss it.' He put his knuckles to her lips and felt their dewy touch. 'It is master of you.'

She shut her eyes, a little thrill passing visibly through her.

'But you know that it often acts in another capacity, don't you?' he said. 'One that is less pleasant, though no less good for you.' He held her chin, stroking the soft skin underneath. 'Can you tell me what that might be?'

'It can . . . it can give pain as well as pleasure,' she whispered.

He gave her chin a little pinch.

'Yes,' he said approvingly. 'Exactly so. What can reward can also punish. Remarkable versatility, I always say. What do you think, pet? Do you deserve to feel its sting tonight?'

'You have said so,' she replied haltingly.

'Yes, I have, haven't I? I said you should be punished. What was it for? I cannot quite recall . . .'

'My wantonness,' she mouthed.

'I did not quite catch your words, pet. Speak up, pray.'

'My wantonness.'

'Oh yes. Your wantonness. You cannot but agree with me that the accusation is just.'

She nodded.

'Then take my hand, pet, and stand up.'

She held on to him, her fingers curling around the side of his hand. He was conscious of the trust and faith that she reposed in him as he pulled her to her feet.

He took her place on the chair and placed her carefully and gently over his lap, her pale bottom now foremost in his line of vision. He had not seen enough of this part of her, he thought, pleased to have her twin moons in such a prominent position. She went over his knee like a lamb. She had clearly been looking forward to this element of the proceedings.

'You are a well-behaved pet,' he praised, stroking the backs of her thighs. Further inside, they were still dewy from earlier activities, lush with that very wantonness he professed to be punishing. The idea that what was about to follow would curtail her sensual desires in any measure whatsoever was, of course, laughable. If anything, it would ready her for another bout. The delightful never-ending spiral of punishment resulting in further arousal, requiring further punishment, resulting in further arousal was one of James' favourite paradoxes, oft-repeated in the pages of his fiction. And now he was able to test its effects in reality.

He lifted one leg, raising her bottom higher, admiring the long, straight slope of her legs and her pointed toes.

'Shall I have to restrain you?' he wondered aloud. 'Does Mrs Shaw?'

'Not as a matter of course,' said Augusta faintly. 'Unless she is minded to be unusually severe.'

'Unusually severe,' repeated James. 'Well, I shall not be so, so I shall allow you the free use of your hands. You may not, of course, use them to defend yourself against what is dealt to you by *my* hand.'

'Of course I will not, sir.'

'Of course you will not. Or you will find yourself tied at the wrists and bent over a chair while I make use of your mistress's cane. What else does she have, by the way? Am I permitted to make use of them?'

'She has quite a collection, sir. Straps, riding crops, flails, the yard rule, the cane. I do not recall all of them. She has placed them all at your disposal.'

'That is kind of her.' James smiled, aware of the incongruity of the concept of kindness in the midst of his erotic cruelty. It was sweet indeed. 'Now, it is time you made better acquaintance with my hand, my pet.'

He raised his arm, calculating at a rapid speed how hard and how fast he should let it fall and on which portion of her helpless bottom.

In the event, he aimed for the lower portion of her cheeks and laid a hard swat square on the right hand side. She snuffled a little but made no cry. He looked at the pink shape he had made on her skin and felt no relief from the constant throb in his trousers. How soon could he have her on her knees, thanking him for his disciplinary measures with her hands or her hot, wet mouth?

Not before he had her bum a uniform sunset shade, he decided, and he got to work eagerly on his self-appointed task, covering her rounded peaches with smart, sharp cracks until his palm stung and she began to whimper and flex her feet with each new blow.

Should he lecture her through this? His characters often did, though how they maintained the presence of mind to form coherent sentences throughout this delightful but desperately arousing task he did not know.

'I sense that you are feeling this now,' he whispered. 'My message is hitting home. Are you learning to curb your lusts?'

If the curbing of lust is the object, perhaps it is I who should be suffering this humiliation.

'Yes, sir,' she said with a small yelp as he laid a solid handprint across both cheeks.

'I hope you are ashamed of yourself,' he continued, adding layer upon layer of fire to her already burning skin. 'A lady of high birth such as yourself, offering her sex to whichever writer of obscene texts has the most attractive voice. You are a trollop, pet, no better than the unwashed whores who stand on the corner of my street opening their legs for every man.'

Augusta panted now, and squirmed her hips. James could see her knuckles whiten as they clung to the chair legs for dear life. Her bottom was a scarlet glow, deeply satisfying to regard. He needed release soon or he might expire.

He delivered a final half dozen, harder and faster than ever, enjoying her wholehearted howl at the last, then he ordered her to her knees.

'Unbutton my trousers,' he commanded gruffly.

She had never done such a thing before, of course, and this was clear from the way she fumbled and tutted as she worked.

'Do you know what I wish for you to do?' he asked softly, helping her with his fingers on hers.

'You have said you will not take my virginity tonight,' she answered.

The final button was loosened and she parted the garment. James had not put on drawers. These were his best trousers and they would need laundering, no doubt, but that was a long way from the forefront of his mind now.

Her hand made contact with his erection and she withdrew it, inhaling sharply, as if in fear.

'No,' he said, taking her by the wrist and holding her still while he adjusted his trousers, the better to free his member. 'You are afraid of it?'

'I just . . . it was a surprise. You are not wearing underwear.'

'No. Do you know what it looks like?'

'Yes, from statues I saw as a small child. And from your own descriptions, in your books.'

'Take hold of it, pet. You will become familiar with it soon enough. Get the measure of it.'

Her fingers crept around his girth, taking a loose hold, as if the warmth of him burned her.

'You can close your fingers tighter,' he said. 'It will not hurt me.'

She clenched them into a fist and he somewhat regretted his words at the twinge this caused. He hissed in a breath.

'Not that tight.'

'You must take pains in your instructions, sir, for I am completely inexperienced.'

'I know, I know. Does it not feel as you expected?'

'I did not know what to expect, sir. It is both softer and harder than I expected, if such a thing is possible. There is an illusion of flexibility, but it is just that – an illusion.'

'Yes. It will not bend.'

'Unbending,' she said, tasting the words on her tongue. 'Unyielding.'

'That pleases you?'

'I have always longed for an unbending man, and now it seems that all men are, at least in this wise, unbending.'

James smiled.

'Then any man would suit your purpose?'

'No, indeed,' she said, colouring. 'Not any man.'

He put his hand over hers and taught her, gently, how to stimulate his senses. Her motion was hesitant at first while she held herself alert for his every physical response, but once she was reassured that her actions gave him pleasure, she settled into a steady rhythm.

He tried to keep his breathing light and even, not wishing to alarm her, but before long the effort expended became too much and he lapsed into chaotic panting and little sighs of rapture.

'My arm aches so,' she said. 'And my wrist. This is a surprisingly difficult task, sir.'

'Do you . . . wish . . . to stop?'

'No. I take pride in my exertion, if it pleases you. I shall not stop unless you order it, even if my arm were to fall off.'

This alarming image knocked James somewhat off course, and he prised her eager little fingers from his cock and took it into his own hand.

'Kneel back on your heels,' he ordered breathlessly. 'I mean to spend upon your breasts. Hold them up for me.'

The sight of them, offered high in Augusta's cupped hands, nipples saucy red, inflamed him to the necessary extent. His wrist working hard, he spurted his male emission all over her creamy mounds, watching as if hypnotised as the translucent jets landed on her flesh then slithered slowly down into her cleavage.

At the moment his seed made its mark on her, she threw back her head and moaned, pushing her breasts yet higher, as if begging for more.

Dear God, that image would be with him tonight.

And oh, how he wanted to dive for her mouth and ravage it, holding her by the hair while his tongue slid sweetly into her compliant darkness. Why would she not allow him to kiss her? It was cruel and strange of her.

But cruel and strange were her tastes.

Instead, he bent low, put his hands on her upper arms and suckled at her nipples, first the right and then the left, flicking them with his tongue before kissing her neck and murmuring words of praise.

'Did I please you, sir?'

'Very much, pet. I want you to keep my mark on you, where it fell, until it congeals. Keep it until you take your next bath. I forbid you to wash it off until then.'

Augusta held a breath then released it with shuddering delight.

'Mrs Shaw will see it,' she said.

'Mrs Shaw will understand.'

'Mrs Shaw will indeed understand.'

James started and whipped his gaze towards the door, where Mrs Shaw stood, in her customary black, looking the pair of them over.

He felt immediately hot with embarrassment at being caught thus by the older woman, with his spent manhood shrinking by the second and his trousers around his ankles.

'Mrs Shaw,' he muttered, rubbing his handkerchief cursorily over the head of his cock before righting his clothes.

'Oh, you are modest,' she said, with a vulpine smile. 'I would not have thought it of you, Mr Stratton. No, Miss Quim, nobody permitted you to rise. Back to your knees, if you please.'

Augusta subsided into her previous position. James saw her dab her thumb into a smear of his ejaculate then lick it off. He was not sure if that constituted breaking his rule or not, but he decided to overlook it, given the way it made his detumescing tool twitch.

'What has passed?' demanded Mrs Shaw, advancing into the room. 'Miss Quim, explain what your new master has done with you.'

'He made me sit on a chair with my legs spread, ma'am, and he touched me in my most private place until I . . . you know . . .'

'Say it.'

'Until I felt the pleasure take me.'

'Do you like his touch?'

'Very much, ma'am.'

Mrs Shaw pressed her lips together and James felt a vague discomfort.

Is she jealous?

'What else?'

'He smacked my bottom, ma'am.'

'Hard?'

'Moderately so.'

'And now you have accepted his male issue on your body? And he has said it must remain there. Well, we must observe and respect Mr Stratton's wishes, must we not? But now it is time you were in bed, Miss Quim.'

She looked briefly and a little sourly at James and explained, 'Miss Quim has a strictly enforced bedtime, Mr Stratton. She is not permitted to be up a minute after nine.'

'So early,' he said, reaching out to touch Augusta's hand, a tender injunction to her not to move yet.

'It may seem early to you, Mr Stratton, but she is subject to fierce headaches and requires a good deal of sleep. I have had the carriage brought around. Miss Quim, to your feet now, look sharp.'

Augusta broke off the contact with James and stood, turning in the direction of Mrs Shaw's voice.

'No, no, Quim, bid your master a good night first. I dare say you don't want a thrashing for bad manners before bed, do you, girl?'

'No, ma'am.' She turned back to James and dropped a deep curtsey, something he had never seen a naked woman doing before. 'Thank you so much for teaching me tonight,' she said, her words heartfelt.

He took her hand once more and kissed her fingertips lingeringly, wishing they were her lips.

'Dearest pet, please believe that it has been my pleasure. And will be again, if you are willing.'

'Next Thursday at seven o'clock sharp,' said Mrs Shaw impatiently. 'Good evening, Mr Stratton, we are much obliged.'

She darted forward and took Augusta by the elbow, leading her bare, semen-splashed form out of the room without so much as a glance back.

Of course she would not look back, James chided himself. She could not see him. Yet he could not quite dismiss the cloud of melancholy that settled around him at the abrupt nature of her departure.

Paulette found him still staring at the door when she entered to escort him to the front door.

'The carriage is waiting, sir.'

'Oh.' He came to, shaking his head. 'Of course.'

He followed her to the vestibule, accepting his coat, scarf, gloves and hat from her one by one.

'You are Paulette,' he said.

She blushed and looked away.

'Yes, sir.'

'Do you like working here, Paulette?'

'It's a very good position, sir.'

'From whom do you take your orders? Her Ladyship or Mrs Shaw?'

'If you don't mind, sir, I'm not to answer such questions.'

He put on his hat, quirking an eyebrow.

'You are forbidden?'

'Please excuse me, sir. The carriage . . .'

'Forgive me, Paulette. I don't mean to land you in any trouble.' He smiled at her, his most charming smile, and her colour heightened. 'I shall see you anon. Good evening.'

'One more thing, sir,' she said shyly, producing the blindfold from her apron pocket.

'I had forgotten.'

She held it out mutely, but he waved his hand.

'I'd like you to put it on for me,' he said. 'Could you, do you think?'

He took his hat back off and bent a little towards her, offering himself.

After letting out a flustered little giggle, she put the length of black silk over James' eyes and tied it in a bow at the back of his head. Her fingers were shaking, he noticed, and she didn't pull the knot half as tight as the coachman did. Presuming that fellow didn't take it upon himself to improve on Paulette's handiwork, James might stand a chance of working out where this bally place was.

'Thank you,' he said. 'You have a much more pleasant touch than that coachman.'

She merely giggled again and opened the door.

James stumbled out on to the porch and negotiated the steps with care, running into the hands of the coachman at the bottom, who guided him to the carriage by his elbow. It wasn't until he was inside the carriage that he heard the front door close.

The horses lurched into life and he waited until they were at the street corner, suspecting a pair of sharp Shaw eyes at an upstairs window, before removing the blindfold. He blinked and tried to read the street sign on the terrace end, but it was too dark and the nearest lamp-post too distant to illumine it.

The houses screamed Belgravia, though, tall and ghostly white in the dim moonlight. Whatever the street might be, he'd lay good money its name started with Belgrave or Eaton.

'Lady Augusta,' he said to himself, peering out at the passing stucco frontages as the coach took a twisty-turny route through the heart of wealth and privilege. 'Lady Augusta *what*?'

He almost forgot to re-don his blindfold until the bright and bustling streets of Piccadilly hove into view. This was where they stopped to take it off.

'Thank you, I shall walk the remainder of the way,' he said.

'Suit yourself,' muttered the coachman, taking the blindfold and shoving it in his waistcoat.

James wandered through the evening crowds, vaguely on course for his lodgings, stopping every now and then to look at some vagary of street life as if seeing it for the first time.

A chestnut seller at his brazier. A legless man propped against a wall, shabby old hat beside him. The bright cherry lips of the girls in the Haymarket, calling to him as he passed. The laughter pouring from the oyster bars. A drunken brawl between two very young, very smartly dressed men, broken up by a pair of peelers.

James skirted it all, different scenes playing before his eyes at intervals. What he had done with Augusta. It seemed, here in the foul, familiar city air, no more than a dream. Ephemeral as gossamer, the memories lingered, pale without their parent sensations. Until he took off his glove and put his fingers to his nose and there . . . there she still was.

Why had Mrs Shaw torn her away from him like that? He

felt strangely *used*. He and the painted girls at the corner were as one. He was a whore, when all things were considered, and no more than that.

How odd it was.

He should not desire Augusta to love or care for him – that was not in the nature of the agreement. And yet he hoped – strongly hoped – that she lay in her bed thinking of him now.

Augusta in her bed, her boudoir, a fragrant, faery place. She would have it smelling of roses and everywhere her fingers fell she would touch the softest and most sensuous of fabrics.

She would lie in a gown of ruffled lace, her hair loose about her on her silken pillow, dreaming of him. And beside her . . . Mrs Shaw.

The strength of the twist at his solar plexus this thought engendered surprised him.

'Do not be foolish,' he whispered to himself. 'She does not and cannot love you. There can be no future in it. You are charged to bring her the pleasure a man and a woman can know, and nothing more.'

Holywell Street was half alive, the second-hand-clothes shops shuttered while the bawdy bookshops stayed open late, thronged with curious browsers, mixing with refugees from the theatres.

His uncle Stratton was waiting for him behind the counter.

'Well?'

'What do you ask me?'

'Are your services satisfactory?'

'I don't wish to speak of it.'

'Oh, come on, lad. At least tell me if we can expect a fictionalised account in your next piece.'

'Uncle, I have said . . .'

James did not finish the sentence, barging through the pop-eyed customers to the hall door.

Annie sat on the stairs, apparently in a state of mild inebriety.

'Are you not working tonight?' he said, picking his way past her.

'Waiting for you,' she said. ''Sides, business is bad just now. Lizzie reckons we ought to try the barracks up by the Palace. Soldiers always want a bit of fun.'

James retraced his steps and sat down beside her.

'Why will you not look for less hazardous work? Practise your reading, Annie. Perhaps you could . . . oh, I don't know.'

'No, you don't know 'cos there's nothing. Nothing what pays like this, when the swells are flashing the tin. It's getting so thin, though. I'll be a threepenny upright before the year's out at this rate.'

'Do not speak so.'

She put a hand on his thigh. He looked down at the flashy rings with their paste gems, the pretty, clean nails that screamed 'prostitute' in this neighbourhood.

'If only I thought you cared, my lovely Jem,' she sighed. 'But your piece of finery's taken you away from me. You belong to another.'

'I belong to nobody,' said James abruptly, standing so that Annie's hand fell hard on the splintered stair, grazing the skin. 'I'm sorry,' he said, instantly contrite, crouching to take the wounded paw. 'Are you hurt?' He took his handkerchief and dabbed at the raw patch, but it was not really bleeding to speak of.

'Kiss it better,' said Annie, and he saw that she had tears in her eyes.

Chapter Four

Every second Monday of the month, a small group of men convened in the back room of Stratton's booksellers; they entered through the side door and took care not to be seen leaving.

James and his uncle waited for them, having provided a small keg of ale and a pie from the stall across the road.

Most of the bookshops of Holywell Street had sprung up in tandem with the old radical-political creed of Chartism. The Chartists had been gone for the best part of fifteen years, but the strange alliance of smut and egalitarian views had continued, a symbiotic relationship feeding one off the other.

'Tell us about your new girl, Jem,' urged one of the cloth-capped, shirtsleeved men quaffing his uncle's beer at a table loaded with obscene magazines.

'What do you know of my private affairs?' demanded James, looking daggers at his uncle.

'Don't take on, lad,' said the elder Stratton. 'You're quite the hero in radical circles these days. An infiltrator. A spy in the class camp. And you don't even have to black boots or shovel horse shit.'

'Quite the reverse,' laughed a fat man in the corner. 'Young Stratton gets his jollies from the quality. What do the Mayfair ladies like, my boy? Up against the wall, same as the girls round here, I'd wager.'

James was embarrassed by the attention, and uncomfortable to boot, but his fury was allayed by the general air of approval and adulation that accompanied his new status as radical playboy rogue.

'It is not something I care to discuss,' he said, to much digging in the ribs and winking. 'Uncle, kindly refrain from spreading this gossip around the neighbourhood. I have taken tea with a young lady in a fashionable part of town, further than that I shall not disclose.'

'It does you credit, lad,' said his uncle, quaffing. 'But it raises an interesting question for debate. Without going into the specifics of young James' situation here, why is it considered shocking for a working man to court a lady? Surely, when all's laid bare, a man's a man and a maid's a maid. There's nothing but this fallacy of blood to keep one from the other.'

'Yes, blue blood, what a ridiculous notion,' agreed James. 'And breeding. What are these noble families? Prize heifers? It is all so ignoble.'

'Many a blue-blood girl has eloped with her dancing master,' observed the fat man. 'But our good and true working girls are fobbed off as mistresses and bed warmers. It seems to me that the women are the true egalitarians.'

'Amor vincit omnia,' said James reflectively.

'If it were only true,' said his uncle gloomily. 'Surely there's a Lord Somebody-Or-Other who'd have your hide, lad, if he knew what you were up to with a girl of that ilk.'

'I don't know about that,' said James, thinking of the malevolent cousins Augusta had mentioned. If they knew of these meetings, surely they would have grist for their campaign to have her declared insane. It was more important than ever to maintain discretion and secrecy. 'I hardly think we will marry.'

'But why not?' demanded the fat man. 'You're good enough for any woman in England. Look at you – strapping young man, with your health and your good looks and as quick a brain as any. More so than those chinless boobies in the House of Peers, at any rate. Any man ought to be proud to own you for a son-in-law.'

James, keen to steer the tenor of the conversation away from his particular circumstances, referred to a pamphlet he'd seen recently, encouraging what it called 'class miscegenation' in order to level the population of Britain to a satisfactory social mix.

A more general discussion of how such a policy could ever be enforced pushed Stratton's own situation once more into the shadows, where it remained until the meeting's end.

James tried to get away before he could be drawn into further discussion of his intimate affairs, only to find the door barred by the fat man.

'I didn't mean to speak out of turn, Stratton,' he half-whispered. 'You must choose your own path in life. Thing is, I had wondered if it might, at some point, cross with the path of my own girl, Maude. You've met her, you recall?'

James blinked and tried to cast back his mind.

'Oh, it was at . . . the Hoxton music hall? I believe? Yes. How is Maude?'

He could not recollect a thing about her.

'She's well, Stratton. She often asks after you. You made rather an impression on her. A good, solid girl from working stock, boy, that's what you want. Somebody who can get on her knees and scrub your front step down, then cook you a good pie for your supper. Never mind your fine lady, good for nothing but embroidery and French. Come to ours for dinner some night, Stratton. You're always welcome.'

'I am not in a position financially to marry—'

'Pshaw, marriage. Maude's mother and I never got a licence. Where's the use? Nobody knows any different.'

'I am a pornographer by trade.'

'You *have* a trade. You're good with words. You can teach. You'll go far.'

'You're very kind.'

'I'm very honest, my boy. Come for dinner.' He nodded and lumbered off into the night.

James' uncle loomed at his shoulder.

'Why must you tell everyone my affairs?' hissed James. 'There is no political motivation to my meetings with this lady – none whatsoever.'

'Are you so naïve as to think that? There is a political motivation to everything. What was said about you being in a position to infiltrate the elite from within – I agree with that. You have a golden opportunity here, Jem. Don't waste it.'

'But what would you have me do? Have myself written into her will? Mix with her relatives and get myself elected to parliament? What, precisely? This is a dream world you are inhabiting, uncle, if you think my . . . dalliance with a woman who happens to be of a higher caste than I will lead to anything but what it is.'

His uncle shrugged.

'Then I hope it will not lead to your destruction, at least.'

'What do you mean by that?'

'I mean, watch your back, nephew.'

Lying fully clothed on his bed, James wondered if he

should abandon his peculiar new acquaintanceship. Would
it not be easier all round if he courted Maude and lived ever
after in two upstairs rooms surrounded by fat, floury babies?
A meat pie, a hot fire and a squashy, soft body in one's sheets.
Did a man need much more than that?

Then he thought of Augusta's unseeing eyes and the
quiver of her mouth as he christened her with his seed.

That story had only just begun. What writer worth his
salt would abandon it here?

The putting on of the blindfold was a ridiculous charade to
James, now that he knew the location of the house, but he
played along with it nonetheless.

He was met at the door, as before, by Paulette, whose
dark blue eyes sparkled at him once the blur of his vision had
cleared.

'And how are you?' he asked, handing her his hat.

'As well as can be expected, sir,' she said, commonplace
enough words, but the manner of their speaking was as
nakedly flirtatious as he had ever heard.

'I'm not sure *what* to expect from you, Paulette,' he
murmured, rendering her breathlessly speechless.

He followed her along the passage, to the drawing room
in which he and Augusta had first been introduced. Paulette
showed him in and then scampered away.

'Good evening,' he said, furrowing his brow and darting
his glance around the handsome red and gold room. There
was no sign of Augusta. Mrs Shaw, in black bombazine,
awaited him alone.

'Mr Stratton. Do sit down.'

He sat close to her, leaning forward, sensing excitement
and danger.

'Am I to attend on Her Ladyship?' he asked.

'Do not refer to her so,' snapped Mrs Shaw. 'Call her Quim. Call her slut. Call her your pet, if you insist on it. But please make no reference to her rank in the outside world. While you are here, we are not in it.'

'As you wish,' said Stratton. 'Then, where is my pet?'

'I have had a great deal of trouble with her this week. She is giddy and heedless. I am not sure you are exerting a good influence upon her, Mr Stratton.'

'I am sorry to hear that, but I imagine the novelty of the situation has perhaps over-excited her. I am sure it is a temporary state of affairs.'

'Temporary or not, it is most provoking. I have had cause to punish her daily and withhold all her customary privileges.'

'Mrs Shaw, you are an excellent disciplinarian, but allow me to deal with her now. I promise you, you shall have your biddable . . . Miss Quim . . . back by the time I leave tonight. Please have her brought down.'

James thought he knew the real source of Mrs Shaw's displeasure. Jealousy. Fear of displacement. It was natural enough, and therefore he would have to work at appeasing her, if he was not to come between the mistress and her . . . other mistress.

'You understand,' he continued in a lower tone, 'that I have no wish to supplant you.'

She snorted. 'As if you could. As if any man could.'

'There, you see, you need have no fear. Pray, send her down.'

Mrs Shaw rose.

'I shall take you to her. Come.'

James moved through the room in the wake of Mrs Shaw's trailing skirts, then he followed her up the main staircase.

Were they going to Augusta's bedchamber? Would he see her in her bed?

Perhaps tonight would be the night to deflower her. Perhaps the white undersheet she lay upon would be stained before he left.

But the chamber Mrs Shaw showed him into contained no bed. It was a large, square room at the back of the first floor whose windows were all shuttered. The gas-lit space was a kind of schoolroom, the wall covered in maps and prints of famous old masters, with indifferent watercolour copies pinned beside them.

A substantial oak table stood by the door, on which was a globe and a great pile of books. Running all the way along the right hand wall was a long trestle bench.

In the centre of the hardwood floor was a solitary desk, at which Augusta sat, wearing a kind of white nightdress.

She looked up when they entered, although of course she could not see them.

'Continue,' snapped Mrs Shaw.

'What is she doing?' whispered Stratton, moving closer to observe the activity in which Augusta was engaged. Her head was bent over a curious type of slate, or rather two metal plates connected by a metal bracket with a narrow space between. On the bottom plate was a great many raised bumps, whilst on to the top plate was clipped a piece of paper, on which Augusta was forming a sequence of dots with a sharp stylus.

'Writing lines,' said Mrs Shaw.

'Writing? What does it mean? What does it say?'

He bent over her and put a hand on her shoulder. He was rather shocked to see that the gown she wore had no back, but simply tied in a bow at the neck.

'It is Braille,' said Mrs Shaw. 'A writing system for the blind. Miss Quim, kindly recite your line for your master.'

She lifted her head and said, in a monotone, 'I must eschew all manner of wilful disobedience and recollect my place.'

James put his fingertips on the raised bumps and let them drift over the repetitive patterns.

'This is wonderful,' he said. 'Could you teach it to me?'

'Oh, sir—' breathed Augusta, but Mrs Shaw cut her off.

'I hardly think it will be necessary. If you wish to learn Braille, try the blind school. There are instructors who charge by the hour. Now, Miss Quim, shall we proceed? How many lines have you managed?'

Augusta put her index finger to the end of a line.

'Eighty four, ma'am,' she said.

'I see. Sixteen short of the hundred. Stand up.'

James stepped back and watched Augusta rise, her white gown falling away to the sides, revealing her bottom. As before, it was peppered with fading bruises and also faintly striped, the evidence of a fairly recent caning. It seemed that Mrs Shaw had had a handy week.

'Now that Mr Stratton is here,' said Mrs Shaw, 'the responsibility for your discipline is transferred to him. I will leave the matter of your punishment in his hands. But, if I may, I should like to witness it.'

James nodded, trying to make sense of the situation. He was supposed to punish Augusta, but how, and for what?

'Might I ask, Mrs Shaw, before we proceed, what you would have done?'

Mrs Shaw smiled tightly, apparently gratified to be consulted.

'Indeed you may, Mr Stratton. For each line unwritten,

I would have given Miss Quim a stroke of the tawse, which you will see on my desk. She is due sixteen. I would probably have given three on each hand and ten on her posterior.'

'I see. Well, I will bear your recommendation in mind. Please, Mrs Shaw, take a seat.'

Mrs Shaw went to sit on the trestle, arranging her skirts with plentiful rustling while James retreated behind the large desk.

'Come and stand before me,' he commanded Augusta. 'Are you able to make your way here unaided?'

'Yes, sir.'

Augusta wended a careful path across the floor, stopping just short of the desk. She clasped her hands beneath her stomach and bent her head.

'I have had some troubling reports of your conduct from Mrs Shaw, pet. Can you make an account of your behaviour for me?'

She twisted her fingers for a moment, then lifted her chin.

'I have been a little lacking in concentration this week, sir. I have not been as attentive to Mrs Shaw as I should have been and, on occasion, I have not obeyed her immediately but dallied and daydreamed the time away.'

'Daydreams and dalliances? What has given rise to these?'

He smiled at the blush that spread across Augusta's cheeks.

'I am a wanton creature, sir,' she whispered.

'I know it,' he said, his voice a low caress. From the corner of his eye, he noticed Mrs Shaw's pursed lips. 'Well, that will not do,' he said, more briskly. 'Will it, pet?'

'No, sir.'

'Do you think Mrs Shaw's suggested remedy a fair and appropriate one? Sixteen strokes with the tawse?'

Augusta's cheekbones twitched and the corners of her mouth turned down.

'It seems a little severe, sir. I have been punished every day this week.'

'I noticed the marks of the cane. For what did you receive it?'

Augusta's fingers curled into claws. 'I do not wish to—'

'Tell him,' interjected Mrs Shaw.

'Mrs Shaw caught me in my bath . . . I was . . . oh, I cannot say it . . .'

'You can,' said James with persuasive authority. 'You will.'

'I was touching myself, sir,' she whispered.

'Touching yourself? In what manner?'

James felt a certain tightness at the crotch. He was rather glad Mrs Shaw could not see it behind the desk.

'In a . . . lascivious manner. Sir.'

'I see. I will need more detail.'

'With the finger and thumb of one hand, I pinched my nipple, sir. Whilst my other hand was occupied . . . lower down. Beneath the water's surface.'

James let the silence speak for itself, demanding to be occupied by further confession.

'My fingers were between my nether lips, sir. I was rubbing . . . my pleasure bud.'

'Your "pleasure bud"?' James bit his lip at the quaint term, trying not to smile too broadly in Mrs Shaw's presence. After all, he had probably coined that very term in the throes of lewd composition.

'Yes, sir.'

'And that was how Mrs Shaw found you?'

'It was not Mrs Shaw at first. It was Paulette, bringing fresh linens to the bedroom. She informed Mrs Shaw.'

'Paulette, you say? So what happened when Mrs Shaw arrived?'

'She made me get out of the bath, sir, and I was not even given a towel. I was made to bend straight away for six strokes of the cane.'

'You were still wet?'

James was impressed. He wondered if he could match the limits of Mrs Shaw's sadistic imagination after all. Perhaps they should collaborate on a novel.

'Yes, sir.'

'That must have been extremely painful.'

'It was, sir.'

'Then I hope you have learned your lesson and your fingers have not strayed where they should not since.'

'They haven't, sir,' she whispered.

James knew that the kind thing to do now would be to drop the subject. But who wanted to do the kind thing? Not him, not Mrs Shaw, and – he would have laid wager – not Lady Augusta.

'Come closer,' he said. 'Lean over the desk and tell me what thoughts occupied your mind while you were so wickedly employed.'

'Oh, sir, I cannot!'

'Oh, pet, you must.'

Mrs Shaw's eyes glittered. She looked ready to salivate.

Augusta bent forwards, resting her bare forearms on the desk. Her gown hung from her neck – Mrs Shaw must have a very fine view of her rear.

James brought his forehead close to hers, so close that he could kiss her lips. How was he meant to keep from doing so? Their delightful curve, their brown-pink fullness tempted him more than he could bear.

But he held off, waiting for her to open them and produce speech.

'I thought of you,' she whispered.

And now Mrs Shaw was frowning, whether because she wanted to hear, or she had heard, was unclear.

'Of me? And what did I do, in these thoughts?'

'Things that you did when you visited. And others besides.'

'Tell me in precise detail, pet, and you may earn a reward.'

'A reward, sir? Of what kind?'

'Of the kind you have wished for.'

James swallowed, his trousers now desperately uncomfortable. The anticipation of Lady Augusta's defloration was cruel in its intensity.

'You will make me yours, sir?'

'You are already mine, pet. I will make you more so. My mark will be on you for the rest of your life and you will be beholden to me for it.'

Her lips, parted and glossy, looked more kissable than ever. She wavered as if she might swoon, her bosom rising and falling with telling rapidity.

'Then I will tell you,' she whispered. 'But you will think me terribly perverse.'

'I? Pet, you have read my books.'

She let out a little laugh of relief. 'Oh, indeed, it is nothing worse than anything you have written. I must keep this in mind.'

'Perhaps I will make a story of it.'

'I think you could, sir. Well, then, here is what I saw in my mind whilst I misbehaved in my bath.'

The tip of James' nose rubbed against hers.

If I don't have a care I will kiss her.

'Mrs Shaw had read me an account of a hanging from the newspaper. I don't like to hear such things, but she will always read them to me. She says it will help to keep me on the path of righteousness, if I know the wages of sin.'

'I see.'

James shivered a little at the thought of the gallows but did not allow the distraction to linger.

'I do not like to think of hanging, but I sometimes think instead of different forms of public justice.'

'Oh, so do I, pet, so do I.'

'I think you will know what I allude to.'

'I could hazard a guess.'

'I pictured that raised platform, around which crowds milled and yelled. Instead of a gallows, there was a form of step stool, rather like one that Mrs Shaw uses from time to time, with a padded seat. Once the crowd has reached a pitch of excitement, I am led out, my wrists cuffed to two burly correctional officers. They escort me up the ladder, where I must face the public. I should mention that I am wearing a gown exactly like this one, which covers my front but leaves my back open to view.'

'Very fitting,' murmured James.

'I can see their faces so clearly. They are full of glee at what they are about to witness. The men make lewd gestures, the women are disgusted by me. Some of them grimace, some of them laugh. I am turned and bent over the step stool. The correctional officers untether themselves from me and link my wrists together in front of me, then attach them to the stool. I will be unable to escape, and now my rear is presented, bare and high, to everybody's eyes.'

What a remarkable visual imagination she had, James thought, for a blind person. He resolved to ask her more about when and how her sight had failed. But first, he would hear the rest of this promising confession.

'There is a cheer as somebody walks on to the platform. I cannot see him, but I know it is you. You are there to give me what I need and deserve. When you come to the front of me, I see that you are dressed all in black. I know that you are a dark-haired man with abundant whiskers. I think your eyes are perhaps blue?'

'They are.'

'And your figure, too, I have a strong impression of its shape and size, gained from our contact of last week. You are above the middle height by some way and you have a great deal of strength, despite a slender frame.'

'You flatter me,' said James, highly gratified by this description.

'Oh, I do not think so.'

James looked down at his long legs and thought perhaps she was not entirely misguided.

'So, I am on the platform with you, you little miscreant.'

The upward curve of her lips and the way she curled her fingers into fists betrayed her pleasure at being so addressed.

'Dressed in black,' she said. 'And you are holding something. It is a birch rod, some half dozen switches tied with ribbon. You place it under my nose and order me to kiss it. I smell it, almost taste it. Most of all, I *see* it. Oh, the sight of it . . .'

She paused to gather herself.

'More wonderful than that,' she murmured, 'the sight of your face. Your expression. It is not cruel, exactly, but it is . . . merciless. You have your job to do and your jaw is set and firm. Your eye knows me for what I am – a disgraceful

wanton who has shamed herself. Yet there is no hatred in
your glance, but a clear understanding of how what you are
about to do will benefit me and be for my ultimate good. You
would not be able to whip me otherwise.'

James rather thought he would, but refrained from stating
it.

'I wish you could see my face,' he said.

'I wish it too. But you have much more to give me than
your face, sir. So much more.'

'And I give it even in your daydreams? Carry on.'

'Oh. Yes.' She blushed. 'I suppose you can guess? You
move around to my rear and you commence thrashing me
with strong, rhythmic strokes. The birch is uniquely painful,
it stings like a swarm of bees. I beg you to stay your hand, but
you are resolute.' She paused, seeming almost to swoon, and
whispered the words again. 'You are resolute.'

'Yes. I am.' James put his hand to her cheek, making her
nuzzle into his palm.

'The crowd bays and roars. You keep at me, and at me,
and at me. I sob words of penitence, to no avail. When I
am thoroughly chastened, and the crowd beside itself with
satisfaction at the severity of my whipping, you put the rod
aside. It is all but broken to pieces anyway. You pull me to my
feet, for I can hardly stand, and turn me so that my front is
displayed to the crowd. They clap and cheer until they are
hoarse, whilst you hold me against you and put your fingers
. . . low down . . .'

'Low down,' breathed James.

Her body stiffened and she shied away from him, putting
her own hand to the cheek he had caressed.

'That was as far as it went,' she said. 'And then Mrs Shaw
came in and caught me.'

James seized her by the elbow, more roughly than he intended. She jerked away from him, but she could not loosen his grip.

'What do you mean?' he said, trying not to display his agitation, 'by fomenting my desires in this manner? You mean to inflame me, don't you, pet?'

'You asked for my account,' said Augusta, her voice small.

He had intimidated her. Guilt made him relax his grip on her.

'I did.' He stood straight again, looking down at her bent figure, forearms still flat on the desk. 'Mrs Shaw did well to cane you for it. Tell me, pet . . .'

He walked around the desk until he stood behind her and then, without warning, slid his hand between her thighs.

'Oh, but you do not need to tell me,' he said, pushing his fingers into her warm depths. 'I meant to ask if your memory had excited you. I see it did.'

He turned to Mrs Shaw, still rummaging between her mistress's legs, and spoke to her directly.

'You do not think it proper for my pet to think of me while she takes her bath?'

'She is wanton.'

'Yes,' said James, withdrawing his fingers and holding them, in their shiny, slick glory, up for her inspection. 'Isn't she? Was it the fact of her self-pleasuring or the fantasy she chose that earned her her punishment, though? That is what I ask.'

'The former, of course,' said Mrs Shaw with a hard stare.

He nodded formally and went to wash his fingers in a jug at the side of the room. Too late, he realised that water was probably for drinking. Not any longer.

Hot-cheeked at his faux pas, he avoided Mrs Shaw's eyes and picked up the strap, a two-tailed Scottish tawse in heavy brown leather.

'You recommended that I give her some strokes on her hands,' he mused aloud, not looking at either woman. 'But I'm afraid I cannot . . .'

'Oh? And why not?' Mrs Shaw sounded indignant.

'I have mentioned, I think, my personal history. I was once a schoolmaster and, as such, had on occasion to use just such a method of corporal punishment on the palms of my charges. I did not enjoy it and I avoided it, but sometimes my superior demanded it and I had no recourse. This may sound odd to you, but I loathed inflicting pain upon those boys. The headmaster said they understood no other language, and it is true that they were rough boys from the worst backgrounds, but it still struck me as cruel. I myself was beaten as a boy and it did me no good whatsoever. I am still the vicious, idle wretch you see today. At least, *you* see me.' He gave a half-laugh, looking to Augusta, who was still bent over the desk, presumably since nobody had instructed her to move.

'I'm afraid I don't understand, Mr Stratton. You are saying that you disapprove of corporal punishment, and yet you have already administered it to my charge and—'

'I disapprove of it for children,' he interrupted, raising his hand. 'And, for personal reasons, the use of a strap on the palms is associated in my mind with the ill-usage of children. Therefore I cannot bring myself to do it in a more pleasurable context.'

'You never whipped a boy's posterior?'

'I refused. And thus I lost my position.'

'How . . . ironic,' said Mrs Shaw.

'Yes, how ironic. Given my predilection for recreational

whipping of the fair sex, I could not perpetrate the same act on a child. The idea was simply abhorrent to me. This was not the explanation I gave to the headmaster, incidentally.'

'I should imagine it wasn't.' Mrs Shaw's tone was vinegar-dry.

'Nonetheless, my refusal to use the cane brought a premature end to my career in pedagogy. I was never cut out for it anyway.'

'Where did you teach?'

James gave Mrs Shaw a long look.

'Why should you wish to know?'

She looked momentarily furious but she soon composed her features and waved a hand.

'I do not, of course. Now, please, may we have our malefactor dealt with? I feel I have been sitting on this trestle for hours.'

James nodded and picked up the tawse. He had never used such an implement before, being familiar with the more straightforward kind of single strap but not this Scots variation on the theme. It should not be difficult to use, though, provided he kept a clear sight of his target and sufficient control of his forearm and wrist.

'Do you understand, pet, that you have earned sixteen strokes?'

Her hips quivered in front of him, her posterior curves so perfectly framed by the shearing sides of the white gown.

'Yes, sir.'

'I will administer your punishment and then the transgressions of the week shall be scored through, and marked off as paid for. We may then start afresh, with our slates clean.'

'Thank you, sir. You are too good to me.'

Oh, I mean to be . . . But he kept the words to himself.

Instead, in an overly brisk tone, he said, 'You must count each stroke, pet.'

He pulled back the tawse, which was heavier than the strap he had used before, and laid it with a hearty crack on the central curve of Augusta's bottom.

She cried out, a suffering little whimper, then counted the stroke.

What an impressive mark the implement made, James noted, a bright red rectangular beacon such as only upwards of a dozen strokes with an ordinary belt might produce. He began to wonder if he had been quite wise in electing to give all sixteen on her rump.

He tried to vary the location of each stroke, working as far down as her mid-thighs in order not to lay things on too thick. Each time she wailed and breathed chaotically and lifted her feet, first the left, then the right, while her flesh absorbed the unforgiving impact. She did not forget the count.

'The Scots tawse is a remarkable thing, is it not?' said Mrs Shaw, the first half-dozen having lit up Augusta's bottom and thighs like London Bridge after the Prince of Wales's wedding. 'But why don't you speak to her as you perform the chastisement? I feel that it makes the effect so much stronger.'

'Perhaps you are right,' said James, drawing back the tawse for the seventh stroke.

'It makes her more amenable, I find, and gives her the inner strength to take a stronger punishment.'

'I shall take your word for it, Mrs Shaw,' said James through gritted teeth, somewhat regretting his decision to allow her to stay. But he saw the sense of her suggestion and, before flicking the leather forward, he put a hand on Augusta's spine, nudging her back into optimum position, from which she had strayed a little.

'You know why are you here, pet,' he said. 'You have displeased your superiors and you must experience the weight of their displeasure.'

He laid the seventh stroke, feeling the familiar drop of the stomach, the sensual rapture that hardened his already considerable cockstand. She took it so meekly and so well, and her helpless little cries inflamed him to near-madness. She was his.

'I will have you behave properly,' he said.

Eight.

A crimson bar, beginning to swell into a welt, rising on her skin.

She wailed, long and low.

'Eight, sir.'

'You will obey Mrs Shaw and myself in every respect.'

Nine.

He could almost feel the throb, causing an answering version in his trousers. Call and response. The stiffness was painful. How was it for her?

She choked, a sound at once high-pitched and guttural, but recovered herself in time.

'Nine, sir.'

'You will act at all times with humility and restraint.'

Ten.

Her knees buckled and her arms slid partway off the desk. A low moan filled the room, followed by a sob.

'I can't,' she whispered.

He rushed forward and crouched beside her, holding her with a hand on her shoulder.

'She feigns it,' said Mrs Shaw, rolling her eyes. 'Do not let the little minx divert you.'

Ignoring her, James spoke into Augusta's ear. 'Have I hurt you too much? Should we cancel the final half dozen? If you wish a postponement . . .'

She shook her head, squeezing out clusters of words between huge breaths.

'Let me . . . collect myself . . . the tawse bites so keenly . . . but if you stop now . . . I will resent you . . . and curse my weakness . . .'

'It is not weakness to know one's bodily thresholds.'

'Yes, it is. Especially when I know that I want you to be cruel and commanding and to whip me through my tears. I know that for certain, my darling Mr Stratton. Please . . . make me resume my position. Speak harshly to me.'

My darling Mr Stratton. How peculiar the words sounded, how jarringly intimate. She wanted him to hurt her and she wanted to adore him for it – perhaps she already did.

Well, he must do as she wished. This was his purpose, after all.

He picked the tawse back up and gave her six swingeing strokes, the hardest yet, plying the strap through tears and screams even though his fist shook and his resolve wavered with each additional stroke. He would not fail her. But God, it was hard. And yet it was also easy. And so beautiful. The strength of her submission to him, in enduring what she thought she could not, impressed him to a degree deeper than mere sensual pleasure.

It was not quite love, as he had experienced it, but it was akin.

When he put the tawse down after the final stroke, his breath was almost as laboured as hers.

'Well done, Mr Stratton,' said Mrs Shaw laconically.

'Thank you, I would be obliged if you would leave us now.'

He put his hand on the desk, palm down, requiring its solidity, watching Augusta's tears pool on the hard teak.

Mrs Shaw gathered her skirts about her but did not rise.

'It would oblige me very much,' reiterated James.

This time she did not hesitate, but stalked from the room, nose held high.

An oppression lifted from James and he felt at full liberty to put his hand upon Augusta's shaking shoulder and crouch to murmur into her ear.

'You have such courage, my pet,' he said. 'You have earned everything you wish from me. Everything.'

He helped her upright and gathered her in his arms, kissing away the tears, working hard to keep his lips away from hers.

'Will you take me to my bed?' she whispered, her clinging fingers gripping harder as if she feared his response.

'Only tell me where it is,' he said.

Her fingers relaxed and her full weight leant into him.

'Lead me to the door and I will give direction.'

Up another flight of stairs the twosome went, and then into a room at the back of the house. The curtains were drawn and the chamber in perfect darkness, so James had difficulty in making out a large four-post bed and a number of heavy mahogany items ranged against the walls.

'I shall light a candle,' he said.

'There are no lights in this room.'

'None?'

'No, they are not necessary.'

'What about when your maid dresses and undresses you?'

'Both Paulette and Mrs Shaw are familiar with my requirements. They do not need light to go about their duties.'

'I see,' said James, although he didn't entirely.

'Yes,' said Augusta, suddenly fierce. 'You see. *You* see. I do not. Who enters my bedchamber enters my world, in all its darkness.'

'Ah,' said James, preventing himself in time from repeating his ill-advised 'I see'. 'That is fair, I suppose.'

She grasped at his wrists, all her earlier ferocity drained. The darkness lent James' other senses an unwonted sharpness; he could tell from her clammy grip and her slight sway that she was nervous.

'If you take me,' she said, 'it must be because you want to. Not because I do.'

'Surely it is important that we both desire this?'

'Yes, yes. I mean, if you are doing this only to appease me, then I release you from this arrangement.'

'That is not the case at all. Not at all.'

'Do you want me?'

'Let me kiss you. I will show you.'

'No, please do not kiss me. If you kiss me, I shall be lost. I shall not be able to say farewell to you, ever.'

He cradled her head on his chest, stroking her hair and sighing, 'Oh, my pet.'

What made her believe that the act of physical union would be any less powerful than the meeting of lips? It made no sense, and yet he must respect her wish.

His hand moved down the warm bumps of her spine and touched the still-raging heat on her strapped bottom.

He shivered with pleasure, his cockstand rising again.

His work, upon her.

'Oh,' she whimpered, shifting against him.

'This is still sore?'

'Very much so.'

'You will not be comfortable upon your back,' he said, almost blushing to be discussing the logistics of fornication with his co-conspirator.

'Do not consider my comfort,' she said softly. 'Take me as you wish. Have your way with me. I want to be overwhelmed.'

'You want me to be forceful?'

She sighed. 'Oh yes.'

'But what if I should hurt you? I have heard that the first time . . .'

'You have never deflowered a girl before?'

'No.'

There was a rather shocked silence.

'Forgive me,' said Augusta. 'I thought you a man of varied experience.'

James stifled an involuntary laugh. 'I have no idea why.'

'Because of what you write, of course.'

'Pet, I have not done the half of it. I have done *some*. Most of my experiments in the sensual arts were undertaken in the back room of my uncle's obscene bookshop with photographic models and actresses. I never went to Oxford or Cambridge but I learned a great deal in that back room.'

'Did you whip girls in there?'

'I am occasionally called upon to whip a girl's posterior for the purposes of taking a photograph of it afterwards, yes. My uncle thinks I have a talent for it.'

'Your uncle thinks rightly,' said Augusta, with a sudden peal of laughter.

She sobered abruptly and wrapped an arm around his neck.

'There is so much of life I do not know. Your experience is a million miles from mine, and yet I feel such an affinity for you.'

'Be reassured,' said James. 'I know what I am about. But I have never breached a maidenhead before and I should like to take it a little gently, if you will allow. Once the deed is done, there can be all the throwing on to beds and ravishing you could wish for. But you will have to be a little patient.'

'Will it hurt a great deal?'

'I hope not. You know there will be blood?'

'I know that.'

'And besides, I must have a care not to leave you with any . . . unwanted consequences.'

'Mrs Shaw says she knows of a procedure to be taken after the . . . it is done.'

'I should prefer to trust to my own judgement on the matter, pet. It is my duty to take care of you.'

She wriggled again against him, as if his words gave her the profoundest pleasure.

'Nobody has ever cared for me, not really,' she said.

'Augusta . . .'

'I am sorry. I should not have said it. Forget my silly self-indulgence. Now, I am yours. Do what you will with me.'

With five and a half feet of feminine flesh to use as he saw fit, James was hard pressed not to reel. He reached behind Augusta's neck and unlaced the inadequate garment that was all she had to cover her. It fell to the ground when he stepped backwards, and he observed her nipples, dark and hard.

'To bed,' he whispered, turning her around by the shoulder. She knew the way, it seemed, for she measured a tread to the right hand side, then climbed on to the mattress on her knees.

'How should I arrange myself, sir?' she asked, kneeling there with her shoulders back and her breasts high.

'Lie on your stomach,' he suggested, having caught sight of a bottle whose label, in the dim light, seemed to have the word '*arnica*' written upon it in a tight script.

He picked it up and saw that the light had not deceived him.

He took off his coat and boots, rolled up his shirtsleeves and climbed on the bed behind Augusta, straddling her over the backs of her knees, to give himself free access to her crimson upper thighs and bottom.

With her legs pressed tight together by his knees, Augusta's virgin orifice was modestly hidden, but James knew it was there, and its unseen presence tantalised him more than if it had been in plain sight. He was very close to making this woman his own, in a physical sense, and the key to her lay within his reach.

He uncapped the arnica and began to rub it into Augusta's hot flesh with sensitive fingertips. She gasped with pleasure and shimmied against his palm. He smiled in the dark and patted her hip.

'Does it soothe you?' he asked.

'Not in the least,' she said. 'If that is my arnica. But your fingers do. They are so unlike Mrs Shaw's fingers.'

'Are they indeed?'

'Yes, she prods and pinches horribly. Yours are kind and yet firm. Oh.'

She melted into a series of low moans.

James smeared the liquid all over her plump, swollen cheeks, then he put the bottle aside and slid a forearm beneath her stomach, inviting her to rise up on all fours. Now her sex emerged from invisibility, still shyly half-concealed, pale pink under the heavier red of her bottom.

James, after a moment of consideration, put his right hand on a pendulous breast while he dampened the fingers of his left and reached between her thighs.

The dampening had not been necessary. Augusta's lower lips were soaked inside, her clitoris fat and greedy for his touch. With giddy relief, James began to rub and massage the stiffened bead, performing the same service for the nipple he held between his other fingers.

'You are wet and ready for me, pet,' he said. 'I think you must have been hoping I would touch you here. Hmm?'

Her only reply was a chaotic hitching of breath and a bucking of her hips, causing him to intensify the pressure on her slippery quim.

'Answer me, pet. Tell me your sex is mine.'

'My sex is yours, sir.'

'What shall I do with it?'

'Take possession of it, sir, make it bear your traces.'

'I should like to hear you beg,' he said, pushing a finger into the space he hoped to more fully inhabit soon.

She yelped and twisted, but he had her fast.

'Please, sir,' she said, panting hard. 'Please have me. I long for it.'

'My wanton pet,' he said.

He could delay no longer. He made short work of losing his trousers and underwear, not troubling to waste time in removing his shirt. His tool was engorged and stiff. When he looked at Augusta's corresponding part, he doubted for a moment that he would ever make it fit. She looked so tight. But nature would assist him, as she already had with the copious lubrication Augusta provided.

He took hold of her hips and pushed her spine downward with a quick shove, raising her bottom higher. Her thighs were trembling already, he noted, and she curled her fingers into the coverlet, clenching two great fistfuls of it. She was so tense her skeleton could have been a metal frame.

He drew a breath and gave her sex an authoritative pat.

'Augusta,' he said sternly.

She inhaled. 'Yes, sir?' she whispered.

'This will not do. Loosen your muscles . . . look . . .' He put his hand between her shoulder blades and kneaded the knitted flesh. 'You cannot clench up or it will scarcely be pleasurable for you. I understand that you are nervous, but there is no need to be. Put your trust in me. Take a deep breath and release it, slowly and completely. Do it now.'

She obeyed gratefully. He felt her unravel beneath his hand, moving from fear to trust in the time it took her to make the ordered exhalation.

'Now then,' he whispered, prompting her to part her thighs wider, rubbing a palm up and down the tender inner flesh. 'Let me see that you are ripe.'

He bent and put his lips to her sex. His tongue reached into her juicy slit and licked a slow, careful line from one end to the other.

She made a sobbing sound and pushed herself back on his mouth.

'Sweet and ripe,' he said before repeating the gesture, ending it with a luscious kiss that sealed his lips around her clitoris. 'You will keep yourself in readiness for me, always, won't you, pet?'

'Yes, sir,' she whimpered.

'Now, keep still and be brave. This will feel a little uncomfortable to begin with.'

He pushed the tip of his prick against that impossibly tiny aperture. She was warm and wet, but it still took him a measure of resolve to move forward and feel the flesh begin to give way to him. How did a maidenhead feel? Was it terribly hard to dislodge, or would he scarcely notice?

'Still, pet, still,' he whispered, pushing forward.

The bud unfurled for him, slick and yielding. He saw the head of his tool disappear into her, a rewarding sight indeed. She wriggled a little, and when he put his hand to her breast he felt her heart bumping in a panic.

'Breathe, my love,' he said. 'Deep and slow.' The chaotic flutter calmed against his palm. He stroked her breast, establishing a rhythm that her heartbeat should match.

Do I do right? Is this how a man should be with a virgin? It is how my characters might be, the less cruel of them.

He eased a little way further in while she whimpered and shook.

'Does it hurt?'

'Not yet,' she said. 'I cannot believe . . . I cannot see how you will not stretch me beyond endurance. Already I can feel that it will become uncomfortable if you advance much further.'

She was right. He had arrived at an obstruction and to seat himself deeper he would need to use some force. This was where the pain would be involved, he supposed, and the blood. He wiped some sweat from his brow, cursing his nervousness.

He would do Augusta no service by being hesitant now. The thing to do was to take it at a swift clip, a clean break through, shortening the moment of discomfort for her.

'Pet, you know it will hurt, but it will not be for long. Shall you be my brave girl now?'

'Oh . . . I hardly know . . . but I cannot go back now. I want you to deflower me.'

'Than I shall. Trust yourself to me. Shut your eyes and hold your breath and all will be undone in a moment.'

He held her tight about her hips, strung up his resolve to its almightiest height, and thrust.

Oh. He felt her rend, but there was no pain for him, only pleasure as he sank into velvet softness and wet warmth.

Her cry was sharp and she almost escaped his grip, but he kept a tight hold and, once he was fully sheathed, she fell forward on her arms, panting hard.

'I'm sorry, pet,' he whispered. 'Was it very painful?'

'The pain was not fierce. It was the fearful anticipation that made it seem the more so. Now there is an ache. Or . . . not an ache. A throb. A rawness, but it recedes in intensity as time passes. I do not know if it proceeds from my flesh or yours.'

'If I withdraw, perhaps you will know,' he offered.

'No, no, do not. For all the smart, I want you to stay inside me. I want to keep this feeling, to commit it to my memory, in case I may never have it again.'

He looked down at the sight of his thick root, implanted inside her, beneath her round, pink bottom cheeks and knew that his offer had not been made in earnest anyway. How could he withdraw from this? His cock would not stand for going anywhere until it had spent itself in this sweet, tight passage. Already it felt so sensitive that he feared he might end this delightful odyssey too soon. It would be as well to take this slowly, even now the walls were breached and fallen.

'Allow yourself to become accustomed to the feeling,' he said. 'Just let me stay here, inside you, against you, a part of you. Know that I have changed you.'

'Oh, yes, you have changed me,' she said blissfully. 'I am altered now, for all time. I am a woman. Your woman.'

He essayed an experimental movement inside her, not a thrust, more a fractional rotation. She sucked in her breath but did not flinch.

'It is sore,' she said. 'What happens next? If it is as your books describe, you must set to work in me.'

'Can you withstand it?'

'I think so. You know I do not mind a little pain.' She let out a little laugh, but it seemed to require some effort still. 'When this is done, I will be happy to feel the proof between my legs for a day or so. I want that, sir. I crave it.'

She could drive him wild with words. They were well suited, he realised vaguely, pulling slowly backwards, ready to take her in earnest. Lovers of words. Words of lovers. Depraved in equal measure, one with desires as dark as the other.

'Oh Lord,' he said, his voice burdened with lust, and then he drove into her. Not as hard as one of his characters might, for he didn't want to chafe her tender passage, but hard enough that she would feel it and cry out.

The sight of his rod of flesh, glistening with her juices, entering the clasp of her cunny, was inflaming in the extreme. He supposed he ought to try and make things last, but there was little realistic prospect of Augusta achieving her release the first time, even if he . . . yes . . . put his fingers to her clitoris and—

She moaned, twisting and bucking in front of him.

He could at least try her.

The fingering of her distracted his mind just enough to prevent him spending in indecent haste. He found her more accommodating now, her muscles no longer clenching reflexively against his thrusts. The pain must be receding. It meant he could drive deeper, relent to his primitive urges.

He cupped her nether lips in his palm and pressed against the soaked split, grinding the heel of his hand into her as he felt his pleasure rise to its peak.

'Taken,' he muttered, losing the sharper edges of his concentration. 'Taken.'

He must pull out now or it would be too late.

It was a cruel wrench, to leave her tight embrace, but he managed to deny himself, removing just in time to shower her bottom with his emission.

This sight, his seed coating her upthrust curves, pale liquid dripping down the fading red skin, was almost a compensation for the necessity of withdrawing. Almost.

He knelt up until the last drop was drained from him, then he lay down on his front, his face beside Augusta's, and turned to her.

'Let me kiss your mouth,' he said.

She let him.

Chapter Five

It could not be love, could it?

James, lying on his bed at dawn, contemplated the cracks in the ceiling plaster, and tried to think. In order to discount love, he must make an inventory of all the components that made up his peculiar bond with Augusta.

There was physical attraction, on his part. Yes, she was handsome enough that she would have caught his eye in the street. Their contract was no hardship to him. As for her, could she experience such a thing, when she could not see his face? It certainly seemed as if she could. Was it his scent, or the feel of him, the tone of his voice, the words he spoke? The words he wrote? What did she feel for him?

He knew also that he liked her and admired her instinct for the right words to say, the right way to present herself in submission to him. Those women that he had been fortunate to hint at this kind of treatment in the past had never hit quite the perfect note. They had been too coarse or too coy, not as forthcoming with their bodies or their expressions of obedience. They had been too ashamed or not enough. Submission, for him, was a very subtle art and he could only assume that domination was no less.

Yet he seemed to be exactly what she wanted too.

And here was where it became complicated. This was the thing they had, the thing so close to love. Affinity. But was it love? How did it differ?

He climbed out of bed and padded over to his desk, taking paper from the drawer and pen and ink from the shelf.

'*It is not, and cannot be, love,*' he wrote.

'*Item: I am flattered by her attentions for she is a lady of fortune and I am scarcely even a gentleman of any sort.*

'*Item: She retains me for a specific purpose, which is to explore the sensations of coupling with a male partner. I am merely that – the male partner.*

'*Item: It is inevitable that strong feelings are aroused by the nature of our dealings with one another – the infliction of pain &c. Those strong feelings do not necessarily imply a meeting of soul mates.*

'*Item: She has stated that she will never marry.*

'*Item: Any public exposure of our connection would result in scandal and ruin for her.*

'*Item: It is impossible.*'

He put down his pen and sighed, washed over with a sense of desolation he had not expected. After a moment of re-reading his words, he returned to his writing.

'*It is, and must be, love,*' he wrote.

'*Item: I think of her constantly and cannot bear the prospect of ending this arrangement.*

'*Item: I am a fool.*'

He then threw down the pen for good and paced about the room for a while, until he heard stirrings from the street outside and determined to dress and buy himself a toasted kipper and a jar of coffee for breakfast.

While he dressed, he thought of his last parting from Augusta.

Mrs Shaw had rapped at the bedroom door and ordered him to prepare to leave in the carriage.

'I want him to stay,' pleaded Augusta. 'Might he not stay the night and leave before dawn?'

James had been almost afraid at the look Mrs Shaw gave him when she entered the room. A blade straight between his ribs.

In the weeks since his visits had begun, James and Augusta had grown closer and tighter, until their bond threatened the older woman's equilibrium. She was jealous of him, it was clear enough.

She spoke more and more cruelly and humiliatingly of Augusta when the three of them were together, referring to her as a 'slave to the male member' and a 'cockslut whore'. At first, James found this rather piquant but now it disquieted him. The words seemed intended to bring Augusta to her senses and make her realise how disgusting men were.

'Have him leave while the milk is being delivered? Are you out of your senses, Quim? You have no say in this. I command you to take your leave of him, or face painful consequences.'

It occurred to James that he could just as easily have forbidden Augusta to banish him from her house. She accepted his mastery of her, and it would be a relief to her to obey his order, which was also her own dear wish. But to set himself in direct opposition and rivalry to Mrs Shaw would not be kind to Augusta. Her desire to have him stay was a foolish whim and no more. The wisest course of action was to leave.

All the same, the look of cold triumph on Mrs Shaw's face

as he walked through the bedroom door, away from a sighing Augusta, rankled in his memory.

What gave her this hold over Augusta? And what if she decided his visits should end?

With vague unease, he shaved and trimmed his whiskers, then he put on his coat and boots and stole down the creaky stairs to the street door.

His uncle stood behind the shop counter already, although he would not open for business for at least three more hours.

'Good to see you up with the lark, Jem,' he said. 'You'll recall that you have a piece to give me for typesetting today. I hope it will not be late.'

'No, uncle, all is in hand,' said James.

'I found this shoved under the door a moment ago,' said the elder Stratton, proffering a folded piece of paper. 'A rum kind of thing – all dots and bumps. No writing. What do you make of it?'

James grabbed it and stared.

'Braille,' he said.

It must be from her.

'Braille? The blind writing system?'

'Yes, the one. When was it left?'

'As I say, a moment or so ago, no more. Jem.'

But he was gone, out into the narrow lane, looking desperately left and right for signs of the messenger.

It was early enough that the street was almost empty and, despite the lowering gloom that never quite lifted – the gift of the overhanging gables – James saw a trim figure in a poke bonnet fingering clothes on the rails that Old Abraham was putting out in front of his rag shop.

He dashed over the cobbles, calling her name.

'Paulette! Is it you?'

She turned, alarmed, and shrank away from the rails, but James put out a hand and caught her elbow.

'Don't go, Paulette. You delivered this to me.' He waved the Braille manuscript in front of her abashed face.

'Yes, I did. And now I must be getting back.'

'So soon? It is early.'

'Early's when the work's hardest, sir. There's grates to lead and steps to scrub. If I don't get back soon, Mrs Shaw'll—'

'Devil take Mrs Shaw. You shall come for a drink with me, Paulette. Please. I would esteem it a great favour.'

Now roses of pink bloomed in her cheeks and she fidgeted with her cuffs.

'I shouldn't, sir, but . . . just a very quick one.'

'Thank you. Just up at Covent Garden, I believe there is a public house that serves at this hour. It will be full of costers but they won't trouble you if you are with a man. Come on.'

'It don't sound very respectable, sir.'

He laughed, drawing her up the lane towards the market.

'Unlike the household in which you serve, Paulette.'

She had no reply to that but a discomfited sniff.

'I wonder what this message can possibly say,' he said, putting the letter in front of his face and frowning at it. 'It was given to you by Lady Augusta, I take it?'

'Yes, sir.'

'To deliver to me?'

'That's right.'

'You appear to know where I live.'

'Her Ladyship knows the name of the bookshop she gets your stories from, sir.'

'And she told you I lived there?'

'No, she didn't know that, sir. Neither did I.'

'You can stop calling me sir, if you please. I am not your master.'

'No, sir. Sorry, sir. It's habit now.'

'I wonder if Lady Augusta told you anything of what is contained in this message?'

'She said she hoped you'd find a way to understand it. Seeing as you mixes with bookish people, you know. But if you couldn't, it was no matter. But she'd wait for you, all the same.'

'Wait for me?'

'I didn't like to question her, sir. She gets out of sorts sometimes, especially when Mrs Shaw's been . . . more than her usual . . . self.'

James smiled grimly to himself. Now he had his little informant in his hand, he would see that he squeezed as much as he could from her.

They arrived at a corner house, a pile of barrows parked outside, from which the sounds of music and loud laughter spilled, as if it existed in a place outside the regular rhythms of life and thought it still half past ten at night.

Inside, raucous costers taking a break from trading their wares mixed with off-duty whores enjoying a post-work nightcap.

'What will you have? I shan't buy you gin at this hour,' he warned.

'Oh, I don't drink. I'd like a ginger ale, please.'

He found a quiet spot for them, away from the rowdiest groups, and sat down beside her in their corner.

She had taken off her shawl, revealing her pristine maid's outfit, drawing a few curious looks from the surrounding drinkers. James knew better than to meet the eye of a tanked-up costermonger, though, and he ignored the attention.

'I wonder if I can count you as a friend,' he said thought-fully, contemplating her over the rim of his glass of warm rum punch.

'Oh, yes, ever so,' replied Paulette warmly. 'I hope you will, sir.'

'You are a good servant to your mistress, I know.'

'Thank you.'

'To whom do you think I refer when I say "your mistress"?' he challenged.

She bit her lip at that.

'Well?' he nudged gently.

'Well, Lady Augusta, of course,' she said, but the 'of course' was far from authoritative.

'Lady Augusta, of course,' he repeated thoughtfully. 'Paulette, who is Mrs Shaw?'

'She is Her Ladyship's companion and housekeeper. You know that, sir, I thought.'

'I wonder if I do. How long have you worked at . . .?'

'Eaton Place?'

He had known it, of course, but it was as well to have it confirmed.

'Yes, how long have you worked there?'

'Only a year, sir.'

'Were you hired by Mrs Shaw?'

'Yes, I was.'

'And when did you become aware of the . . . curious nature . . . of the household?'

'Oh, Mrs Shaw made it plain before she employed me, sir.'

James' eyebrows shot up.

'Did she indeed? You knew about their . . . connection?'

'Yes. That was why she picked me from, from . . . where she did.'

'And where was that?'

'Oh, sir, you will think badly of me.'

'Paulette.' He put a hand over hers and tightened his fingers. 'I couldn't think badly of you. Look at how I am situated. Look at the manner of life I lead, here among the worst scoundrels of the city. Look at how I have come to know Lady Augusta, and understand that there is nothing you can say that will shock me.'

'But you're a gentleman.'

'I am not a gentleman. I can dress the part and speak the part but I am certainly no better than you when we are reduced to our bare essences.'

'You don't believe that, do you?'

'Most assuredly I do.' He bent his head closer to Paulette's. 'Whisper it.'

She looked, for a moment, as if she might break down in tears, then she turned her lips to his ear and said, 'The charity home in Little Ormond Street, sir. The Society for the Improvement of Fallen Girls and Women. The Fallen, as they calls it.'

She turned her face away immediately and made to stand, but he held her by her upper arm, preventing flight.

'Don't run away,' he reproached. 'I know what that place is and I do not judge you.'

'Truly?' She was tearful now, and he handed her his handkerchief to blot out the falling drops.

'You have my word, as a not-quite-gentleman.' He paused, allowing her a moment to collect herself, then persisted with the line of enquiry. 'So Mrs Shaw deliberately sought out staff from amongst the ranks of the . . . penitent fallen?'

'We are all from there, sir, at Eaton Place. She knows we'll turn a blind eye to what goes on, you see.'

'Yes, I do see,' said James, ruminating on the phrase 'to turn a blind eye' and finding it ironically apt in the circumstances. 'Everyone is blind in that house, to one degree or other, but Mrs Shaw. She is the one who sees.'

'I suppose, sir, in a manner of speaking.'

He abandoned his efforts to make her leave off calling him 'sir'. Besides, it was pleasing to his ear.

'And she is intent on keeping me blind, too. Sometimes with blindfolds and sometimes by other means. She fears Augusta's attachment to me, don't you think?'

'I, sir? Oh, I cannot say.' Paulette looked a little afraid now and she looked about the bar room as if expecting Mrs Shaw to loom from the fly-spotted mirror with the Tanqueray Gin monogram.

'Where does she come from? Do you know anything of her past?'

'Nothing, sir. I should not dare ask.'

James smiled, a little cruelly, at that.

'Does she ever whip you, Paulette?'

Paulette's cheeks and neck flooded with deep pink.

'Oh, she does? She's a scoundrel, if a woman can be called such a thing. You know, I rather admire her. But I think her hold on Augusta an unhealthy one.'

'Do you?' The girl perked up at this, looking at James with a species of adoration.

At once he saw that this girl viewed him as a saviour; the one who would deliver her from the depredations of the tyrant. *Well, this could be of use to me.*

'I rather think I do,' he said. 'And we can't have her whipping you, can we, Paulette? That's simply cruel.'

'There's nothing we can do about it, see,' she said, wringing her hands. 'Else we'll get packed back off to the

Fallen without characters. She can say anything – that she caught us with the coachman, anything – and then the Fallen won't even have us back. And then we're on the streets again. Do you see, sir? Oh, please don't mention my name in any of this. You won't, will you?'

'Of course not, my dear.'

She pinked more pleasurably at his epithet and moved closer to him.

'I still think you're a gentleman,' she said.

Their confabulation was broken up in a most disorderly manner by a brace of staggering women in *maquillage* and low-cut gowns.

'Oi, Jem,' said one, then she stopped short, peering at Paulette. ''Ere, it's Polly, ain't it?'

'Paulette,' she said fiercely, then she stood to go. 'I must be off, sir. I'll be missed directly and then heaven knows how Mrs Shaw'll take on.'

'Oh, very well. Good bye, then, and we will speak again soon, I trust.'

'I hope,' she said, dropping a half-curtsey before fleeing from the unwanted company.

'Jem,' said the prostitute urgently, recalled to the original matter. 'You've got to help us.'

'Help you? Excuse me, I'm not sure I have the pleasure of your—'

'You're a pal of Annie's, ain't you? She's always talking about you. Anyone'd think you were sweethearts.'

'Yes, yes, I know Annie. What of her?'

'She's been took,' proclaimed the second tart dramatically, waving her gin glass so that some of the precious dew spilled from it.

'What do you mean, "took"?'

'She got into an argument with a punter two nights back, down by the barracks. He wanted something she didn't want to give 'im and he cut up rough, but she wouldn't have him. Anyway, what happens today but he turns up with a rozzer in tow, points the finger at her and accuses her of having the pox.'

'This unsatisfied customer? Reported her to the police as suffering from a venereal disease?'

'If you want to put it like that. Rozzer drags her off to get her examined by a doctor, but she refuses and he says they'll lock her up for three months till she agrees to it! Oh, can't you go and help her out. They listens to gents like you.'

'It's a fucking laugh, this Contagious Diseases Act,' said the other bitterly. 'Any bastard can say what he wants about you. I ain't having no doctor shoving his hand up my cunny. It's not right.'

'Unless 'e pays yer,' the first one prompted.

'That's different. That's business.'

'So,' James cut into the debate, 'you're telling me that Annie is imprisoned somewhere, pending a medical examination she refuses to agree to?'

'Yes, thassright.'

'Where?'

They shook their heads at each other and shrugged.

'The lock hospital,' one suggested.

'Where's that?'

'Harrow Road.'

James stood, a hand clasped to his brow, his thoughts circulating painfully through his head.

'Then I shall go there. Thank you, ladies.'

He strode out of the pub. As he hastened around the corner of the table where he had sat, he knocked a piece of paper to the floor, where it stayed, getting trodden into the muddy, tacky floor by the weight of dozens of feet.

Harrow Road was not close at hand, so he hailed a cab at the corner of Seven Dials and tried to recall all he had read in the press about the Contagious Diseases Act.

A controversial measure passed in the preceding year, it aimed to protect the sexual health of the nation's servicemen by subjecting the women who serviced *them* to regular medical examinations.

If the women refused, or agreed and were found to be infected, they could be confined to the Lock Hospital, which specialised in venereal disease.

An imposing three-storey building taking up a good portion of the land on and around Harrow Road, it struck nonetheless a little of fear into James' heart when he alighted from the cab and faced it.

Here, but for the grace of God, go I.

He had been fortunate, he acknowledged. As a younger man he had not been as cautious as he was now wont to be and, fresh as a face and clean as a frock might be, he now recognised that that was no guarantee of freshness and cleanliness within.

He made his way through the portal arch and turned into an office area on the right of the building, where sat a grizzled old fellow with tired eyes and rumpled neckcloth, making notes in a large ledger.

'I say, I wonder if you could confirm that you have a friend of mine confined here?' opened James, trying to suppress the shudders that always overcame him in any medical establishment. He had had a morbid fear of physicians ever since he broke his ankle jumping from a wall as a boy.

'A friend?' The man looked up, lugubrious in voice and expression. 'The men's hospital is in Dean Street.'

'No, the friend is a lady.'

He laughed at that, as if it were the most amusing thing he'd heard in weeks.

James bit down on his rising impatience.

'She was brought here last night.'

'Does she owe you money? She won't be earning much tonight.'

'I'm not a ponce,' exclaimed James, his temper bursting through his scant restraints. 'If that's what you mean.'

'Begging your pardon, sir, I didn't mean to imply any disrespect. We've had rather a large number of well-dressed gents inquiring after patients since this new rule came in, that's all.'

'It's a shameful rule.'

'Yes, sir, so they all say. What's your friend's name?'

'Annie . . . or Anne, I suppose . . .' He stopped, realising that he had never known her surname. A twinge of guilt disturbed him. He was familiar enough with her to put his prick in her mouth, yet he had never thought to ask her full name.

'Yes? Anne what?'

'I don't know,' he admitted. 'She's my neighbour,' he added defensively when the man seemed about to break into another cackle.

'Well, if you don't know her name . . .'

'Would she not have given her address? For your records?'

James tried to read the words upside down, but the script was not an easy one to decipher.

The man humphed a little, but relented with a resigned, 'What's the street name?'

'Holywell Street, Strand.'

'Oh yes?' He gave James a quizzical look, obviously knowing of the area's ill repute. 'All right. Let me see.'

While the man scanned his ledger, James looked out through the back window, into a large yard. A woman on crutches was taking the air, accompanied by a nurse. She had the most fearful face, half eaten away by the ravages of syphilis.

He shut his eyes, nausea gripping the pit of his stomach. Nausea and fear. What if he had it, unknown and unrecognised, and it festered within him, biding its time . . .? He should never have been so reckless. Never again.

'Ah yes,' said the man with a triumphant air. 'One of a shower brought in a few hours back. Gives her name as Anne Alice Sparrow, aged twenty-two, of Holywell Street, Strand. Ah. She's refused an examination, I see.'

'I can vouch for her. She is free of infection.'

'It isn't as easy as that, sir. She's been remanded for examination and they won't let her go until she agrees to one.'

'Then she's a prisoner.'

'More or less, if that's how you want to put it.'

'It's an outrage. Let me see her. You can't keep her here like a caged animal.'

'No visitors allowed, sir. You'll have to wait for her to come out – that's if they find her clean, of course.'

'But what if she never consents to the examination? I'm sure I wouldn't!'

'Then we'll have the pleasure of her company for the next three months.'

James was momentarily tempted to seize the fellow by his high collar. Did he not understand how appalling this was?

But it would help nobody if he got himself arrested, so

he stood still for a moment, willing the gathering rage to subside.

'This will not end here,' he said calmly. 'I mean to see my friend and take her home, and I will take steps to ensure it.'

'Best of luck to you, sir,' nodded the man, making it clear by the ostentatious polishing of his monocle that the conversation had concluded.

'Good day,' he said.

'I hope you succeed,' the man added, arresting his departure for a moment. 'It's playing havoc with the business of the hospital, all these girls hauled in every night. We don't have the capacity, but neither do we have the right to refuse 'em. If you could see your way to having a word or two with Lord Palmerston on the subject, we'd all be much obliged. Good day, sir.'

Outside, on the pavement, James considered this. Lord Palmerston might not be an accessible ear, but he had an idea that there were other people who would be.

He turned in the direction of Bloomsbury and headed for Little Ormond Street and the Society for the Improvement of Fallen Girls and Women. Here, he saw, he had the opportunity to kill two birds with one stone. He could put himself forward as an advocate against the Contagious Diseases Act, which he knew them to oppose, and he could perhaps find out a little more about their relationship to Mrs Shaw.

Furious thoughts filled his head as he strode the London pavements, at such a pace that he cannoned into a number of street vendors, including a butcher's boy who put up his dukes and challenged him to fisticuffs. But James merely flapped a hand and paced onwards, already halfway through a letter to *The Times*, if only he had a pen and paper.

Ripe words from the butcher's boy sailed unheard past his ears.

At the corner of Little Ormond Street, he signed off with a rhetorical flourish and gave each tall Georgian house his complete attention as he read the plaques by the doors. The Fallen took up half of one side of the street.

He was not sure if it truly had a vaguely mournful air or if he projected it on to the building himself, knowing the histories of blight and misery that lay behind the stones. It was not, perhaps, quite as shiver-inducing as the Lock Hospital, but it still laid weights on his heart as he ascended the steps.

Perhaps he should seek a bed here himself. Was there a Society for the Improvement of Fallen Men and Boys? For if the offering of sexual services constituted fall and ruin, then was he not himself fallen and ruined?

But he was in no mood for riddles or paradoxes.

The maid who answered the door stared at him as if afraid.

'I . . . wish to speak with a member of the Society,' he said. 'Is there somebody I could see?'

'If you are not a doctor, you mayn't come in,' whispered the girl. 'Unless you have an appointment.'

'I have no appointment, but I have urgent business. I entreat you, please ask if anybody is free to speak with me.'

'Oh, I shouldn't,' she said, wringing her hands, but after a moment she seemed to think better of her hesitation and bade him wait a moment.

Presently, a handsome, well-dressed woman of perhaps forty years appeared at the door. When she saw James, she frowned.

'What can your urgent business be, I wonder?' she said.

'May I come in and tell you?'

'No. I am extremely busy. But you may make an appointment, if you wish. What is your concern?'

'My friend and neighbour has been forcibly removed to the Lock Hospital. I wish to lend my voice to your campaign against the Contagious Diseases Act.'

'You would like to become a patron of the society?'

'I . . . yes, I think so. That is, I am not rich and can offer only my *voice*, as I have said, but . . .'

'Oh, yes, moral support is all well and good. Though, of course, many would argue with the *moral* part of that. What influence do you have?'

James opened and shut his mouth, then said, with perfect authority, 'I am a journalist.'

'The press?' The woman's eyes lit up. 'Are you perhaps free this evening, Mr . . .?'

'Stratton. James Stratton. Yes, I am available.'

'Then come back after seven. I can receive you then.'

'Thank you, madam.'

'My name is Mrs Edwards.'

'I am obliged to you. Until this evening, then.'

He tipped his hat and observed how her face lost its somewhat sombre cast when she smiled, which she did before closing the door.

He couldn't help wondering if she was a friend of Mrs Shaw's. There was a likeness in dignity and demeanour between the two women.

He stopped dead halfway along Long Acre and slapped his hand to his forehead.

Augusta's message!

Where was it? And, more to the point, *what* was it?

He had no luck at the tavern and was forced to shrug his shoulders and return to Holywell Street empty-handed.

'Do you know of any blind men, uncle?' he asked abruptly, pushing into the shop, which was mercifully empty of customers.

His uncle looked up from the pictures he was regarding with an eyeglass, as if he were a Hatton Garden jeweller inspecting diamonds, and shook his head.

'I'd pity them if I did,' he said. 'For he'd never be able to look at these. See, James, new pictures from Lusher's studio.'

James waved his hand, impatient.

'Never mind that,' he said.

'You surprise me, nephew. You usually enjoy his work.'

'Did you know that Annie has been taken away?'

'Taken away? What do you mean? Little doxy owes me a week's rent.'

'I'll pay it. She's in the Lock Hospital. They won't release her until she consents to a medical examination of an . . . intimate nature.'

Thomas Stratton tugged at the ends of his moustache and shook his head, as if rebuking his nephew for mentioning such subjects. The fact that he held in his other hand a collection of lewd daguerreotypes did not apparently strike him as ironic.

'Unfortunate,' he said. 'But an occupational hazard, I'm afraid.'

'It never used to be. And it shouldn't be now.'

'Since when did you become so involved with the rights of whores?'

'I am involved with the rights of *people*, uncle. All people. Not just those society deems worthy of notice.'

His uncle raised his eyebrows and put the pictures back on the counter.

'Where's that piece you owe me?'

'Oh . . . that. Look, could it wait until tomorrow?'

'No, it could not. Your client is calling this afternoon. I suggest you shut yourself in your room and glue yourself to that desk until it's done, or you'll be seeking alternative accommodation. Perhaps you can go and join the whores at the Lock Hospital, since you enjoy their company so much.'

James spent a thunderous three hours writing a story, savage even for him, in which a woman forced to prostitute herself took revenge on society by whipping a rich client until he bled. This, fortunately, would be entirely to this particular reader's taste. He tied a furious knot around it, marched downstairs and threw it on his uncle's counter, just as the customer in question arrived at the door.

'Good afternoon,' growled James, passing him on his way to the street.

He didn't wait for the client's surprised tipping of hat or return of greeting but proceeded up the street, back to Covent Garden.

The market had ended for the day, save for the usual cabbage leaves and orange peel blowing around the cobbles and settling in the gutters. What could be seen of the sky was overcast and soon the rain would turn all into stinking mush.

In the pub, trade was desultory, the costers having gone home to bed while it was yet early for most of the whores. He called for a brandy and water and then another, and another again, until he recollected that he had an appointment with Mrs Edwards, who would no doubt refuse to admit a drunken man into her sanctum.

He spent the remainder of that afternoon in walking up and down the city streets, anxious to clear his head, which was in a tempest of ire and frustration and, at the back of it, a yearning for Augusta that would not let him be.

What could the message have said? He had half a mind to hotfoot it to Eaton Place and demand entrance. But of course, then they would know that he knew the location and presumably that would alter matters significantly.

Well, perhaps it was time that they *were* altered.

Now could not be the time, though, for it was close to seven o'clock.

He turned back to Bloomsbury and was on the Fallen House step promptly, with peppermint on his breath and determination in his heart.

He was shown by the same shy girl he had seen before into an office to the side of the lobby. The building was eerily quiet. He looked about him, expecting to see the eyes of fallen women upon him, but there were none.

'Mr Stratton,' said Mrs Edwards, rising from her desk, where she had been occupied with correspondence.

'Thank you for receiving me, Madam,' he said, bowing before taking his indicated seat. 'Your kindness is much appreciated.'

She smiled, a formal kind of smile.

'What do you know of our work?' she asked.

'Very little. I have heard of groups of people walking the streets in search of girls to save – I presume that those with whom they find success must reside here. If that's the case, then they are very quiet.'

'Our women live in a separate building behind this one, but the upstairs rooms are used for learning during the daytime.'

'What manner of learning?'

'Reading, writing. Very many of these girls have not received a whit of education in their entire lives.'

He thought of Annie.

'My friend is one such. I have myself given her lessons in the alphabet.' He coloured faintly, remembering how those lessons frequently ended.

'Ah, the friend of whom you spoke.'

'Yes, she who lies even now in the Lock Hospital, quite friendless and alone.'

'She will not be alone. The Lock Hospital is always over-crowded and now more than ever.' Mrs Edwards permitted herself a modest smile.

James didn't consider her remark very amusing, but he bit back his retort.

'Yes, but you are in sympathy with her plight, are you not?'

'I am indeed. As are many others. We will be happy to add your voice to the dissenting chorus. Unfortunately, those in government seem disinclined to accept our point that a fallen woman is still a human being entitled to dignity at present. But I am hopeful that, with God's help, we will prevail.'

James wasn't sure whether God had a great deal to do with it, but he nodded vigorously.

'I shall write an article,' he said.

'That would be marvellous,' said Mrs Edwards, warming a little. 'To which newspaper are you attached?'

'Oh, none, that is, I am freelance.'

'I see.' The moment of warmth passed into memory.

'I have had pieces in the *Examiner* and *Lloyd's Weekly*,' he hastened to add. 'And shall have many more.'

'Nothing in *The Times*?'

'No. That is, not yet.'

'You are an ambitious young man, I suppose.'

'I am both ambitious and able, I hope.'

She sat back and surveyed him. What a quietly powerful presence she radiated, James thought. She was like a queen, and something like Mrs Shaw, though without the malevolent aura.

'Well, you have a chance to prove your mettle, Mr Stratton. Write your piece. Sell it to *The Times*, or one of the popular magazines. *All The Year Round*, perhaps. The fact that you are personally acquainted with a victim of this vile piece of legislation will perhaps count against rather than for you, but it will pique interest. Of course, you must not be blunt but allusive or it will not sell to anybody. But I'm sure you don't need me to tell you that. No words that would be deemed unfit for a lady's ears.'

She sighed.

'I am not often the best judge of such things,' said James with a rueful twitch of his lips.

'Then perhaps you should give it to me first, for my approval. Come to me tomorrow – I will show you around and introduce you to some of the girls.'

'Thank you. I will. In the meantime, is there nothing that can be done for Annie?'

Mrs Edwards shook her head.

'The law is the law, until we are able to unmake it. There will be no rioting in the streets, but reason will be our weapon, Mr Stratton, reason and compassion.'

'This is an age of reason,' said Stratton, 'but I am less confident that it is one of compassion.'

'And I also. But do not despair. Would you like tea? I cannot offer anything stronger, for we practise temperance here, but tea . . .'

'Oh, no, that will not be necessary. I do have a question, however . . .'

She had already risen to call for the maid, but sank back into her chair at his request.

'About our work here?'

'About a former resident.'

Mrs Edwards did not speak, neither was her expression encouraging, but he ploughed on nonetheless.

'Her name is Paulette, or Polly. She was hired from here to work in a house in Eaton Place by a woman named Shaw.'

Mrs Edwards' face became hard and closed; her words came as from a grindstone.

'If, after all, you are here to enquire after some sweetheart—'

'No, that is not it. Not at all.'

'Then what is it you wish to know?'

'The woman, Shaw. Are you acquainted with her?'

'She is one of a number of patronesses who have given our girls respectable places.'

'So you know her personally?'

Mrs Edwards was silent awhile.

'I will open this house to you tomorrow on the condition that you will write a sympathetic piece,' she said.

'Yes, of course, but—'

'I am not well acquainted with the name you mention. I cannot assist you further and, even if I could, I would not think it proper.' She rose. 'Tomorrow, then.'

'Oh. Yes. Tomorrow.'

He took her offered hand and shook it across the desk, then watched as she rang for the maid.

Darkness had fallen as he took a south-westerly path towards the Strand, but at Holborn he reconsidered his route and walked along Shaftesbury Avenue instead, crossing Seven Dials into Soho and beyond.

In Eaton Place the shutters were closed but light illumined the cracks between wood and window frame and he thought Augusta must be sitting upstairs, waiting for him.

But it was not his day to visit, and Mrs Shaw would not expect it. What had that note said?

He went to the rear of the Palladian row and through a stone arch into the mews. These were still populated here and there with a few ostlers and some carriagemen awaiting their masters and mistresses from whichever fine gathering they might be attending in one or other of the houses.

In the windows above the stables, candles flickered, the families of the ostlers preparing for the night. The sparse light it cast on the ground led James to the back of Augusta's house. There seemed no way to it other than through the carriage house, which was shut up for the night.

Looking around, he made sure nobody observed him before lifting the latch gently from the door. It was not locked. He slipped inside and made his way past the carriage and a row of snorting horses, breathing in the aroma of rotting straw and horse manure, before coming out through a back door into a small formal garden area.

The house loomed above him like an aggressor, demanding to know his business. He kept to the shadows, tracing his way around the wall until he reached the steps that led down to the kitchen. If he could find Paulette . . .

Peering through the glass in the door he saw that the kitchen was in darkness. A movement caught his eye, but it was merely a cat yawning and stretching in its basket.

He sat on the bottom step and raked his fingers through his hair. This was a stupid mistake. What on earth was he thinking of? He ought to go home, go to bed, come back on Thursday, at the usual time.

But if he went to bed, he would lie awake, wondering about the message, fretting about Annie, revisiting the endless frustrations of the day.

What was the worst result that could derive from coming here and being found out by Mrs Shaw? She was not, after all, mistress of the house. If Augusta wished to see him, then how could her companion and housekeeper prevent it?

All the same, if he caused a rift between them, then he might precipitate a crisis in all of their lives. Was he prepared for this?

Was he prepared to continue in his role of . . . of whatever he was? He looked down at himself. Surely he was more to Augusta than male flesh ordered up for her pleasure? But perhaps he was not. It seemed that the time had come to find out, at any rate.

Moving around the large glassed bay of the ballroom, he came to the other side and found – Could this be true? – a sash window open just an inch or so at the bottom. The room it looked into was a small chamber of the breakfasting sort, not that James had ever sat in such a room himself. It was in darkness, the furniture outlined in the gloom. He put his palms upward beneath the window and forced it higher.

Once inside, he tried to recall the layout of the house. All was silent, but that was not to say that everybody was asleep. He knew from Augusta that Mrs Shaw liked to send her to bed early and exhausted and then stay up half the night in her first-floor study. The staff slept at the top of the house and could not be expected to hear him creeping about down here.

Nonetheless, he had to take his courage in both hands and hold it tight in order to cross the big polished expanse of the ballroom knowing that, should somebody come in, there was nowhere to hide. When was this room ever used? Had Augusta ever danced?

All the same, it was in perfect condition, reeking of beeswax and festooned with *jardinières* full of fresh flowers, as if company were expected at any moment.

He reached the staircase, heart tight in his chest, and tiptoed up, listening out for the merest creak. At the top, he looked in the direction of Mrs Shaw's study. The door was shut. He crept closer and bent to look through the keyhole. Only unrelieved blackness met his eye, but this may only mean that the key was in the lock. All the same, the room was quiet, no scratching of nibs or rustling of paper to be heard.

He straightened up and walked past the 'schoolroom' towards Augusta's bedchamber.

At the door, he put a hand over his mouth, suddenly nauseous.

This was lunacy. Even if she were alone, he would terrify her. But he had not come all this way and taken all these risks to turn tail now. Whatever had been in that message might have been crucial. Life and death could hang upon it. Unlikely, of course, but still . . .

He turned the handle, as slowly and carefully as he could with a trembling and sweaty hand.

All was darkness and silence within. He shut the door, blessing the well-oiled state of the handle, and stood against it, accustoming himself to the gloom.

'Somebody is there. Who is it?'

The clarity and purpose of the voice shocked him so that he shivered.

Augusta had not been asleep at all. But of course, she had no lamp lit, for there was no need – he had forgotten.

'It is I, pet. Do not fear.'

'Oh! You have come.'

The joy in her voice impelled him towards it. She was not in the bed but sitting close to the window in a little chair upholstered with Chinese silk.

'You expected me?'

'Of course. But I did not hear you ring.'

He took her hands and pulled her to her feet, holding her against him for a moment before seeking the liberty of a kiss, which – Oh, wonder of wonders! – she granted.

'The note you sent – it was an invitation?'

'You did not manage to translate it? I felt sure you would know somebody who could do so. I have been sitting here waiting for your step in the street that I might go down and open the door to you.'

'You would know me by my tread?'

'I would. I know your boot soles so well.'

'So soon!'

'I love to hear them. So you did not understand my message but you came anyway?'

'Via the back. A window was a little open.'

Augusta laughed, a high, excited sound – it seemed to James that she was more than a little giddy.

'Hush, Mrs Shaw will hear us.'

'Oh, but that is why I invited you. Mrs Shaw has been called away for a few days, on family business. She does not expect to return until Tuesday.'

'I see.'

'The letter was merely the address, and the information about Mrs Shaw. Could you not have found somebody to read it? Mrs Shaw says you live in a street of booksellers.'

'Alas, none of our books have sold to blind customers. Other than yourself. But could you not have told Paulette?'

'I am not always certain of her allegiance. She fears Mrs Shaw and owes her this place too.'

'But you are her mistress?'

'Am I? Sometimes it seems—'

'You gave Mrs Shaw her position of authority over you because it pleased you to do so. She is not your mistress in fact.'

'The lines have become so blurred of late, my love. And since I have met you . . .'

They kissed again and James led her to the bed, on which they sat to continue their conversation.

'Am I then to hide from your servants? Am I a secret, not to be revealed?'

Augusta's fingers twisted against his.

'It is not what I would wish but . . .'

James slid his hand around her waist, noticing that she wore only her nightdress.

'And what would you wish, Augusta?'

'Oh, call me pet, for that is my name when you are with me.'

'Very well.' He sighed, feeling not quite an entire man, constricted as he was by the role she chose for him. 'What would you wish, pet?'

'I would wish to be yours.'

'But you are mine.'

'To be yours alone, and to have no care of what the world might think.'

James was silent, laying her head on his shoulder and smoothing down her long braid of hair with his palm as he thought about the peculiar position in which he found himself.

'You mean to tell me that you love me?' he said at last.

'Don't speak it,' she said. 'Don't refer to it at all if you cannot say the same.'

'Pet, I have come here for you. I have broken into your house! How can you think I have no regard for you?'

She nuzzled her forehead in the hollow of his shoulder.

'I have no way of knowing,' she said softly. 'I cannot see your eyes. And I have nothing in the way of experience. I have never loved, or been loved before.'

'Oh, pet, *never*? I am not sure I can believe that. What of your parents?'

'I was a disappointment to them. When I lost my sight, they lost their hopes for me.'

'How old were you, when that came to pass?'

'I was but a child of six or seven.'

'And had you a blow to the head? Or what was the cause?'

'I don't remember. A blow to the head apparently. I simply . . . don't know.'

'A life without sight. I have tried to imagine it but, notwithstanding my gifts in that direction, I find it defeats me.'

He held her cheek, looking steadfastly into her unseeing eyes. How different would this feel if the eyes were lively with warmth and desire? Would his regard for her be stronger? Was he such a weak specimen of a man that he allowed himself to be swayed by this one deficiency?

'I'm not sure I completely understand what love is,' he said. 'But I have felt close to it at times. Now is one such time.'

'You are telling me that you are faithless.'

'No, I am not faithless. I am not.'

'Give me your faithless kiss again.'

Her lips were so soft. He felt the curves of her body

through the nightdress, and the warmth of her turned his head. What was love more than this raw need for her, this want that never quite lost its edge, day after day and all through the night?

And yet there could be no future.

His blood swept all such reservations aside as it rushed through him, impelling him to consider only the present. She was here, in his arms, ready to accept whatever he had to give her. It could be days or weeks before such a precious chance came again, or it could even be the last time. There was nothing to do but follow the commands of their bodies.

'Take off your gown,' he murmured, moving his lips to her ear. 'Or raise your arms that I might do it.'

Mutely she obeyed and he uncovered her, noticing how her skin seemed to gleam in the darkness.

'Your lips are mine,' he said, taking them once more while his hands made a feverish transit of her curves.

'These are mine.' He held her breasts and kissed them each in turn, tonguing the nipples until they stood as stiff as could be.

'And all of you is mine.' He pushed her gently to her back, dipping his hand between her thighs, which she parted without demur.

'Do you know this to be true?' He crouched over her, urgently needing to possess her, to drive home his point.

'I know it,' she breathed. 'I know I am yours. You may do as you will with me.'

But did she mean it? And what did she mean by it? He pushed the question away, to be asked later, afterwards, once the insistent nag of his loins had been sated.

He threw off his coat and wrenched his neckcloth from his collar, interspersing the shedding of each garment with kissing and fondling, sometimes languid, sometimes savage. She plucked at his buttons, helping him with his waistcoat, rising up to meet his lips and teeth, wrapping her leg around him to keep him close.

'Here is my body,' she whispered intensely as she tugged his shirt from his waistband. 'Here is my self. It is for you.'

He took her wrists and pinned her down, kissing all over her face and neck and then down to her breasts. His lower body, still in trousers, ground into her, giving a foretaste of what was to come.

'Don't,' he growled, 'make offers you cannot honour. If you tell me you are mine, you must mean it.'

'I do. I do mean it.'

He freed himself from his trousers, then ordered her not to move a muscle while he dealt with what remained of his clothing.

She lay rapt, chest rising and falling quickly, arms above her head with the delicate, vulnerable sides of her wrists upwards. So pale, like blank white paper. He wanted to blemish her, put his mark on her, write his history into her skin.

She was one of his erotic fantasies made flesh, risen from the page. What should he do with her? The array of options was dizzying. What should he do with her *first*?

He knelt up, braced his arms beneath her knees, drawing them up and wide apart, then swooped down to taste the sweet juices in their downy nest.

She shuddered and cried out, half rising.

'Hush, lie down,' he ordered, raising his face for a moment.

'Oh, what are you doing to me?'

'You have done this before?'

'Nobody has done it to me, though Mrs Shaw has ordered it done to her.'

'Then Mrs Shaw is very selfish. Hush now. Let me take my fill of you.'

With a tremble of a sigh, she lay back down and devoted herself to receiving James' oral attentions. He meant to be thorough and to take her to her peak at least once, or twice if it could be effected. The taste of her was surprisingly clean, a pure effusion of liquid desire, and he laved enthusiastically. She had so many hidden crevices and furrows to explore and he performed his task without reservation, pouring hot breath on to her most intimate parts. Her pearl was fat and rich and it seemed to grow still bigger against his tongue. He bathed two fingers in the flowing juices and then set to thrusting them slowly in and out of her while he licked.

Her ever more desperate squirms made him smile and suck all the harder on her bud.

'Oh, too much, it is too much, I shall . . .'

She writhed like a dervish and he put his free hand firmly on her hip, gripping it. His fingers continued with relentless rhythm and his tongue drew firm strokes across her clitoris until, seconds later, he scented victory and held her tight while she came undone, all the struggle leaving her body until she subsided into the deep peace of completion.

At which point he started licking her again.

'Oh, you mustn't,' she gasped. 'It is too much, too much . . .'

He broke off to warn her. 'Do you tell me what I must and must not do, pet?'

'No, but, oh, I shan't be able to bear it!'

'You shall bear it, because I shall make you. You know this, don't you? Hmm?'

'Oh . . . yes . . . but . . . *argh!*'

Enjoying her pitch of pleasurable discomfort, he went at

her with a will. She bucked and thrashed like a snake pinned by a predator, but he put a stop to that by turning her over and smacking her behind until his palm prints glowed red.

She settled down for him after that and resigned herself to being licked and tasted and probed until he had satisfied himself that she was completely tamed.

Her second spending was a great triumph to him and he heaved a long sigh of contentment into her poor, over-stimulated folds.

He lay upon her and kissed her own flavour into her mouth, long and ravishingly, his hands in her hair. He knew that she would refuse him nothing now, her will quite bent to his by the force of the pleasure he had wrung from her.

'Turn over, my love,' he whispered.

He helped her on to her stomach and kissed the back of her neck, nipping at the soft flesh that he found when he pushed aside her hair.

With one forearm beneath her stomach, he raised her gently to her knees, keeping her spine sloped downwards and her face in the pillow.

'All is dark,' he said, running his hands up and down her thighs. 'Do you know what I am going to do to you?'

'I do not,' she whispered.

'I could do so many things – I am almost unable to make a choice.'

'Do you mean to chastise me, sir?'

'No, pet. I am pleased with you. You called for me. You did well. You have had your reward and now I mean to take my pleasure.'

He took his member in hand and introduced it to the slippery passage between Augusta's legs, so temptingly displayed for him. It was easy now, after that first time, to glide into the well-lubricated sleeve. She gripped him, warm and tight, and he shut his eyes to let the sensations burst individually in the darkness of his consciousness. He moved one hand to her breasts and toyed with them while he established his rhythm, languidly at first. Once he was past his first foray, he moved the hand back to her rear and stroked smoothly along the crease. She made sweet little gasps with each thrust into her but she seemed to have no objection to his further explorations in that other furrow. He dug deeper with his fingers, spreading her cheeks that she might more fully accept him. This was the boldest move he had yet made, and she yielded to it without the least demur.

Her ready submission inflamed him all the more and he grew rough with his handling of her, pounding at her flanks like a man possessed.

'Pet, have you ever taken anything up here?' he asked, pressing his thumb against the tight opening that marked the final destination of his examinings.

'Oh, sir, no, sir.' She squirmed violently, as if only now noticing what he had been about.

'Truly? Mrs Shaw has never opened you here, with any foreign object?'

'No, indeed. Oh heavens. Is it possible? You cannot—'

'I cannot,' he spoke over her, 'call myself your true master until I possess every part of you.'

She inhaled sharply. He continued to beset her with firm thrusts while his thumb rested against that contested aperture.

'Can you not?' she asked, her voice small and meek.

'Indeed I cannot. I intend to breach you, once you are fully prepared. No part of your body is to be your own. Do you mind me, pet?'

'Yes, sir, oh but it is so—'

'I will measure my pace, do not fret. Take time to feel this pressure upon you and to imagine how it will feel when I push down. Think of it, pet, for that day will come, and soon. Think of it.'

His head was becoming light and he knew his end was near. He should withdraw before it was too late.

He twisted his thumb against her clenched ring and enjoyed one last thrust before making the hated retreat. He finished himself at furious pace, splashing his seed upon her proffered bottom, still holding her between her cheeks with his thumb well pressed down.

She sighed, then moved her hips, as if asking him to increase his pressure.

'Did you like that, pet?' he asked in wonder, removing his thumb instead. 'Lie down. I want you to keep my seed upon you until it dries, yes, like that. Keep still.'

He picked up his waistcoat from the side of the bed and rummaged for his handkerchief, using it to wipe himself clean before lying down beside her.

'You did not answer me,' he charged her, kissing her nose and then her lips. 'Are you ashamed?'

'I have never been so used,' she said. Her eyes were shut and he kissed their lids. 'You bring me into a deeper sense of my own self. I cannot resist you yet I sometimes feel you will lead me to my destruction.' She paused, then whispered, 'Yes. I am ashamed.'

He stroked stray hairs from her brow then laid more kisses upon the smooth skin there.

'Shame becomes you,' he said. 'You should embrace it.'

'I do. You know that.'

'Yes. You won't deny me what I demand of you.'

'I could not.'

'Then we will work upon that. I will prepare you. But what will Mrs Shaw think?'

Augusta flinched at the mention of her name.

'Oh, Mrs Shaw,' she sighed. 'Be careful, my angel. She is jealous of you. Having brought you into my orbit, she now wishes to banish you from it. She will not succeed – she has not the authority. She is, at the root of things, my employee. But she will try.'

'If you accept that you are in fact her mistress, you can tell her how to act.'

'She would not then stay. She is proud. She accepts her role here because it gives her the illusion of being mistress of the house.'

'An illusion only.'

'Sometimes it becomes more solid. Sometimes I hardly know myself who is mistress and who servant.'

'When did you engage her?'

'After my mother died. I was sixteen.'

'Excuse my ignorance in such matters, but how did you choose her? Your condition places certain restrictions on you. I suppose you interviewed her?'

'I did interview her. I had my then housekeeper place an advertisement for a lady's companion. She read me the replies and I interviewed on that basis.'

'What was it about Mrs Shaw that drew you to her?'

'She understood exceedingly well how my blindness limited my life and she gave a very good account of how she might be able to help. She was so brisk, so competent – she almost took the choice from me. Which was what I secretly wished for.'

'You chose her because of her domineering manner?'

'Oh, my love, I suppose I did.'

'What became of your housekeeper?'

'She found another position. There was no love lost between her and Mrs Shaw and she felt usurped.'

'Mrs Shaw has altogether too much influence on the running of this household.'

Augusta laughed and pressed herself closer to James before kissing his cheek.

'Do you laugh at me?'

'You speak so much as a husband might. It is as if we lie here in our marital bed, squabbling over what to pay the butcher. I am not altogether averse to it.'

Her final sentence sounded so wistful that James experienced a fleeting sense of guilt. This was what she wished for, yet it was not in his power to offer it.

'Just because you have no sight, does it mean you can never marry? I am sure many blind women make happy marriages,' he said.

'Many blind women with the whole world of men to choose from. I used to dream of finding a husband, if only to spite my cousins who would then be debarred from the inheritance. But I cannot dance, so I cannot go to balls, so I cannot . . .' She ended with a sigh, then took James' hand, threading her fingers with his. 'But I do not care if I can have you. We have a marriage, of a sort, do we not? If it is the most I can hope for, then I shall make the best of it.'

'We have the principal advantage of marriage, which is the pleasure of company,' he said.

'Will you stay with me until morning?'

'Yes.'

'You must take care that you are not seen when you leave.'

She lay quiet in his arms for a spell, then half-sat up. 'How did you know the address?'

'Mrs Shaw's wiles to keep me blindfolded were unsuccessful. She might use your lack of sight to wield power over you but she will have no such advantage over me, trust to it. I do not think she always means you well, pet.'

All was so still. Holywell Street was never so quiet after dark – it was almost noisier then than by day. Cats fought and so did people on the slimy cobbles beneath the overhanging gables. Drunken laughter and singing blew on the wind from the nearby public houses and footsteps, footsteps, footsteps all night long.

What on earth would Augusta, so used to the graveyard quiet of Eaton Place, think of it?

'I depend on her so,' said Augusta after a long pause. 'I have come to rely upon her for so much.'

'I think she has orchestrated your dependency. She fears me because I dilute it.'

'No. I do think she fears you, but not for that reason. For another and tenderer one. She loves me and I do not love her, or at least, not with that species of passion I seem able only to feel for a man. You are that man, and I love you.'

'You should not. I am unworthy.'

'My heart has no knowledge of worth or reason or convenience. It wants its way, and its way points to you.'

'But how can it be, pet? How can it ever be?'

'Oh, I don't know. I wish I did. For tonight, I am content just to sleep in your arms, as true lovers do.'

He held her spooned against him and stroked her hair until she drifted into sleep. Before dawn, he woke her with kisses, mindful of the need to get away from the house unnoticed.

To come to consciousness beside a warm and welcoming body in clean sheets was a new experience for James, who had tended to take his pleasures as he found them, which was usually somewhere inconvenient. The absence of bedbugs or cockroaches in the linen was refreshing.

They tangled and tussled, lip to lip, luxurious and drowsy, until James was sheathed in his mistress's clutch. They rolled across the rumpled bedclothes, hard at rut, trying not to exclaim out loud for fear of disturbing a servant.

'You must never forget that you are mine,' whispered James, putting a hand over Augusta's mouth to silence the ecstatic cries that threatened to pour forth.

Her mouth may have been muffled but there was no mistaking the way she pulsed around him, her body stiffening momentarily before the tide overcame her. He waited for her to stop writhing and become perfectly pliable again before indulging his own pleasure, withdrawing first and spilling across her pale belly and thighs.

'And now my day has begun well,' she said dreamily, amid kisses.

'I hope it shall continue so.'

'Oh, must you go?'

For he had risen and poured water from the pitcher into the ewer on its stand.

'I must. I'm afraid I have business to attend to today.'

'More stories to write?'

'No. Not that kind of business.'

He wondered whether to tell Augusta about Annie and the Fallen House, but a desire to keep the sordid minutiae of his life separate from his time with Augusta made him hesitate, then dismiss the idea.

He splashed cold water over his face and used the

washcloth to clean his naked body. It felt a little disrespectful to do this – it was Augusta's washcloth after all – but he was loth to dress and take to the streets in his sticky, grimy, post-coital condition. His day's growth of beard and whiskers would have to remain, but he must remember to shave before going to the Fallen House, where a respectable appearance would be required.

'What kind of business then?'

'Oh, immensely dull and trivial business. Money matters,' he said vaguely. 'Errands for my uncle. That sort of thing.'

'Your uncle owns the bookshop, does he not?'

'Yes.'

'Have you always lived there?'

'For the most part, since my parents died.'

'Was that a long time ago?'

'My entire life. Both of my parents died when I was very young, not above four years of age.'

'How unfortunate. At least I knew my parents, even if they left me too soon. What manner of people were they?'

'They were not of the kind you would mix with.' He paused in the tying of his neckcloth. '*I* am not of the kind you would mix with.'

'And yet I mix with you most willingly.' She laughed, a little wickedly, inflaming his desires afresh. But there was not time to sate them now.

'I am glad of it.'

He buttoned his waistcoat, brushing it down where it had crumpled from long lying on the floor.

'You will come tonight,' she said. 'I shall wait for you.'

'Expect me,' he said.

He went over to kiss her a lingering goodbye, then he put on his coat and boots and left.

Chapter Six

'Do you have some further idea of where you might submit the piece?'

Mrs Edwards sipped at her tea, and James felt the weight of expectation heavy on his shoulders.

'I had considered the *Piccadilly Clubman*. I feel that the family magazines will consider this story unsuitable for the female readership and the newspapers are perhaps unready to extend sympathy towards those who have chosen an immoral mode of existence. Immoral as they would see it, anyway.'

Mrs Edwards did not appear pleased with this.

'The *Piccadilly Clubman* is not a respectable publication.'

'It is read by respectable men, though, many of them influential and likely unaware of your work. These women to them are something to be bought and then forgotten. To know otherwise might awaken some consciences.'

'I would still prefer *The Times*.'

'Who knows but that *The Times* may pick it up if it causes enough of a stir in the *Clubman*.'

'Well, perhaps there is something to be said for that argument. Have you finished your tea?'

James nodded his assent and Mrs Edwards led him back into the entrance hall, then up the stairs.

'Our schoolroom and workshops,' she said, indicating a number of doors.

The first of these, a back room, was well lit and contained a half dozen of women, all working at some form of tailoring.

'We aim to teach our residents means of obtaining honest employment once they are ready to return to the world,' said Mrs Edwards. 'As you see, they all wear a uniform, and that is what they are making.'

Each woman was indeed identically dressed, in a blue serge frock of exceeding plainness and a white apron. There was some fancy stitching on the apron bibs, no doubt for the purposes of teaching such skills as pintucking and embroidery. Modest white caps covered each woman's hair and James thought he had never seen such a homely group. Did they not miss their paint and finery?

One of them pricked her finger and exclaimed, holding the wounded spot with its tiny bead of red to her lips.

James stepped forward and offered his handkerchief but the girl stared away from him with glazed eyes and said nothing, even when he urged her to take it.

'Leave her. They are instructed to have no commerce with gentlemen, under any circumstances,' said Mrs Edwards. 'You mean well, but you will do more harm than good. These girls have made excellent progress and do not need to be set back.'

'How do I set them back if I offer them a kindness?'

Mrs Edwards spoke in a lower voice. 'They are learning to master their fleshly impulses. Over the course of their licentious careers, a certain kind of response to male attention becomes ingrained in their natures. This must be erased if they are ever to prosper in respectable society.'

'You think they will want to, to . . . ply their trade with me?'

Mrs Edwards pinched her lips and gave a sharp nod.

It struck James as unlikely but he put his handkerchief back in his pocket and followed his hostess to the next room, where millinery was in progress.

In the large schoolroom at the front of the building, women sat on forms, as his boy pupils had done. It struck him as inappropriate and a little humiliating for grown women to be treated as schoolgirls and he fought down a rising sense of unease as he watched the mistress, a strict and unsmiling figure, drill her pupils.

'What do they learn?' he asked Mrs Edwards.

'The essentials. Reading, writing, arithmetic. There is only so much we can inculcate into such decayed minds.'

'Decayed?'

'Moral atrophy leads to intellectual decay, Mr Stratton. Don't you think?'

If so, he thought, then I am an idiot.

'I am not sure of that,' he demurred. 'I'm sure plenty of these women are perfectly bright, if given a chance to show it.'

'They don't need to be bright, Mr Stratton. They need to be good.'

After leaving the schoolroom, they returned downstairs. They exited the building through a locked back door and crossed a small courtyard hung with washing.

'Don't look at the smalls,' implored Mrs Edwards, chivvying him along to a low shed-like building, one of a complex.

It contained a laundry and a kitchen, the first so powerfully filled with steam that James felt himself quite faint with the heat. Women bent over large coppers, pushing swirls of linen around with wooden tongs.

Next door smelled strongly of boiled cabbage, causing James to put a hand to his mouth lest he should retch. This was what workhouses were like, he thought, or at least, it was how he had come to imagine them, from his reading of *Oliver Twist* and similar fare.

'We think it very important that our residents learn household skills,' she said. 'Many of them are quite unused to washing their clothes – they come to us riddled with lice – and have existed on oysters from street stands. If they can cook and clean and wash, perhaps there is a chance they might find a husband.'

James kept to himself the observation that, given they could also fuck, they were pretty marriageable already in his view.

'There is a small infirmary occupying the corner of the yard. Now, the chapel,' said Mrs Edwards briskly, relieving him of the necessity of inhaling any more cabbage-rotten air, and then crossing the courtyard once more.

It was a balmy day already, but inside the corrugated metal chapel James could almost feel the remnants of winter in the air. How frigid this edifice must be on the coldest days of the year, and how stifling on the warmest.

A dozen women knelt on makeshift hassocks, surely sewn on the premises, prayer books clasped between their folded hands, heads bowed.

'Everyone must spend one hour of the day in silent prayer and reflection,' whispered Mrs Edwards. 'Peace is something many of our girls have never known from birth to the day they arrive here. Their lives have lacked the spiritual dimension – this is our greatest gift to bestow.'

James thought that regular meals and a clean bed were probably bigger inducements.

Crossing the courtyard on the way back to the house, he asked, 'How long do they typically stay here?'

'As long as they like. In general, it takes about a year for them to become suitably accomplished to seek employment.'

'But they are free to leave at any time?'

'Of course. This is not a prison, Mr Stratton.'

'It is as highly regulated as one.'

'These girls need order. They come from chaos. You must know that. What of your friend in the Lock Hospital? It is outrageous that she should be confined there, of course, but in the long run, she is probably better off there than on the streets.'

Privately, James was not sure he believed this. He could hardly picture Annie in a place like this at all. She would rebel, weary of the constant round of labour and the eerie silence. What manner of girl could go from such a tempestuous life to one so regimented?

'I wonder,' he said, re-entering the office, 'if you would grant me some interviews with your inmates? It would be most illuminating, for the purposes of the article.'

'I'm not sure why. As I understand it, your article will be against the enforcement of the Contagious Diseases Act. I am happy for you to publicise our cause and give an account of our charitable function, but it is window dressing to the main thrust, surely?'

'I think if people can see how your charity benefits and changes the girls who avail themselves of it, they may be more kindly inclined. It is important to give the girls a human face. It is too easy and too tempting to think of them as mere ciphers, and to thus dismiss their suffering.'

Mrs Edwards contemplated his words, frowning.

'I take your point,' she said. 'However, we have an inviolable rule against mixing of the sexes here.'

'What about your chaplain?'

'He is never alone with them.'

'What about a doctor?'

'I would always be in attendance at any medical appointment.'

'What of the Hippocratic oath?'

'Oh, these girls are not . . .'

She trailed off. James could have sworn she had been about to say 'people'. What a peculiar woman she was, campaigning for the rights of prostitutes, and yet seeming to have every bit as much contempt for them as the remainder of society did.

'They need an advocate,' she said, less hastily. 'They are happy for me to be on hand.'

'Will you not consider my request?'

'Oh, I don't know . . . perhaps if I could be present . . .'

But James wondered if the women's accounts would be entirely freely given if their forbidding philanthropist were in earshot.

'I understand that you are uncomfortable with the idea. Please don't put yourself to trouble on my account. I am only thinking of what will sway the public's attitude with the most force.'

'I know you are. I understand. You must let me ponder the proposition. Come back tomorrow and I will have an answer for you.'

'Thank you. But may I now ask some questions of you?'

'For the article?'

'Of course. What else?'

'You seemed very interested in whether I knew some

female of your acquaintance yesterday. I wondered if you had
a more personal agenda in mind.'

'Ah.' James looked down at his lap, feeling caught out.
'Mrs Shaw. You said you did not know her?'

She paused, just a moment too long, before replying,
'That is right.'

James knew it would be folly to pursue the issue. He
interviewed her instead on the subject of the charity's history
and antecedents. Any attempt to delve deeper into her
personal life was blocked, graciously but unequivocally.

He left the building knowing a great deal about its bricks
and mortar, but almost nothing about the woman who had
caused the foundations to be laid.

But it was in a spirit of optimism that he crossed the
Bloomsbury streets, thinking of lunch and the work he had
to do to meet his next deadline. If Mrs Edwards would not
let him interview her inmates, it was of no moment. He had
recalled somebody who would do every bit as well.

Thus it was that, some hours later, his hand cramped from
scribbling, he found his way through the mews once more to
the square of land at the rear of Augusta's home.

This time he did not enter via an open ballroom window
but descended some back steps to a little laundry yard, empty
of washing on this late weekday and eerily quiet. He wondered how many staff Augusta employed. Someone to cook,
presumably, and a coachman, Paulette and another maid. Was
there anyone else? It was a large house for one girl to keep in
order.

His question was answered when the unfamiliar face
of a young girl, perhaps fifteen or so, appeared around the
doorway and screamed.

'Oh, do not be alarmed, pray,' he said, moving swiftly forward. 'I don't mean to frighten you. I'm looking for Paulette.'

'Are you?' She still looked terrified, her plump face bright red and her eyes threatening tears.

'Yes. Is she in?'

'She's upstairs, working. You'll have to come back later.' She looked him up and down after brushing a tear from her eye and added, more confidently, 'Are you following her? She don't have followers, you know. Mrs Shaw'd kill her.'

'Well, there's no need to say anything to Mrs Shaw, is there? And no, I'm not a follower. I'm a distant relative. Look, I'd rather not go away. Do you mind if I wait in the kitchen?'

'It's not permitted, sir, to have menfolk below stairs.'

'Are there no male servants in the household?'

'Only the coachman, sir, and he lives in the mews with his wife and family.'

'Paulette did not mention this. It is an unmarried lady that she works for, is it not?'

The girl looked over her shoulder, as if anxious to get back to her labours.

'That's the owner of the house, sir. But she don't give the orders.'

'Oh?'

'She's got a companion, sir, Mrs Shaw. She rules this roost.'

'Perhaps I should go away now, in case she should catch me.'

'She's away, don't worry.'

'Then could I not come in and wait?' He calculated his most appealing look and directed it with earnest intensity at the girl.

She faltered and he knew he had won his way.

'Just for a moment,' he said, consolidating his position with a pensive curl of his lip. 'I shall tell nobody if you do not.'

''Cept Paulette . . . oh, she's all right. She won't say anything. Come on then. Lucky Mrs Ringer's out for the afternoon.'

'Who's Mrs Ringer?' He sat down at a trestle table and watched the girl pick up a pudding basin and attend to its contents with a hard-working arm.

'She's the cook. Since it's only Her Ladyship in the house tonight, she's taken herself off to the pub, sir. Left me and Paulette to it.'

'She drinks?'

'Gawd, don't she?'

'What does Mrs Shaw think of that?'

'Oh, she don't know. Not yet. I can't see it staying secret much longer, mind, the rate she's been polishing off what's in the cellar.'

'Have you been here long?'

'No, only since Easter.'

'You're very young. I suppose this is your first place?'

She paused in her pummelling of the pudding bowl and James saw her shoulders tense, though he couldn't see her face.

'Yes,' she said. 'It is.'

'Like Paulette,' he said, leaving the implication hanging in the floury air for the girl to snatch up or wave away.

'I don't know about Paulette,' she said, taking to the pudding bowl with renewed vigour. 'I'm just a good girl what wants a quiet life, sir.'

She was a mere child, perhaps something like Annie had been when she first embarked on her debauched career. James felt a brief pang, an ache of the heart, and decided, despite his journalistic curiosity, to leave her be.

Paulette was perhaps ten minutes more and time passed slowly in that dark back kitchen with only the clatter and thump of the maid's efforts towards cookery breaking the monotony.

'Oh, heavens, what are you doing here?' she cried, standing with her back to door as if she feared Mrs Shaw might rush through at any moment and discover them all.

'I came to see you, Paulette,' he said, standing and smiling in what he hoped was the manner of a distant but affectionate relative. 'For it has been such a long time, has it not?'

She frowned, then caught the tendency of his glance towards the other girl and nodded.

'Oh yes. A long time. Too long.'

'And I have important family news which I must impart to you in private, if that can be managed.'

'Yes, yes. Come into the, uh, the pantry. Excuse us, Bess.'

She led James into a large, cool room lined with shelves and dense with the smells of different foods, like a very small grocers shop. She shooed out a couple of flies and shut the door behind them.

'What is it?' she hissed. 'I wonder what on Earth you might want from me?'

'Today I paid a visit to the Society for the Improvement of Fallen Girls and Women.'

'You . . . why?'

'I am writing a piece for the newspapers. However, Mrs Edwards is reluctant to allow me to interview any of her . . . her . . .' He was not sure how to put it.

'Prisoners?' said Paulette with unexpected and explosive bitterness.

'You know, I think that might just be the word.'

'I'll say it is. Food's better in prison, though, or so I'm told. And your thoughts are your own.'

'Whereas at Little Ormond Street . . .?'

'Every minute had to be accounted for, from getting up at five to going to bed at nine. When we weren't working we were praying. We weren't allowed to even chat to each other, in case we talked about our old ways and were tempted back.'

She shivered, though it wasn't particularly cold in the pantry, just a few degrees cooler than the rest of the house. It was dark, though, the only light coming from a grille high in the wall.

'Mrs Edwards runs a very orderly house.'

'No better'n the workhouse. I wish I'd have gone there instead.'

'But you have this position now, as a result of your time there.'

'Yes, for what that's worth.'

'You aren't happy here?'

'Happy? What's happy got to do with it? I'm off the streets and I'm earning a wage. That's about as much as a girl like me can hope for.'

James found her matter-of-fact acceptance of a poor lot in life sobering. He wondered if she was ever tempted to get her ribbons back out and head for the Haymarket.

'Mrs Shaw takes on staff from that refuge because she knows they will know the ways of the world and will not be too shocked by what they see happening here – that's what you've given me to understand.'

'Yes, that's right.'

'Does Mrs Edwards know Mrs Shaw has this in mind?'

The question gave Paulette pause.

'I shouldn't think so. No. She couldn't know it, could she? She don't approve of, what's that word the clergy use, fornication. I suppose if she knew it was all going on between ladies she'd be twice as horrified.'

'You suppose. Do you like Mrs Shaw?'

'No, Lord, no. Why all these questions about her? You aren't going to write about her, are you?'

'No. Of course not.'

'And is that . . . all . . . you wanted with me?'

Her look now was unmistakably bold and he could picture her up against a wall in the Strand or sitting on a gin palace stool looking over a garish fan.

Come hither.

He would never see that look on Augusta.

It doesn't matter.

But he was uncomfortably tempted, and felt sweat break on his brow.

'I don't know. Paulette . . . what do you think of things here?'

'You want to talk about them upstairs,' she sighed, rolling her eyes. 'I'll have to wait a while longer for someone to whisk me away from all this then.'

'I'm sorry.' He gave her a rueful smile.

'Oh, stop it with your doe eyes. Just 'cos we hardly ever see a nice-looking fella around here don't mean you can play us all like fiddles.'

'But I am curious. When did you find out how things were here?'

She folded her arms. 'Well, let me see. Mrs Shaw did drop a few hints in the cab from the Fallen House. She said, "I require a particular class of girl" or something like that. I asked her what she meant, and she said, "A woman of the world, Paulette, who doesn't shock easily." You can imagine, that got me interested. Thought I might be going to a high-society brothel or something and she'd pulled the wool over Mrs E's eyes. I said, "I ain't going back to prostituting myself,

Mrs Shaw, not for no one." She took umbrage at that but she still didn't really explain what she meant. It wasn't till I had to serve tea to Lady Augusta in her bed the next morning that I realised.'

'What did you see?'

'You love the dirty stories, don't you? I've heard about you. I know what they sell in that shop of yours.'

'Yes, quite. So?'

'I'm not sure I should tell you. Might get you too excited. Don't want to find myself ravished here amongst the flour and honey . . . do I?' She bit her lip coyly.

Oh, the minx! She was like Annie. Annie. Where was she? The thought of her plight dampened his rising ardour and he was able to hold up his hand.

'All right, perhaps I shouldn't have asked.'

'Oh, no, I'll tell you,' she said hurriedly. 'Don't go. I went in there with the tea tray and, oh my goodness, I dropped it, didn't I? Cups, saucers, hot tea . . . scalded me ankle.'

'What did you see?'

'I saw Mrs Shaw sitting there on the bed with her feet wide apart and in between them there was Her Ladyship's stern end, bright red it was, bent right over while her face was right in Mrs S's bush.'

'I . . . see.' The visual accompaniment to this little vignette imprinted itself powerfully in James' mind, and once again he was plagued with the surge of lust.

'No, you don't. But I did. Shocked, I was. Near fainted, poor modest girl that I am.'

'Really?'

'No.' She winked. 'Plenty of the girls round my part of Lambeth were up to that caper. Not me, but I've seen it.

Gents will pay extra for a show like that, which is a bit of luck if you don't feel up to the other.'

'I daresay it is. So you knew from that moment that there was a Sapphic attachment between your mistress and her companion?'

'I'll say. I caught it, too, for breaking the china.'

'Caught it?'

'From Mrs S. She caned me.'

'She does this to *you*? And to the other girls in the house?'

Paulette was downcast now, her shoulders hunched.

'What can we do about it, sir? We don't like it but—'

'It isn't on,' he said. 'You shouldn't have to take it.'

'No, but we do.'

'You'd like it if she left, I assume?'

'I'd hang out the flags. Oh, don't tell me you're trying to get rid of her? Oh my life, you'll have your work cut out but there ain't nothing I wouldn't let you do to me if that day ever came.'

He smiled and patted her cheek, buoyed by the flirtation.

'I'll bear it in mind. And now I ought to go or our young friend out there will begin to have suspicions—'

'Oh.' She put a hand on his sleeve, suddenly uncharacteristically diffident. 'Before you go . . . I don't like to ask but . . . it gets so lonely here and it's such a long time since I felt a man's arms around me . . . would you mind?'

'Not at all.'

He let her step into a tight embrace, resting his chin on the top of her head while she burrowed into him with happy little sighing sounds.

He wished there were more he could do for her, and perhaps there could be. He needed only time.

That night, on entering Augusta's chamber, he did not go to join her in her bed but instead shut the door quietly behind him and waited for her to speak.

'My love?' she said tentatively, sitting up and drawing the bedclothes around her.

'Augusta,' he said, tightening his grip on the rattan cane he had collected from the schoolroom on his way.

She inhaled, a little fearfully.

'Why do you call me that, sir? Have I displeased you?'

He walked across the room and back, purely for the effect of stringing out her tension with the measured tread of his boots on the wood.

'I'm afraid you have,' he said.

The way she swallowed stirred him more than was convenient, but hang convenience. He took a breath, steadied his head.

'How have I offended, sir?' she asked, her voice very small now.

'You allow Mrs Shaw to beat your servants.'

Augusta clearly had not been expecting a real accusation. Perhaps she had thought he would construct some trumped up charge for her to play along with. But her face flooded scarlet and she slumped, her head on her knees.

'Oh,' she whispered.

'Well?'

'I have delegated matters of staff discipline to her, yes.'

'Yet you know her to be a sadist who takes pleasure in inflicting pain. Is this the action of a responsible mistress, Augusta? I am disappointed.'

'You know the roles of mistress and servant are not clear-cut in this house.'

'I know who is employer and whom employed. You pay her wages.'

In the silence that followed, James lit a candle. He ought to be able to see what he was doing.

'Then, yes, I should be held accountable,' said Augusta at length.

'You should.'

Her eyes followed the sound of his voice and she raised her head towards him in mute query.

In response, he held out the cane until its slender tip pressed against her cheek.

She gasped and reached up to touch it.

'Stand,' he said.

Recoiling from the cane, she cast aside her bedcovers and put her feet on the floor. James helped her up, then, with a hand at her elbow, walked with her to the end of the bed. Releasing her, he placed the end of the cane in the small of her back and pushed it very slightly.

'There is a footstool directly in front of you. Bend and place your hands upon it.'

She obeyed, her nightgown rustling about her legs. Beneath it, James saw the outline of her twin rounds, parted by a crease. They were well delineated but, all the same, the gown would have to be lifted.

But before driving his point home with the rattan, he would make it verbally.

'You have permitted Mrs Shaw to exert an undue influence upon you,' he said. 'An influence that casts its shadow over the entire household.'

'I have come to depend upon her.'

'This is weakness, Augusta.' He swished the cane for emphasis and was rewarded by a flinch. 'I understand that she has introduced you to pleasures you had only dreamt of but it does not make her your saviour, nor your mistress in fact. But it was easier for you to let her hold sway. It took the burden of decision-making off your shoulders. Am I right?'

She nodded, those shoulders dolefully low.

'In giving yourself the luxury of irresponsibility, you have brought unhappiness below stairs, Augusta. You may deserve the full force of the rod, but do you think Paulette does?'

'N-no, sir.' Her contrition was genuine, he was sure of it.

'No, sir. She does not. And yet you . . .' He hesitated. He'd been about to say 'turn a blind eye'. 'You put your hands over your ears and pretend you don't hear her cries. Paulette is not like you, Augusta. She does not need to be whipped. But you do. Don't you?'

'Yes, sir. I do.' She let out a breath of something like rapture.

'Then let us proceed.'

He lifted her gown swiftly to her waist. She was unmarked, not having received any form of severe chastisement for over a week. He liked a blank canvas best of all and took a moment to imagine all the different ways in which he could paint it.

'One day,' he said, tapping the cane very gently against her thigh, 'I should like to birch you. I should take you out and make you gather the rods under my supervision. Perhaps I should thrash you then and there, out in the open. What would you think of that?'

'I never go out of doors any more. I have never been to the country.'

'Never?'

He retracted the cane, astonishment diverting him from his disciplinary path.

'No. I have lived always in London. I used to go to the

parks, but it has been some time since I went anywhere at all.'

'Why?'

'Mrs Shaw frets that I will become lost.'

'You are lost,' he said quietly. 'Very lost.'

He gripped the cane tighter, recalling his resolution.

'There is something to be discussed once your correction is complete,' he said. 'Now brace yourself, I will give you ten. You will count.'

Each stroke raised a glorious welt, straight and true from the broad centre of her bottom to the crease of her thigh. She was brave under the lash but she could not bear it without some protest, hissing and wailing and stamping her feet, first one then the other, in quick succession.

James revelled in the sensuality of his work, the sound of the air whistling as if in fear of the descending rattan, then the smart crack as it met her skin. Her twisting spine, her bending neck, the weal forming into a firm and constant reminder of its presence. She would sit gingerly for a day or so, and remember what had been done to her at his hand. And, oh, the power vested in that hand!

She counted between gritted teeth.

At nine, she declared that she could not bear it.

'I wonder if Paulette could,' he said.

'No, you are right. I deserve this. Lay on the last stroke.'

'I will make it the hardest.'

He did so, wincing himself as the rod swiped across her bottom, fascinated at Augusta's capacity for absorbing and embracing the pain.

She burst into tears and sobbed out the ten.

He supported her trembling body straight away, holding her against him, whispering hushes into her hair.

'I had not realised,' she said, still weeping, 'that the

servants suffered. I had not given them a thought. I am a poor kind of mistress.'

'No, you are not. You have been, but no longer, I trust?'

'No longer.'

'The lesson is well learned.' He kissed the tears from her face. 'And now I cannot be stern with you, as I intended, and make you take your place in the corner. Come and lie on the bed. On your stomach, I think.'

He helped her climb back on to her bed and lie, gown still raised above her striped rear, with her face in the pillows while he rubbed at her shoulders and neck.

Her residual hiccupy sobs soon relaxed into sighs.

'You care for me so well,' she whispered. 'Better than Mrs Shaw.'

Something like fear stilled his hands. Perhaps he should end this. Was it not kinder, after all, to end it now? Yet how could he? How could he leave her? If his body did, his mind and heart would not follow. There was a danger here that he could not quite put his finger on, but of an acuity he had not fully perceived until now.

'I will fetch some salve,' he said.

'There is no need—'

But he was on his way to the medicine cabinet before she could finish. He needed some cool air, something to still his racing thoughts.

He went into the schoolroom and threw up the sash, breathing in great lungfuls of the mild early-summer night. The heat of the day had caused the rubbish in the mews and the kitchen yards to smell rather high. In winter, it would be smoke. One simply exchanged one miasma for another in this town.

He thought of Annie, behind a heavy door in the Lock

Hospital. She would think she'd been abandoned. He thought also of another girl, one long absent from his life, of where she might be and what doing and with whom.

But to think of that was useless.

Here he had, in this very house, a lovely and willing woman who adored him, because of his peculiarities in taste rather than despite them. She had asked him here as an arrangement of sorts, but it seemed much more than that now.

Yet it was an impossible situation. There was no question of a more permanent attachment and the spectre of Mrs Shaw loomed above them, no matter how much closer they moved to each other. They deceived themselves if they thought this could ever last. He deceived himself. And she must know it . . .

He put the window back down and went to the medicine cabinet, selecting the required unguent from its ranks of bottles and jars.

Take your pleasure with her and leave. Do not expect more.

In the bedroom, Augusta lay so quiet and motionless that he thought she might have fallen asleep. When he sat on the edge of the bed, she yawned.

'I thought you had gone,' she said, somewhat piteously. 'I couldn't bear it if you left me like this.'

He took the lid off the jar and dipped his fingers into cool cream, which he rubbed carefully into the uppermost welt, regardless of her hiss and wriggle.

'When Mrs Shaw returns,' she said, 'she will ask me how I came by these marks.'

'And what shall you tell her?'

'Oh, she will guess correctly before I say a word, I'm sure.'

He let his slippery finger glide along the stripes, while the cream sank into each hot, hard line.

'Do you fear her response?'

'I think she will punish me. She may forbid you from visiting.'

'She cannot forbid me anything. She is not my mistress. Nor is she yours. If you wish for me to visit, then I will visit.'

He watched the shift of her shoulders as his greased fingers moved lower. More and more cream he applied, until it was thick and shiny on her skin, over the rounds of her buttocks and on the tops of her thighs.

She made no resistance when he dipped his hand between them, indeed, she parted her legs in welcome. He slicked the tender skin until it shone, but took no notice of her subtle attempts to divert his fingers to her nether lips.

He stopped just short each time, his knuckles whispering against the tendrils of wiry hair, but refusing their damp invitation.

When she moaned and pushed her bottom up, he laughed and withdrew his hand entirely.

'Have you earned such reward, pet?' he teased.

She muffled her frustration into the pillow.

'I think not, heedless one,' he whispered. 'But I can show you another way.'

And now he dipped each finger, and his thumb too, into the cream and inserted his hand between her still-burning cheeks, plumbing that mysterious depth she had not yet yielded him.

'Oh.' Her little quiver of surprise and alarm did nothing to relieve the stiffness in his trousers. He had written of this act so many times that it felt infinitely familiar to him. But he had never done it. No woman had ever granted him that licence.

Would she really . . .? Could he be close to this?

He put a hand between her shoulder blades and continued

his probings, shallowly at first, until she seemed to unbend and breathe again more easily, more heavily.

'I have told you before,' he said, 'that I want to be master of every part of you. Do you recall?'

His forefinger reached the tight pucker it sought and held itself, very gently but with confident intent, against it.

'Yes, sir,' she said, so quietly and meekly that he almost missed the words.

She was going to let him. He bit down on his lip, hard. He had to keep his head.

'And do you accept that this will mean my taking you, here.' He pushed, as against a button, and felt her clench tight.

'Can it be done?' she asked, fearful.

'It can, of course, be done. I gather you may find it uncomfortable, but what's a little discomfort after a sound thrashing?'

She kicked her feet at that, in a helpless bid to protest.

'I'm sorry. That sounded unsympathetic. But you will take what I give you, and you will be grateful for it.'

She exhaled and clawed at the sheets. That had been the right thing to say.

'I will prepare you thoroughly,' he promised, slightly regretting the necessity. He would be more than happy to take her as she was. But the ground must first be laid. 'Like . . . so.'

He pushed again with his forefinger and she flinched and thrashed.

'No,' he said, holding her more firmly and straddling her legs so that they could no longer kick. 'That is not the way it is done, pet. You must unclench and embrace the intrusion. It is much easier.'

Or so my characters always tell the women they seduce. But is it?

'Now lie still,' he whispered. He dug down. The tough little ring that had seemed so determined never to open for him yielded a mite.

'Oh, it is too hard,' wailed Augusta. 'My body does not do as it is bidden. It is not natural.'

'That is what makes it such a prized gift,' said James. 'That is what makes it the most precious surrender I could ever desire.'

His words seemed to stir Augusta to greater determination and she pushed her bottom up a little, signifying that she was open to him and his will, whatever it might require of her.

'For you,' she said under her breath. 'No other.'

He forged forwards and his finger popped through that barrier with surprising ease, the cream having its hoped-for effect. Now he was held tight in that dark place, having breached it walls, he was not sure what to do next. He wriggled his finger, exploring the stretch and texture of its environs. Although narrower than her other passage, it was of a similar feel. It would grip him so beautifully.

'Well,' he said, twisting himself in to the knuckle. 'What now, my pet? You have my finger in a very private place, do you not? What does it feel like?'

'I am a most abandoned creature,' she moaned.

'Oh, you are.' He twisted it again. 'Does it not hurt?'

'No, there is no pain as such. It is strange and not entirely comfortable but . . . as you wish it . . . I must accept it . . . I will accept it all . . .' The struggle with her breath was due to the insertion of a second finger.

James wondered at the capacity for enlargement such a tiny aperture possessed. Surely then it *was* possible.

'And now there is some little pain,' she said. 'I am not constituted . . . for such . . . activity . . .'

'Remain calm,' he said, far from calm himself but grateful now for his capacity to seem steady and well ordered when his blood and other parts were raging. 'Open to me. Submit to me.'

Here was where the test would lie.

If she protested once more of pain or fear or any other unpleasant condition of mind, he would stop and leave the subject for another time.

But if she did not . . .

'Open,' he repeated, his voice now very low and supernaturally calm. 'To me.'

She breathed a sigh and he felt her shoulder blades loosen beneath his hand.

Yes, this could be done. He scissored his fingers as wide as he could and a mild whimper was her only plaint.

'Now,' he said. 'I shall remove these fingers and replace them. You should, I think, kneel up . . . yes.'

She obeyed straight away.

He watched her maintain that position while he stood and undressed, as quickly as he could to placate a fear that she might change her mind while he was not touching her.

Once naked, he loaded his fingers once more with cream and added to the superabundance already in evidence between her scorched cheeks. For additional ease of transit, he rubbed some also along the length of his erect member, trying not to be too enthusiastic in his manipulations lest he should over-stimulate himself and put a premature end to this adventure.

He took a hold of her hips, deliberately firm, as much to convince himself that this would be well as to persuade her. She could not have confidence in him if he had none in himself.

He had written this scene a dozen times.

He knew what to do.

Be master of yourself.

He knelt behind her and let his prick slide into the well-oiled cleft, feeling its way until it found that little knot his fingers had already attended to.

'Mine,' he said, prodding it with his tip. 'Mine for the taking. Tell me so, pet.'

'Yours for the taking,' she said, but he could hear the nervousness behind the assertion.

'You must keep that in the forefront of your mind,' he said.

He moved his thumbs to the centre of her buttocks and used them to draw her cheeks wide, granting him greater ease of access.

He was primed and ready for the push. All it would take was a little nerve. A little faith that he would not damage or overset her. But was he too cruel?

She wriggled, very slightly, but the movement shifted his alignment so that it was perfect. Her assistance gave him heart.

And now, should he make one bold stroke forward, or should it be a slow, creeping sort of thing? Absurdly, Tennyson's *Charge of the Light Brigade* popped into his head and he had to stifle a laugh. The valley of death indeed.

Do or die, boy.

He pushed.

She gasped and snuffled and jolted under his hands, but she did not tell him to stop.

Her clamp around him was so gloriously tight. It was the most inexpressibly pleasurable feeling, something he had tried to imagine for so long and now he was doing it, and it was so much better.

'Oh *Lord*.' The words escaped him, strained and quivery.

Augusta pushed back on him, taking that first inch magnificently.

Looking down, he was lightheaded at the sight of his fleshy staff disappearing, slowly and inexorably, into that ever-stretching chamber.

As he reached the halfway point, she twitched violently and showed some signs of distress. He held himself still and asked her, firmly, what was amiss.

'It hurts now, oh, it is too big.'

He had known this point would be reached, though, and he knew it could be overcome.

'Push back on me, pet, and I will take you past this. It is but momentary.'

'I cannot.'

'You can. You will.'

She did.

The moment of her absolute possession was upon him and he felt he ought to be experiencing some momentous mark of the occasion, like a vision or the sound of angel voices. But no, it was sufficient in itself that he should be in this position, feeling this velvet clamp on his manhood while his testicles rested against the curve of her bottom. Here was the peak of his mountainous sexual ambition. He must plant his flag in it.

'You know now,' he whispered, 'that you are mastered.'

'Yes, sir.' She sounded far away, somewhere in a dream.

He put his hands over her breasts, holding them firmly.

'Wherever you are and whatever you do, you can never forget this moment and what has been done to you.'

'I know,' she breathed. 'Oh, how I know it. I never wish to forget it.'

'Tell me how it is for you.'

'It is both uncomfortable and painful and yet I treasure the sensation more than anything. Especially with the sting of the rod still upon my cheeks. Whatever you chose to do to me . . . whatever . . . I could never deny you. I am yours.'

He buried his mouth in the tender part of her neck, sucking lusciously. *Take my mark.* When Mrs Shaw saw it, and the stripes of the cane, and glory knew what else, oh, what sweet uproar there would be.

My message to you, madam. My message to you upon Augusta's buttocks and her neck and wherever else I may choose to print it. Read it. Take note of it. She is mine now.

His blood surging with this fighting spirit, he commenced the business of using her in earnest. His strokes were slow and gentle to begin with, accustoming her to this strange new brand of pleasuring, until her measure of stretch was sufficient to let him abandon some of his caution and take a more vigorous tack.

She made a deal of noise, the vocalisations similar to those she uttered under the lash. This fired him even more, but at the same time he wondered if she could derive pleasure from what he did. Would she reach her crisis this way? It was surely not nature's way.

Nature seemed to place no such obstacles in the path of his own heightening excitement, however. This was all too exquisite and could not be held back for long.

The consciousness of what he did, coupled with the unfamiliar and delightful tightness and Augusta's perfect acquiescence brought him all too quickly to completion.

How sweet to be able to fill her with his seed and know that no unwanted consequence would be borne nine months hence. He held Augusta tight around her middle and thrust hard until every last drop was spilled, filling her to the brim.

'Please,' she gasped. 'Stay within me. As long as you can.'

She prised his hand from her breast and moved it lower, across her belly and down.

Oh, so the erotic satisfaction of this act was not his alone. She was wet below and the bud of flesh was beautifully fat.

'You are a wicked creature,' he murmured into her ear. 'I have half a mind to refuse you. But such pleasure . . . it has mellowed me.'

He rubbed and rubbed at her, pleased at the way his cockstand maintained itself for longer than he would have expected. When she reached her peak, he wanted her to be fully sensible of the length and width of him inside her.

It did not take long to carry her to the edge and when she tipped over it, her exclamations were so passionate and so loud that he feared the servants might hear.

He put a hand swiftly over her mouth and let her pour her raptures into his palm, feeling the honeyed heat of her coat his other, lower-placed fingers.

Now, only now, could he slowly withdraw his semi-tumescent member.

She whined a little as he pulled out, finding it more uncomfortable than the seating, which he had not expected. Indeed, she seemed to clench at him, trying to hold him inside her. A swift unsheathing foiled her in this and he held her hips for a moment, preventing her from falling flat on to the bed.

He wanted to see the void he had inhabited. He particularly wanted to see it glisten and drip with his seed, while the livid streaks of the cane framed it on either side. That called for a daguerreotype, if only he had the equipment to hand.

He took it in, committing its particular singularities to memory, for a heartfelt moment. Then he released her and let her lie on her stomach – her only alternative, after what he had dealt her.

When he lay beside her and stroked her cheek, he found that it was wet.

'You are weeping. Pet, why do you weep? Are you hurt – beyond that which is our custom, I mean to say.'

'I am more than hurt. I am slain.'

'Augusta.' His reproach was gentle and he leant over to kiss her where the salt drops lay.

'How can I not love you? How can I ever live without you?'

'Perhaps you will not have to.'

'How can it be? How? Kinder to me by far if you had never come and I had never known you.'

'Do not say so.'

'No, you will not agree, for you have a lovely arrangement, don't you? A weekly spree with no need to fear that you will be held to any account.'

'Augusta, you misjudge me.'

'It is what Mrs Shaw says. She is always right about men. Always.'

'She is not right about this man. She is quite wrong.'

'Then prove her so.'

James laid his hand upon her neck and held it between finger and thumb.

'How?'

'Be my lover in truth. Not merely twice a week.'

'What do you mean? What do you want of me?'

She was quiet awhile.

'No,' she said at last. 'Perhaps I should not ask it of you. Perhaps I do not dare. For if you say no . . . then what . . .?'

'Augusta, if what you want is within my power, then . . .'

She drew a deep breath before speaking more.

'I shall start with an attainable goal. That is sensible, after all. I should like you to take me to the Cremorne Gardens.'

'The Cremorne?'

'Yes, that is what I said.'

'I don't care for your tone but I shall let it pass this once.'

'I am very nervous.'

'I grant you that. Why do you want to go there? Most of its amusements will be sadly lost on you, my love.'

'Oh, I know I won't see the lamps or the fireworks. But there is music, isn't there? And dancing. I should so like to dance with you.'

'I am rarely called upon to dance. I'm not sure I remember the last occasion.'

'Come down to the ballroom! We will waltz.'

'Pet, you are a little feverish, I think . . .'

'No, I am quite well! Is it such an outlandish request?'

James lifted his hand from her and sat straight, clearing his thoughts.

No, he supposed it was not. And Augusta had spent too long sequestered. A small expedition might do her constitution the world of good.

'You should take some air outside these walls,' he conceded.

'Yes, air, I want to breathe air. I want to smell things, sweet or rank, I don't care which. I want to feel the bodies of strangers pressed against mine. I want ladies skirts to brush my hem and gentlemen's elbows to jab my ribs. And I want to hear their voices – all those conversations, all those lives, everything I've been kept away from. Just for one night, dearest James. I may call you James, mayn't I?'

It seemed a momentous permission to grant.

'It is my name.'

'I have always called you sir before.'

'I know.'

'Then you do not mind?'

'You complicate my life, Augusta. I cannot say I don't mind it. But there is nothing I can do to simplify our circumstances.'

'You sound cross.'

'I am serious, that is all. I cannot untangle the threads.'

'Then do not try. Take me to the ballroom. Dance with me.'

He stood and took her hand, drawing her up on her knees then to her feet.

'Aren't you a little stiff for dancing?' he teased, seeing how the recent caning affected her gait.

'I do not mind. I shall dance through the sting and the pleasure of being in your arms will be all the keener for it.'

'Do not expect great expertise. I think yours may be the first ballroom I have entered.'

'You must have danced before?'

'At places like Cremorne and the Argyll Rooms. Nowhere you might consider respectable.'

'Oh, I have heard of the Argyll Rooms. Are they not terribly louche?'

'Rather.'

They had reached the foot of the stairs now.

Ahead of them, the gilt-edged double doors to the ballroom stood, as if inviting James on.

'We shall have no music,' he said, approaching them.

'We shall hear it in our heads.'

James doubted it, but he found, once he had Augusta in a dancer's hold and cast off with his right foot, that she was right. There was music in his head, some Viennese waltz he had heard at the Argyll Rooms, and its buoyant rhythm kept him in step as he whirled Augusta around the perimeter of the darkened room.

She melted in his arms, leaning back as if in a swoon, but her feet kept pace with his, belying her appearance. Upon her face, a smile of ecstasy more profound than he had ever seen during the throes of passion. She seemed to be approaching the pleasures of life in a reverse fashion, he thought. While most people progressed from childhood games to dancing, or gaming, or flirtation and only then negotiated the heady delights of physical love, she had taken a backwards route. Did this mean that she found more exquisite satisfaction in the scent of roses on a summer night than in anything he did to her?

Strange, if so, but not altogether beyond comprehension.

He saw, all at once, how pitifully neglected she had been and anger kindled in his breast.

The music in his head came to an abrupt halt, violins suspended in mid-phrase, and he pulled up sharp, so that she cannoned into his chest, laughing great gasps into his face.

'Is the waltz over so soon?' she exclaimed.

'For tonight,' he said. 'But at Cremorne, we will waltz all night.'

'Oh, I look forward to it so!'

'You should sleep. You will over-exert yourself. Come.'

She followed him, and when they were in bed, she curled into his side, happily.

'You care for me so well,' she whispered.

'It is time somebody did,' he replied.

Chapter Seven

His day had been unusually productive. He had managed to procure an interview with a junior governmental aide on the subject of the Contagious Diseases Act, and Mrs Edwards had allowed him to attend the morning chapel service with the women.

Thoughts of the thunderous sermon alternated with anger at the politician's apologism for the roughshod over-riding of the working girls' rights. He decided he would bring it up at the meeting tomorrow night with his fellow radicals, though he doubted they could be persuaded to take up their cudgels on behalf of mere women. They were generally much more preoccupied with their 'brothers'. Except those 'brothers' involved with Mr Marx and his International Workingmen's Association, whom they regarded as hated rivals, despite espousing approximately the same set of beliefs. James had flirted with the idea of throwing his political lot in with the IWA, but knew that his uncle would never forgive him, and blood, after all, was thicker than water &c &c.

He took, as usual, the tradesman's entrance into Eaton Place, assisted by Paulette, whom he slipped a sovereign and a peck on the cheek before finding Augusta waiting for him in the drawing room.

'You rob me of my breath,' he said, the gallantry falling awkwardly from his lips and making him glad she could not see his cheeks, warm with the rush of blood there.

'I am sure I do not,' she said, laughing, a picture of delight.

'I have brought you this.' He handed her a red rose, cut down for a corsage. 'Shall I pin it for you?'

'Oh, please do.' She laughed again, a little shrilly. 'Lord, how like a courtship scene in a novel this is. I feel quite . . . eligible.'

'You *are* eligible, Augusta,' said James, fastening the flower to her silk-clad bust. 'You are beautiful, young and wealthy.'

'I am damaged.'

'You must stop thinking of yourself in that way. You must stop thinking that you can expect no more from life than the crumbs it tosses in your direction. You are worth more.'

'Even when you say sweet things you sound as if you are scolding me. I do love it so.'

'I *am* scolding you. I shall continue to do so until you take my words to heart.'

Her heart. The rose lay red beside it, complementing the midnight blue of Augusta's gown.

'You may scold all you like at Cremorne,' she said, placing her hands in his, 'but you can do no more, with all those people round about. I can speak and behave as I will, with impunity.'

'You are quite sure of that, pet?'

'Oh!' She squeezed her fingers between his. 'You would not dare . . .'

Already she had him hard. He would have to distract her from this line of thinking, and smartly.

'You will need a wrap. The air is cooler now the sun is almost down. Let us find one.'

'Are we to walk there?'

'We can hail a cab.'

'A hansom? Oh, I have never travelled in one.'

'Then you have never lived, my dear.' James laughed, selecting a wrap that went well with Augusta's dress.

'No,' she said, subdued. 'I have never lived. Until I met you.'

The responsibility of it chilled him again. He was not fit for the position she granted him – the man of her dreams. He could not be that man. How could this ever be reconciled?

For this one night, he told himself, *I will be that man.*

And then, he decided in a rush of blood to the head, he would break this off. He would leave while he still could, and while he had done her no lasting damage. Or perhaps it was too late for that? All the same, the situation was impossible, quite untenable, and he should withdraw before further wreckage to their hearts was sustained.

But could he leave her?

You must.

One night, one last night, and with luck it would be enough to show Augusta that she could emerge from Mrs Shaw's shadow and live her own life according to her own lights. Then, at least, he could say he had been of some service.

Augusta was thrilled at the feel of the pavement beneath her shoes, tapping her feet and then stamping them once she had been helped down the steps.

'Will it rain?' she asked, turning her face up to the skies. 'Did you bring an umbrella? Oh, how long it is since I was rained upon – I almost hope it will.'

'It will not rain. I could wish it were a little warmer, but the clouds are neither low nor dark this evening. Here is a cab – hi!'

He guided her up on to the seat and instructed the cabbie to take them to Cremorne Gardens, which commission was set to without a word.

'Oh, how bumpy the roads are. This is rather painful – you know why.'

She blushed and he recalled that her bottom would still be welted from the recent caning. Again, an uncomfortable stiffness in his trousers drove him to attempt a change of subject.

'You will speak to Mrs Shaw about her disciplinary methods with the servants, I hope.'

Augusta sighed and turned her face from him.

'I know I should. She is not the easiest person to approach . . .'

'Nobody knows that better than I do, pet, but you must broach the subject. You cannot allow poor Paulette to suffer. It is wrong. And while you are about it, you must make her take you out, as we are going out now. You cannot live out your days as her prisoner.'

'Oh.' Augusta turned back to him, her face a little stricken. 'You sound as if . . .'

'As if what?'

'It doesn't matter.' But she was silent for the rest of the short ride, and her hand lay limply in his, as if she had withdrawn herself from him.

She wanted more from him, that much was clear. Which of them would suffer most from their separation? Of course it would be her, of course it would. She had so little else in her life. But was he to blame for that?

He could give her one wonderful night. He should stop
this harping on about afterwards and concentrate on her
pleasure. Take the moment and live in it, live a life in one
evening. He owed her that much.

'Should you like to dine first, or dance, or perhaps a walk?'

He took up her listless hand and put it to his lips.

She brightened, laying her head upon his shoulder.

'Shall we walk? You can describe everything we pass and
then we might take some supper. With champagne.'

'Of course, champagne. But not too much. We can't have
you falling over on the dancing platform.'

'I shall be safe if I am with you.'

'You must keep close to me always, pet.'

'Do not loosen your grip on me.'

He swallowed nervously and the cab joined a lengthy
rank all along the Chelsea Embankment.

The pavement was thick with people moving this way
and that. Away from the Gardens, seeking cabs or omnibuses
or paddle steamers, were the respectable families with their
tired children – some crying when they dropped their ice
on the ground or lost hold on a balloon, some sleeping in
parental arms, some bounding and leaping with enthusiasm
at all they had seen and done.

In the other direction, towards the gates, swarmed swells
and eager office boys and ladies impeccably clothed, in the
hope of becoming profitably and impeccably unclothed later.

'Hold tight,' said James, assisting Augusta's descent. 'It
is very busy. Have a care, sir, the lady is blind!' He spoke
irately to a passing youth in a loud waistcoat and cravat
combination, but the youth merely made an obscene gesture
and rushed onward, whistling at a gaggle of young women
ahead of them.

'They behave better once inside,' James promised Augusta, weaving through the crowds with her on his arm. 'For the most part. The dancing platform can be . . . an experience.'

He paid two shillings at the gate and at once the clamour receded, now that the struggle with the departing families was at an end.

If only Augusta could see the lanterns, strung through the bushes and along all the pathways – how magical it always seemed. They were lately lit, the dark having fully fallen within the last ten minutes, and the moths and bugs of summer night lazed about them, spotting the glow.

'Tell me,' prompted Augusta. 'Where are we now?'

'We are in a fairy garden, lit by the glow of monstrously bloated fireflies.'

'Oh, you liar. You can say anything to me, can't you, and I will not know it to be true or false.'

This hadn't occurred to James and he wondered at the possibilities it might afford.

'What if I told you that everyone about us was quite naked and engaged in acts of the most sybaritic debauchery?'

'You would be telling an outrageous falsehood! Please. I do so long to be able to see what is before us through your eyes.'

'Actually, I am not so far from the point. Matters can become quite . . . fleshly . . . among the hedgerows as the witching hour approaches.'

'I daresay you speak from experience, do you?'

'I couldn't possibly answer that.'

She tapped him on the forearm with her fan, then leapt and clung to him as a bell rang loud and clear a few feet from them.

'What is that?'

'It signifies that we are to follow the group we are with to another part of the gardens. It prevents the possibility of bottlenecks, I suppose.'

'And where are we walking to?'

'We are strolling, in the company of various well-dressed people, along a broad, lamp-lit path bordered on both sides by flower beds and ornamental trees – I don't know the genus. I'm a poor botanist.'

'But you are a writer.'

'I should make more of a descriptive effort, shouldn't I? Very well, they are a little taller than I am and willowy with a narrow, silvery leaf.'

'Perhaps they are willow, if willowy.'

'Perhaps. There is no moon overhead, for it is cloudy. And now we approach . . . something. I know not what. Ah. A bandstand. Do you hear the music?'

'Is this the dancing platform?'

'Oh no, they have a full orchestra there. This is a small band and they are playing . . . is it by Schubert?'

'It is a serenade of some kind. Hush, listen.'

The music was lulling and sweet, a fragile melody played on strings and harps. It conferred such an air of fanciful mysticism on the open clearing where they stood that James half-expected nymphs and sprites to circle the tree trunks hand-in-hand.

'I haven't heard music like this in an age,' whispered Augusta. 'My own poor efforts at the piano have been the sum of my recent experience. Oh, this is bliss.'

James put his hand on hers and squeezed her fingers, shutting his eyes in a kind of anguish.

Don't think about leaving her.

At the ringing of the bell, they moved on to the theatre, jostling for seats near the stage.

'What manner of performance will it be?' Augusta asked once they had found a space together.

'A burlesque of some sort is the most usual thing, or a harlequinade. Ah, here is the harlequin. And, of course, a chorus of girls in short skirts is *de rigueur*.'

'Do you see their legs? Are they shapely?' asked Augusta in a mischievous whisper.

'Not as shapely as yours,' he replied, playing the gallant again.

'But you cannot see mine.'

'Not yet.'

She gasped delightedly. 'I hope you don't have wicked intentions for me, sir.'

'I always have wicked intentions for you.'

He felt her thrilled shiver against his arm and stole it around her waist, observing that he was not the only gentleman thus entwined.

'I must describe the scenery to you,' he murmured in between yelled lines of dialogue and answering bellows from the audience. 'The backdrop is a somewhat crudely painted representation of a set of mountain peaks. I think they are supposed to be the Alps, as some of the chorus girls wear dirndl skirts in the Swiss peasant style. Oh dear, and here is a yodelling song.'

The audience were encouraged to join in with this, but James eschewed the baying and held Augusta tightly, hoping that the noise and confusion weren't overwhelming her.

'There is a waterfall – a real one – and, oh, I was not aware that polar bears inhabited the Alpine lands but . . .'

'A real polar bear?' Augusta clenched against him.

He laughed.

'Oh, no, no, my love, not a real one. Not unless polar bears wear white nankeen trousers on their four very human-looking legs. Alas, the polar bear has caught the heroine and borne her away – Harlequin must enlist the help of these rather comical mountain soldiers.'

'What is everyone laughing at?'

'A piece of business – I cannot describe it – it makes fun of Lord Palmerston.'

A loud bang, the report of a stage gun interrupted the commentary. Amidst raucous laughter, ridiculous drama and hurried musical numbers, James lost the thread and was unable to narrate further. It was clear enough what was happening, he imagined – chaos didn't need much in the way of description.

After a finale of incomprehensible proportions, the pair was borne along once more in the slipstream of the crowd, next ushered into a room in which a variety of novelty acts followed one upon the other, of increasing degrees of grotesquerie.

James found that the constant describing had dried his throat and suggested taking supper, perhaps in the Cremorne Hotel or in the supper boxes by the dancing platform.

'Oh, by the dancing, please,' Augusta cried, so there it was that they repaired, hand in hand now, breathing in the perfumes and cigar smokes and sweaty underarms of all who passed.

'This is almost too much,' said Augusta, sitting down across the table from James and putting her fingers to her temples. 'I wonder if I am a little over-stimulated. I feel a headache coming.'

'Perhaps we should have started with something a little gentler,' mused James. 'A bazaar or a restaurant.'

'It is like a deluge of sensation. I am unused to it, that is all. I am having a lovely time, please don't think otherwise. To hear so many voices – and the laughter! And the feel of the air from all those skirts, all those feet, and the cool of the night on my skin. I am part of the world again.'

'When was your last expedition?'

'Oh, before Mrs Shaw. I was fifteen, I think. We took a picnic to the river. Oh, how I long to do that again. Shall we? Shall we lie in the long grass and let the sun warm our faces and . . . oh, shall we?'

James coughed and took a draught of the horribly sweet sherry the Cremorne called its house beverage.

'What prevents it?' he said, trying to be non-committal without giving away his resolution.

'Nothing. Nothing must prevent it. Oh, everything will be so different now, James. I will stand up to Mrs Shaw and be mistress in my home again. And with you . . . I no longer have the taste for her. It is only you I want, only you I crave.'

You must not.

'You are my brave pet. Should you like some of this sherry?'

'Did we not say we would drink champagne? Call the waiter. Call for champagne. I will pay.'

'You will not.' But he called the waiter, wincing inwardly at the thought of paying the bill. He would have to write a great many words next week.

The pop of the cork made Augusta squeal with glee and clap her hands.

'Listen to that froth – the popping of the bubbles. It is enough to gladden the most downcast heart, is it not?'

No.

'And the taste . . . nectar.'

'Cheers. Let us drink to future happiness.'

'Oh yes. Future happiness.'

The glasses clinked but James could not look at Augusta as he drank. She celebrated where he could not. A leaden heaviness lay at the pit of his stomach, a dread that thickened his head and made his limbs slow down. The bottle of champagne, seductively curved, stood between them on the white cloth, mocking him. She would be happy without him, it was absurd and vain to suggest otherwise. She would meet another man, a man of her class and standing, who would understand her just as well as he did . . . Except that was hardly likely. How could Augusta reveal her exotic tastes to a potential bridegroom? It hardly cropped up in the course of drawing room pleasantry.

'My love,' he said, and then he could think of nothing to say that would not reveal his inner struggle.

'Yes, beloved?'

'You deserve the greatest happiness,' he said lamely.

She seemed almost disappointed by this. She had leant forward, her eyes dancing as if they had regained their sight, her lips pouting as if begging to be kissed. Now she subsided back into the chair and took another sip of champagne.

'James,' she said, 'do you love me?'

He could answer this truthfully, at least.

'I believe I do,' he said.

And now a contented smile lit her face, uninterrupted by the arrival of the waiter with the food.

'It is such an unusual and intimate set of experiences we have shared,' she said, bending over the plate to divine its contents by sense of smell. 'I think one can scarcely engage in such activity without the precipitate giving of one's heart. Do you?'

'You are right. The necessity for trust, for honesty, for absolute understanding of the other's needs, forces the hand of the affections, so to speak. Before one knows it, one is . . . embroiled.'

'Embroiled? Like these vegetables.'

He smiled. 'No, those are simply broiled, my love.'

'I am embroiled. So deeply – so surprisingly. I did not expect it. Did you?'

'Not in the least. I was hired, you recall, to provide a service.'

'I fear I have taken more from you than you intended to give.'

I fear you have.

'I could not know that you would be so intoxicating.'

'Intoxicating. Ah.'

She drank more champagne, then lifted the glass aloft once more.

'To love,' she announced, and James observed the couples on the surrounding tables, watching them with indulgent eyes.

'To love,' he echoed.

Aphrodite, you heartless jade.

The strains of a popular Schottische drifted over from the dancing platform nearby. It was like the beginning of a death knell to him, the signal that the evening would be over in an hour or two, and then he would make his farewell to Augusta. Could he say the words to her?

'Have you loved before, James?' asked Augusta, causing the melancholy thoughts to dissolve in a ferment of unwelcome memories.

'I?' He played for time, looking towards the dancers on the platform, unable to discern individuals among the heaving, weaving mass.

'I don't know whom else I could be asking, do you?'

She essayed a playful tone, but he could hear the urgency that underlay it as clearly as the bell that urged the pleasure-seekers through the garden.

'Some time ago,' he said, quietly enough that he hoped she would take the hint.

Her face was blank; her fingers toying with the stem of her glass.

'Loved and lost?' she said.

'Yes.'

'You don't wish to speak of it, do you?'

'No.'

'Have you ever spoken of it?'

'Augusta, you know my wishes and you flout them.'

If only his voice carried the authority of his words. But the memory had temporarily unmanned him and he knew she would not be convinced.

'This is not a game any longer, James,' she said. 'I am not your creature to be commanded. Not while we are here, at supper together, as lovers.'

'It has never been a game to me.'

'Oh, it has. That first time . . . no matter. What I mean to say is this. I feel I must know you, my love. I must know everything about you. I must be able to understand you, or I shall live in darkness more encompassing than that which my blindness casts upon me.'

'Perhaps I cannot be known.' This had been a mistake. He should never have brought her here.

'You can, you can. Tell me all, James. Tell me of your

birth, your childhood, your boyish enthusiasms, your family. I want to hear it all.'

'There is very little to tell, and champagne does not at all suit it.'

'Oh, my love. Should we drink bitters?'

'Yes. We should drink bitters. And salt tears.'

She reached for his hand, but missed her target. He took them up, squeezing her fingertips as if he would crush them.

'My father died in jail, a debtor. My mother died of gaol fever – typhoid, you know – when I was but four years old. I was born in the Queen's Bench.'

'Oh, you were not!'

'Indeed I was. Born in prison. Gaol babe.'

'And . . . you lived there?'

'Until I was four years old, yes. After that, I lived with a foster mother in Southwark for a time. My Uncle Stratton at length undertook to have me educated in his own singular way.'

'The uncle with whom you live now?'

'The same. He taught me my letters in the back room of his shop, amongst the drawings of half-clad ballerinas and bound Venuses. I became his messenger and errand boy, carrying packages of obscene material to all the debauched of London. I was quite a favourite. I only escaped from some houses with my virtue because I had learned to box.'

'Your virtue? Oh, whatever do you mean?'

'I was a pretty boy, Augusta. There are men who appreciate such. And women, too, truth be told.'

'You mean they tried to make love to you?'

'Some tried to make love to me. Some were a little more forceful than that. I was invited to some interesting parties. I learned early on to decline such invitations.'

'Your uncle . . . did he not protect you?'

'Had I told him, I suppose he might. I never told him, though.'

'Why not?'

'I suppose . . . I don't know. I suppose I was ashamed. I thought, as I was often told, I brought such attentions upon myself. Oh, you look so shattered. Don't fret, my dear. I grew up quickly and learned how to conduct myself.'

'You were a mere child.'

'Mere children sweep the chimneys, my love.'

'Well, that is so, I suppose.'

'Besides, I was handsomely tipped and able to save myself some money. I was thirteen, or thereabouts, when one of my uncle's best clients, a well-known classical scholar, offered to give me free lessons at his home.'

'But did he expect your love in return?'

'No, he expected nothing. He hoped for it, I am sure. But he never pressed himself upon me. I think he derived his greatest pleasure from teaching me. And I derived pleasure from learning, and so I will always regard him fondly, even if, in some way, he was satisfying a hidden baser urge by bettering me.'

'So this is how you pass so readily as a gentleman?'

'Yes. I am well-read, if ill-everything-else.'

'Are you still acquainted with this gentleman?'

James paused. The champagne tasted too acidic and it caught at the back of his throat.

'We have since parted company,' he said. 'Ten years ago, in the wake of the Obscene Publications Act, when my uncle's shop was raided and shut up, and he imprisoned for a spell.'

'Your benefactor abandoned you? But he was a customer of your uncle's – was he afraid of taint by association?'

'No. He took me in, while the shop was out of commission. I was seventeen at the time.'

'Did he . . . importune you?'

'No. But his wife did.'

'Oh, heavens!'

'I'm afraid I . . . succumbed to temptation. We were discovered together and I was thrown out.'

'And what then?' Augusta's cheeks were pink and she leant forward, her fist tight around the stem of her glass. This was better than one of his stories for her, he observed.

'As I have mentioned, I gained employment at a national school. I did not much care for teaching and it was a relief to me when my uncle came out of prison, opened up his shop again – in the guise of a respectable bookseller – and I was able to revert to my former mode of living.'

'And ever since then . . . ?'

'I have lived among pornographers and whores. Not to put too fine a point on it. And you might look down upon them, but they are, many of them, richer in their hearts and their souls than most of the high-born people I have known.'

'I look down upon nobody,' said Augusta. 'Since I cannot look. Do not presume to know my mind.'

He smiled, but it was a melancholy smile. Why could she not be cold and disapproving? Why did she insist on keeping his love warm and alive in his heart?

'If you are disreputable,' she continued, 'then I have no use for reputation.'

'You should,' he said. 'For such as you, it is important.'

'Not for long. James . . . we could leave London. We could leave England. Live on the continent – travel, or settle somewhere temperate and anonymous. I have the means, if you are willing.'

He thought his heart might stop.

'Leave?' he echoed. He had never dared accept any possibility of their togetherness, had not felt able to bear the inevitable disappointment he had learned was congruent with airy speculation. If life had taught him one thing, it was that pleasure was fleeting and incompatible with his hard reality. In that, he was just the same as everyone who drudged a dishonest living in Holywell Street.

'Yes,' breathed Augusta, warming to her theme and knocking back the champagne in a couple of swift gulps. 'Oh, my champagne is gone. Will you pour me another glass? Yes, we can leave. Who is there to prevent us? Mrs Shaw? Why, she is a hireling. I am answerable to nobody else. I shall sell the house – I hate the place, anyway – and we will go to Rome, to Venice, to Paris, to . . . oh, say you will. Say you will come with me. We could even marry!'

'We could not,' said James with a swift intake of breath. 'No, that is one thing we could not do.'

She waited for him to put down the champagne bottle.

'Why not? No, don't answer. Don't tell me. We needn't marry. We can simply adopt the same name, for our travels, and nobody will be the wiser. If that is your wish, dearest James.'

'It is not my wish, but it is all I can offer.'

'Then . . .' She swallowed and bent her face to her glass, as if its fizz might revive her failing spirits. 'Am I to understand . . . no, do not tell me.'

'I have a wife,' he said gently.

Chapter Eight

'And she lives?' Augusta's sightless eyes glistened. They might not see, but they could still weep.

James took his handkerchief and reached across to dab the gathering glimmer at the corners.

'I don't know,' he admitted. 'I think, if she were dead, some effort might have been made to trace me. I have kept watch on all the newspapers.'

'You don't know where she is?'

'No.'

'Please, put your handkerchief away, I am well. This was the love you did not wish to speak of?'

'Yes. But I should tell you. You have made me such a handsome and generous offer – it is ungenerous of me to hoard my secrets from you, even if you may hate me for them. You deserve to know.'

'Please tell me about her. Tell me whom I must eclipse.'

'Augusta, it is not a case of eclipsing her.'

'Then whatever it is I must do to replace her in your heart.'

'You have a place in my heart. You are precious to me, so

very precious. I have never had such intensity of communion with a woman. I have never known one who shared my dark proclivities to such an extent—'

'Oh, don't! Don't make it all about the bedchamber. I shall hate myself.'

'Why? You should love yourself, as I love you. It is nothing to be ashamed of. It makes you mine, and me yours.'

'But I suppose what you felt for *her* was on a higher plane?' Augusta's voice was bitter, tight with jealousy.

'I shall not speak of it if it upsets you so.'

'James! I shall leave here, leave you, if you will not tell me.'

He felt that she meant it.

'Very well. In the briefest possible terms: She was a chorus girl at the Olympic Theatre, which stands on Wych Street and has a stage exit on Holywell Street. I would see her there, leaving every night with her companions. I was, at the time, barely twenty-one years old.'

'And you are now twenty-seven? It was not long ago.'

'It seems very long ago, to me. Her name is Ellen. Was. Is. I know not. I would contrive to be, each night, in the public house they sometimes visited after performing. I haunted it, although she would only come in perhaps one or two nights of the week. I became a little . . . unhinged . . . with the need to possess her. I pursued her remorselessly. At first she would make fun and then it became a kind of game – she would avoid me, but it was clear that she expected me to follow her, to chase her. She took pleasure in it. It became a consuming affair, for both of us.'

'I should so like to be courted like that,' sighed Augusta.

'She liked the courtship well enough. It took almost a year but at length I wore her down and she consented to marry me. Why I ever thought myself a suitable husband, I don't know. I earned, then as now, very little and had only my room above Stratton's bookshop to call a home. But she said yes. I didn't question it.'

'A life of poverty, with love, is still a good life.'

'You might think so, Augusta, but I advise you to keep a close hold on your money. Our life was not a good life. I wanted Ellen to stop working at the Olympic, but she would not. The end of our little game of chase was the end of her feeling for me – I suppose she had not expected her affections to fade as soon as she was caught, but they did. She had no genuine love for me. One night, three months after our wedding, she did not return from the Olympic. I have not seen or heard of her since.'

Augusta was silent for a time.

'Was there nobody you could ask? Her friends, the other chorus girls, the theatre manager?'

'I asked everyone I could think of. She had left the theatre with a gentleman. They were to dine at some rooms on the Strand. Nobody knew what happened after that, nor yet the gentleman's name.'

'I suppose he installed her somewhere as his mistress?' Augusta hazarded.

'I suppose you may well be right.' He drank the remainder of the champagne. 'I was too young, and she was too beautiful, for a life spent in Holywell Street. You see me now, a sadder and a wiser man. Yet not so sad.' He took her hands again and kissed her fingertips. 'For you have revived my spirits.'

'We are star-crossed,' she said.

'Had Juliet been blind and Romeo been married, and both been of a class apart. It is to be hoped our story will not end so, however.'

'What an anomaly you are. The gaol-born gentleman. The schoolmaster who spared the rod – but only on his pupils. The married man with no wife. It is all terribly *romantic*.'

'Until you live it.'

'Yes. I am sorry. I was insensitive.'

The pause that followed was almost too full for James to bear. He wanted to get up and pace furiously up and down. Could he leave the country with her? Would his pride let him live on her money? Did he, after all, love her enough? What obstacles stood in his way?

Augusta was first to speak again.

'If she were to come back . . .' she said.

'Ellen?'

'Yes.'

He looked up to the clouds above, which were clearing, revealing pockets of starlight.

'I do not think it likely,' he said.

'But if she did.'

He shook his head. 'She is my wife,' he said. 'But that does not mean I must take her back. I am not the same man now as I was then, and she is not the woman I dreamed she was.'

'She is your past.'

'Yes. I wish I had not such a past, but I cannot erase it. What I can do is look to the future, and marvel at the possibility that it might contain you.'

'It must contain me. Mine must contain you. We could leave tomorrow, before Mrs Shaw returns. I need only go to the bank and make a withdrawal for the passage.'

'Augusta, do not act in haste.'

'I have thought and thought about it.'

'We have known one another two months.'

'It is long enough! Is it not long enough for you?'

'I have some affairs to settle before I can leave town.' Annie's face, her cheeky grin replaced by distress, lodged itself in his mind and would not be moved.

'You can write your stories anywhere in the world and post them to London.'

'Those are not the affairs I have in mind. I must file this piece on the Contagious Diseases Act. I must see that my neighbour is released from the Lock Hospital.'

'Oh, your neighbour!' cried Augusta, frustrated. 'Are your whores and chorus girls always to come before me?'

'Augusta, I will not have you speak so,' he hissed in a furious undertone.

She was meek straight away, casting her face down to the table.

'Forgive me. I spoke rashly. I am merely anxious to know my own future.'

'My love, let us give ourselves time to consider this decision. If I am with you, whether in London or, or the East Indies, or anywhere, I am well. If you fear Mrs Shaw's return, you needn't. You are perfectly within your rights to dispense with her services.'

'Oh, I could never . . . I would far rather just leave and never have to deal with her again.'

'It is the coward's way, Augusta. I know you better than that. If you wish, I can be with you for the difficult interview.'

'Oh, would you? I could do it if you were by my side.' She shuddered briefly.

'Of course,' he said softly. 'And I think, if we leave, Paulette should come too. What future has she, if thrown back on her own resources?'

'I would give her a character. You need not be the personal

saviour of every fallen woman in London, you know. Leave
it to Mr Gladstone.'

James bit back a sharp retort.

'You know nothing of their lives, and you should thank
God for it,' he said, more mildly.

'Oh, let's not quarrel. Not on such a night as tonight,
when I am so full of hope and love and elation. You do love
me, do you not?'

'I do. I cannot expect to thrive without you.'

'Nor I without you. Oh, why did I not seek you out
sooner? We could, even now, be sitting beneath palms on
some southern shore.'

'Or drinking Madeira wine in Madeira.'

'Or walking hand and hand through some scented garden
on the Amalfi coast.'

'Or listening to a real German band in Germany.'

'Or lying abed, anywhere at all, it would matter not
where.'

'Yes, that last is my favourite, I think. But we can do that
here.'

'Here? At Cremorne?' She giggled coquettishly.

'If we wish it.'

'You are a devil! Oh, will you dance with me? I do so love
this tune.'

The music, seductive and shimmering, drew them to
the platform. James held Augusta tightly in his arms, so she
needed only to rely on the movement of his body against
hers and the rhythm of the band to dictate her steps and
cast off into the waltz. Now that there were others on the
floor, he was self-conscious about the figure he cut, but
after a time it became clear that the other dancers were all
absorbed in their partners, or in trying to remain upright

after a few too many of Cremorne's special beverages.

Her waist strained and twisted against his hand and her bosom was pressed to his lower chest. If only she didn't wear so many petticoats, he thought he would be able to feel the heat flowing from her sex. Her initial stiffness melted by degrees until she was content to be led around the floor, so complete was her trust in him.

Not for the first time, James tried to imagine how blindness must feel. Would he be able to let another be his eyes? He felt a profound sense of responsibility – the confidence she rested in him was humbling. For all she knew, he could be making faces of revulsion every time he spoke to her. He could be a fortune hunter, cold, hard avarice in his eyes – she would never see it.

Then it was that a disquieting question occurred to him. Was it him she loved, or the escape he represented? Perhaps, after all, she had been playing him and conspiring to free herself from the implacable grasp of Mrs Shaw.

But then, would this possibility not have occurred to that sharp-eyed lady?

Rings within rings within rings of possibility spun in his head, making it ache. Heavy perfumes and beer fumes added to the fug of his brain until he had to draw Augusta aside and stagger from the platform before he swooned like a girl.

'Kiss me,' she sighed, once the press of bodies on all sides had thinned out and they were among the bushes and box trees behind the platform.

'The way you swore only the man you loved could kiss you?' he reminded her. What a victory it had been, the first time she allowed him to touch her lips. Surely she had meant this? Surely such profound sentiment could not be counterfeited?

'Yes, yes, and it was you. At last, it was you. Kiss my lips, my love, and know that they are yours, that all of me is yours.'

A tree bark of suitable width and smoothness presented itself before him and he manoeuvred Augusta against it, still in their dancer's clasp. Her fingers pressed into the back of his neck as he bent his head, clearing now that the air was less heavy, and took her lips with his.

He lifted the little hand that he held clasped and fixed it high above her head, against the tree trunk, holding her in thrall. Her bosom heaved against him, fast as the breath he was stopping up with his mouth.

You are *mine*, he insisted to himself. *You mean this.*

With his hips he imprisoned her in position, her legs clamped between the tree and his solid form. She made no effort to escape her plight but showed that she welcomed it, pushing her pelvis into him and darting her tongue between his lips.

He feasted upon her, ravenous, as if the Cremorne supper had gone uneaten. He bit and sucked and probed every inch of her warm, wet mouth until she made tiny mewls of protest in her throat. He released her for a second, during which she gasped, 'My breath!' and then caught her again.

The hand that had been around his waist slipped under his jacket and stroked the silken back of his waistcoat. Her knuckles ran lightly up and down his spine. He growled and fixed his teeth to her lower lip. The hard knot of his erection pushed into her stomach and he parted her legs with an importunate knee.

'Dearest, wickedest love,' she panted, released for another brief intermission. 'You can have no idea what a wanton creature your pet is.'

'Yes, I can.'

'But what if I told you I had neglected to wear anything beneath my skirts tonight?'

He grew faint again, leaning his head on the bark, pressing his lips to her ear.

'You cannot untell what you have told me,' he whispered.

'No,' she said, quivering.

'And, now it is told, I cannot unhear it.'

'No.'

'And, now it is heard, I cannot but act upon it.'

'I cannot stop you.'

No, she could not stop him, and he made this clear by lifting up her skirts so that her pale bare legs trembled in the new moonlight.

'Put your arms about my neck,' he ordered. 'And hold tightly.'

She obeyed, with a shuddering laugh, as if afraid of what he had in store for her but knew herself powerless to evade it. He clasped the backs of her thighs in each hand and lifted her feet from the ground until her legs were wrapped around his waist.

She yelped but he silenced her with another kiss, even more brutal than its predecessors.

'Take what you are given,' he muttered into her ear, pushing himself hard against her so that she was firmly pinned.

She clung with monkey-like tenacity while he unbuttoned and unbraced and released his stiff cock from its trammels.

'I suppose you are wet enough,' he wondered aloud, as much for her benefit as his, for he knew how she loved to die a thousand shameful deaths under the lash of his tongue. He jammed his crotch into hers and rubbed her juices all over his shaft. 'Oh yes, I see that you are. Of course you are. You are empty without it, are you not? Incomplete unless filled to the brim with what I have to give you, are you not, pet? Answer me.'

'Yes, sir, yes, it is true, I long to have it in me, always.'

The words spurred him to action and he buried himself, swiftly and sharply, inside her tight, willing sheath. The stroke was bold and she cried out, needing more of his masterful silencing treatment, his tongue mimicking the other member, deep in her throat.

No gentle build-up now, no caressing, no easing into coition. Instead a shocking rhythm from the start, thrusts that slammed her against the tree and made her hold on to him so tight that her arms and legs shook with the effort of it.

She buried her face in his neck, trying to muffle the unearthly sounds issuing from her throat. When he felt her teeth on the sensitive skin there, all thoughts of drawing the coupling out were driven from him. She made him lose control of himself, she made him mad. It was impossible to take her hard enough. If he could slam her right through the tree's bark, he would, but he had to content himself with filling her with his seed, letting it pour, hot and plentiful, into that tight little quim that belonged to him.

The deed was done before he considered its implications.

'Oh,' he breathed, laying his forehead on her shoulder. 'Oh, I should not have—'

'No matter,' she whispered, finally releasing his neck from the clamp of her pearly little teeth. He would be marked. He must wear his collar high tomorrow.

James' knees could no longer hold out and he sank down to the ground, still connected to Augusta at their most intimate juncture. They clung to each other like ceramic figures on a mantelpiece, if ceramic figures in such an improper pose could exist, as if fused together.

'But what if you should—?'

'No matter,' she repeated, kissing his cheek and nibbling at his earlobe. 'We are leaving here.'

James still privately felt that, however far they travelled from London, their circumstances were less than ideal for bringing a child into the world. But it could not now be helped and, with a little luck, they might escape that eventuality all the same.

'I love you so, James,' she said.

'And I you. But I was a brute. Was there pleasure in it for you?'

'Oh yes. Very much pleasure.'

They kissed fervently and were still so engaged when a rustling from the bushes close by disturbed their post-coital embraces.

Augusta broke off, having heard it first, and James looked up to see a pair of men he did not recognise, in the company of a uniformed police officer and . . . James stared.

'Mrs Shaw.'

Chapter Nine

'So you see,' she said to the accompanying men. 'It is as I told you.'

James pulled hastily out of Augusta and tried to wipe himself on the grass before correcting his attire. His lover had stiffened and cried out with dismay on hearing Mrs Shaw's voice, turning away and hiding her face in the tree's bark.

'I see,' said one of the men, shaking his head. 'Dreadful business. Full-blown nymphomania.'

The other gentleman merely folded his arms and nodded.

'We have had our suspicions for years,' he said.

'Oh, how dare you!' Augusta turned her face back to the company and hauled herself to her feet.

Seeing that her legs shook, James took her elbow, holding her steady.

'How dare you, Rupert,' she repeated. 'Are there no depths to which you will not stoop? And you, Mrs Shaw! You, to conspire with him against me. For shame!'

'This is one of your cousins?' James asked, though he felt he already knew the answer.

'Yes, we share a bloodline, though we have little else in common, including simple humanity.'

'See how she raves,' gloated Mrs Shaw. 'She is unhinged by her excesses.'

'Constable,' said the other man, whom James supposed some kind of asylum quack. 'Seize the patient.'

'Leave her,' snarled James, standing in front of Augusta. 'She is as sane as you are.'

'The corrupter does not wish to lose his prey,' observed cousin Rupert.

'Move aside, sir, or consider yourself under arrest for obstructing a police officer in the course of his duty. Not to mention gross indecency.'

'Yes, arrest me,' cried James. 'I am guilty. But leave her.'

'Mr Stratton,' said Mrs Shaw, stepping towards him with a smile made of razor blades and hate. 'If you value your liberty, leave us now. If not, I am sure the constable here will be able to raise some assistance to deal with you. Nothing will stop us from doing what is best for poor Augusta, least of all a backstreet pornographer.'

'I will not let you take her.'

Mrs Shaw signalled to the policeman, who blew his whistle loudly.

Realising that his time for reasoning and remonstration was short, James turned to the cousin.

'I know, for Augusta has told me all, that you covet her inheritance and you have no scruples in the lengths you will go to in order to obtain it. I suppose your pocket doctor does not know this? Do you, doctor? This man wants Augusta's money. His motive is avarice and greed. Meanwhile, Augusta has the full control of her mental faculties and is guilty of no worse crime than falling in love. Do you treat your patients for love, doctor? Do you consider it an illness?'

'Of course not, but the only women I know who would behave as Lady Heathcote has are prostitutes and nymphomaniacs. She is certainly not the former and so I have no hesitation in diagnosing the latter.'

'But you are wrong!'

'Oh no, young man, I am very seldom wrong and you yourself show some alarming signs of an overly passionate disposition.'

'Do not presume to diagnose me, sir; I am a healthy man as she is a healthy woman. We do no more than act on God-given desires.'

'Oh, so it's God's fault now,' said Mrs Shaw with a waspish laugh.

'Jezebel,' spat James, seeing the reinforcements advance through the dark shrubberies.

Augusta clung tighter than ever to James, feeling perhaps that the time when she would be wrenched from him came close.

'You will not,' he vowed, 'you will not take her, not while I stand.'

'Step aside,' barked the constable, braver now with his comrades at hand.

'Augusta, my dear,' said Mrs Shaw, her voice all false tenderness. 'Come to your loving Mrs Shaw.'

'I love him and only him,' she cried. 'You do not love me. You are in league with my enemies. How long have you been plotting with them?'

'You see, she has such a dark imagination,' said Mrs Shaw, turning to the doctor.

'How can I be imagining what is here before me! I

would say I could see it with my own eyes, but of course—'

'You might consider,' said Mrs Shaw, still speaking to the medic, 'the possibility that her blindness is entirely hysterical. I have always thought it so.'

'I had a blow to the head!' screamed Augusta.

Rupert laughed. 'So we see.'

James leapt forward and laid him out with one well-placed fist. Augusta, still clinging to him, staggered and became disengaged. In a moment, the doctor had hold of her, Mrs Shaw providing reinforcement at her shoulder.

James wheeled around, lunging towards them to try and retrieve Augusta, but the police officer and his cronies were all around now and they leapt on him, knocking him to the floor and pinning him down until he could kick and flail no longer.

By the time they raised him to his feet, handcuffed and bleeding from the lip, Augusta had been taken.

'What is the charge?'

Uncle Stratton looked quite bilious as he stood on the other side of the barred holding cell at Walton Street police station in Brompton.

'Affray. Resisting arrest. Public indecency.' James quoted the list with dull resignation.

'And all this happened at the Cremorne Gardens? Where you went with the young lady you have been so secretive about?'

'Yes.'

'The thing is, James, I've been warned to stop you poking your nose in affairs that don't concern you.'

'Warned against? By whom?'

'I had a visitor – the lady in black who first enquired for

you. According to her, you are to forget everything that you
have seen and heard if I value my livelihood and my home.'

'She threatens the shop?'

'I believe so.'

'She is Satan in black bombazine.'

'She is convincing enough for me. James, I urge you to
do as she says. Take whatever the magistrate hands down and
then come back to Holywell Street and put all this behind
you.'

'I thought you believed in social justice.'

'I do, boy, you know it.'

'I have seen the most hideous of injustices. I cannot allow
it. I must rescue that woman, Uncle, or I cannot live with
myself.'

'Rescuing women. One day whores, the next, aristocratic
ladies. You cannot fight these people, lad. The odds are
stacked too high against you.'

'I don't care what you say. I shall act according to my
conscience. Uncle, you must back me. I cannot stay in here
while she . . . they could be doing anything to her.'

'They'll let you go once they've set a date for your court
appearance.'

'In the meantime, they might be . . . *ugh*.' James shuddered. He had visited the Bethlem hospital as a curious
younger man and, although he supposed Augusta would
be shut away in some more private, genteel establishment,
the treatments would probably vary little from what was
available to the poorest lunatics. An image of his love,
strapped to a bed covered in leeches, made him blanch
and turn away from his uncle, his hand over his mouth to
suppress the rise of bile. She would not even see what they
were about to do to her.

'I can't lose the shop again,' pleaded Uncle Stratton. 'Be reasonable, James.'

'Am I to be reasonable at the expense of the woman I love? Be reasonable on your own account, Uncle. You ask too much of me.'

Uncle Stratton wrung his hands a few minutes more then left, shaking his head.

James went back to the stone bench he had been sharing with a variety of drunks and thieves and laid his head against the wall, shutting his eyes.

His head ached and he had not slept a wink since his arrest the night before. His mind raced with the knowledge of Augusta's terrible predicament and he found himself alternating horrible imaginings of her fate with rage against Mrs Shaw and cousin Rupert.

Had this been their object all along? To have Augusta shut away in an asylum so that Rupert could assume power of attorney over all her wealth? Something must be in it for Mrs Shaw – a share of the money, he supposed. But how long had the plot been laid? Had she always been Augusta's foe, or had Rupert made advances to her? It seemed unbearably cruel on the part of Mrs Shaw to introduce Augusta to the world of sensual pleasures and then use that to entrap her.

'She should be in the asylum,' he muttered. 'She is unnatural.'

'Wossat you say, boy?' An old drunk in the corner raised his threadbare hat. 'Speakin' ill of a lady, is it? I hopes not.'

'No lady,' muttered James.

After a miserable, painful hour spent in a hell of his own contemplation, James was finally allowed to succumb to sleep. His dreams were disturbing, of ripe red lips and fat leeches, barred windows and bared breasts. The jangling of the locks woke him abruptly and he did not understand the words of the officer with the keys until he spoke them a second time.

'Stratton, you're out. Look sharp.'

He swayed a little on his feet, his head still full of swooping strangeness, and stepped carefully across the cell to its door, which was opened only enough to let him squeeze through.

'You're to present yourself at Westminster Police Court on Friday next at one o'clock sharp to answer charges,' said the police officer who had arrested him, failing to meet his eyes. 'These your belongings? One fob watch, one wallet containing sixteen shillings and sixpence, one silk topper, one jewelled tie pin.'

'Yes, they are mine.'

'Sign here then. You know where the Westminster court is, do you? Vincent Square.'

'I will attend.'

'Best not forget, eh? Next Friday. I'll be there to give evidence against you. Keep your nose clean in the meantime.'

'Are you personally acquainted with Mrs Shaw?'

'I said, keep your nose clean.' The officer gave him a sharp look.

'Or did you happen to be on duty in the vicinity of the Cremorne Gardens?'

'Let's get you out of here.'

'You have witnessed a crime – a most monstrous injustice. A lady as fully in possession of her wits as you or I, locked away in an asylum by malevolent relatives. Can you stand by and let that—'

Stratton found himself unceremoniously shoved through the door and down the steps of the station, landing ignominiously on his hands and knees on the pavement, eliciting huffs from passers-by.

It was a moment or two before he could collect himself. His head ached and his body was sore in all quarters after the desperate struggles of the evening. He was famished, having turned down the gaol-house breakfast, and he thought one of his fingers might be broken.

But that was mere background irritation compared to the huge canker of fear and despair pulsing in his breast. How was he to find Augusta? How was he to save her?

'Jem? Oh, Jem. It's you, ain't it?'

He looked up and saw, through a fog of pain and bleached light, a familiar face looming down.

'Annie,' he said, surprise lending springs to his legs. He scrambled upright and stared. 'Do I see aright?'

'Your uncle said you was here. I came down soon as I could. What have you been up to, you silly boy?'

Her hand on his bruised cheekbone was soft and tender. He put his own hand upon it, holding her there for a moment.

'You are not in the Lock Hospital?' he said, feeling stupid at the obviousness of the remark.

'No. I let 'em do their worst in the end. It was that or never get out of there – or so they said. I couldn't stand it no more.'

'You should not have to submit to such an indignity. It is an outrage. There is a lady in Liverpool to whom I mean to write.'

'It's all finished with now, Jem. Never mind me. What's happened to you?'

He felt as if circles span around his head, little satellites, giving him glimpses of visions.

'I ought to eat something,' he said.

'Oh, well, come on. Hyde Park ain't far. We'll get a potato

and eat it by the lake, shall we? And you can tell your Annie all about it.'

On a bench beneath the leafy canopy of the park, James and Annie sat eating their potato and watching the ducks in companionable silence until Annie swallowed her last morsel and took a breath.

'So, then. Your uncle didn't have much to say to me, except "Where's me rent?" Who's been spoiling your lovely face?'

'I need your help, Annie,' he said, vestiges of an idea having formed somewhere in the chaos of his head.

'*My* help? What can I do? Tell me what's gone on.'

'I can't. If I say too much, there may be a price to pay, heavier than a few cuts and bruises. But you can help me.'

'What would you have me do?'

'There is a house not far from here – a very grand house in a very grand part of town. It would help me enormously if you could visit that house – the back door, the servants' entrance – and ask to speak to your cousin Paulette.'

'I don't have a cousin Paulette.'

'No, of course. But I need to see her, most urgently. It is more important than I can say. Will you try?'

'Well, I s'pose,' said Annie dubiously. 'What's the address?'

'Fifty-six Eaton Place. The back entrance can be approached via the mews behind it. There is a cook and a young girl, a scullery maid, her name escapes me. Knock on the kitchen door and ask to speak with Paulette. I would give you a note, but she cannot, I think, read. When you are alone, ask her to name a time and place when we can meet, as soon as can be arranged. Today is best, tomorrow may already be too late.'

'Too late for what?'

James shook his head and held out his hand. 'Too late,' he repeated, his voice cracking.

'All right, all right, lovey. Deario. I ain't never seen you like this. That address again?'

He repeated the address, and the mission.

'And will you wait here?'

'I will wait here. If you can return with her, so much the better. If not, just remember the time and venue she names.'

'Right. No time like the present then. And I wouldn't be doing this for anyone but you, you know.'

'I am sensible of it. Thank you. You will have my undying gratitude.'

She winked. 'I'll have to think of something to do with that.'

Annie rose and pecked James on the cheek before bustling off over the ripe green grass, her crimson gown, far too fancy for the daytime, catching every eye.

He was asleep on the bench when she returned, pumping him by the arm to rouse him.

'Oh, how could I have slept?' he chided himself, trying to dismiss the blur from his head by shaking it vigorously. 'Did you see her? What news?'

'She can't get away this morning but she has an errand to run in an hour or so. She can meet you in Eaton Square Gardens at three o'clock. She says to wait if she ain't there on the dot.'

'Of course, of course. Three o'clock. I hope it is not too late.'

'She seemed very frightened. She thought the scullery maid might be on to us. Said something about her having a lot of strange cousins.'

James clasped his brow, trying hard to think in competition

with the throb that threatened to burst through his skull.

'Come on,' said Annie, motioning him up. 'Let's get you home. You could do with a lie down, by the looks of you.'

'I need to go the apothecary. A tot of laudanum in some brandy. I can scarcely see through this headache.'

'I've got a bottle in me room, lovey. Come on.'

The temptation to lie down on Annie's bed, amongst her garters and ribbons and pots of rouge and discarded petticoats, and dream the day away was immense but James knew that he must do his utmost to remain alert and awake. To miss the meeting with Paulette was out of the question.

So he stayed just long enough to swallow a measure of brandy mixed with laudanum, screw up his face at the odd sickly-sweet fire of it, and let Annie stroke his forehead for five minutes until the worst of the pain began to recede.

'I mustn't sleep,' he said, resisting Annie's attempts to draw him down into her arms.

'But I've missed you. You need to rest, Jem.'

'If I sleep now, I will not wake. Better that I walk the streets until the hour of my meeting is nigh. Thank you, Annie, for all your kindness. I don't deserve it.'

'You still owe me undying gratitude,' she pointed out, a mite sulkily. 'I might want to collect.'

'Another time,' he promised, kissing the top of her head and hastening through the door.

The streets, usually his wide domain, which he traversed with confident ease, seemed different today. Narrower, darker, dirtier – and threatening who-knew-what around each corner. James found himself looking sideways and watching his back, passing clear of alleyways and archways. Every eye that met his was assessed and glared at in return, every street vendor pressing against him earned a sharp oath.

In one night, the city had turned against him, and now it was his enemy. He found himself thinking everybody was in on some huge conspiracy against him, and all knew of Augusta's misfortune, and his part in it.

If it weren't for me. The words tortured him, running incessantly through his head and yet he knew that Mrs Shaw and Rupert and the rest of their coterie would have found a way to entrap Augusta in the end, with or without him.

Passing an art gallery, he saw a watercolour scene of a garden in the south of France, and the thought of how he and Augusta had sat making starry-eyed plans for European travel scant hours before made him stop and crouch down by the window and have to shut his eyes until the wave of despair passed.

Where was she now and what were they doing to her? He did not dare think of it. The brandy and laudanum sat uneasily with his bile and he did not want to risk the indignity of vomiting on the street. No, he must think only of freeing her from whatever imprisonment she suffered.

They would have to leave the country as precipitately as could be arranged. A mail train to Dover, a boat for hire. As for bringing the guilty to justice, well, that seemed too formidable a task. Let them have her money, let them have her property. To bring all to light would harm Augusta's reputation anyway. If she could be free and with him, they might live as peasants treading grapes in the French vineyards for all he cared.

Without having realised where his feet trod, he found himself before the Society for the Improvement of Fallen Girls and Women in Little Ormond Street.

Perhaps Mrs Edwards would care to know what manner of woman her friend Mrs Shaw was? Perhaps she should be warned not to send any further unfortunate girls to that house in Eaton Place? Perhaps he could extend the scope of his article about the Contagious Diseases Act to encompass the shameful treatment of women in general?

All these on his mind, he hastened up the steps and rang the bell.

'Mr Stratton wishes to take a moment of Mrs Edwards' time,' he told the maid, who looked a little alarmed to see him. 'Excuse my face,' he said, essaying a rueful smile.

She came back a moment later.

'I'm afraid Mrs Edwards is busy, sir.'

'Afraid, are you? No doubt, living in a prison like this. Step aside – I will see her.'

He had marched across the hall to Mrs Edwards' office before the maid could cry out a warning.

Two women bent over Mrs Edwards' desk, examining a document closely. When he entered the room, they looked up. Mrs Edwards gasped in affronted wrath while her companion's eyes narrowed to gimlet proportions.

'Mrs Shaw,' said James, low and with precise enunciation.

'Mr Stratton, you were not invited in,' said Mrs Edwards. 'Kindly leave us.'

'You know this woman well?' he asked of the refuge keeper, indicating a thumb in Mrs Shaw's direction. 'You know what a great friend she is of the unfortunate?'

'Get out. I will call for a police officer.' Mrs Edwards went to the window and pulled up the sash.

'Where is Augusta?' demanded James of Mrs Shaw, who merely stood, smirking slightly, on the other side of the desk. 'What have you done with her, you evil bitch?'

Mrs Edwards began to wave frantically out of the window.

'Hold, Patricia,' said Mrs Shaw calmly. 'This fellow need not detain us.'

'Augusta. Tell me where she is or I swear I'll take you by the throat and—'

'Hush! Such a passionate young man, aren't you, Stratton? I've told you, haven't I, Patricia, what interesting tastes he has. How he treated my poor little Augusta – drove her to nymphomania.'

'You lie!'

'But what if I were to tell you, Stratton, that you have done a great many people a great deal of good?'

'What?'

Mrs Shaw waved downwards at the document on the table.

'My share of Lady Heathcote's fortune is rather substantial – the Heathcote cousins tried to palm me off, of course, but I am not a woman to be trifled with. I held out for my thirty per cent. I feel I earned it, after all those years with that silly little trollop.'

'You have sold her! Thirty per cent? Thirty pieces of silver! I hope and trust you will meet the same end as that miserable traitor.'

'You dare to cast moral opprobrium on me, Stratton? You, who are no better than a common fortune-hunter? Better the money should go where it now will – towards this refuge and the unfortunates within – than straight into your pocket, as you designed.'

'It was never my design,' cried James, beyond self-command now. 'I am here now because I care for her – because I *love* her, with her fortune or without it. Tell me where she is and I will take her away from you and all those who wish her harm. We will never make any claim on the money. We will disappear and you will never hear from us more.'

Mrs Shaw laughed scornfully. 'A poor effort from a man of such imagination, Stratton. No. Remove yourself now unless you have developed a taste for the hospitality of the police cell. Go and comfort yourself that Augusta's loss is the immeasurable gain of so many young women less fortunate than her.'

'Who on earth could be less fortunate than Augusta at this moment?'

'I see a police officer, a pair of them,' said Mrs Edwards, still at the sash. 'Shall I cry murder, Millicent?'

'Let us give the young man one final chance to leave of his own accord.'

Defeated, James backed out of the room, but before he left, the slightest thread of an idea occurred to him, and he spoke again.

'Well, you have done your worst,' he said. 'You have her money and I must throw in my hand. Well played, Mrs Shaw. You have won the prize. At least, I suppose, I gave Augusta some pleasure before you laid down your cruel cards on the table.'

'You did,' she conceded, and her face reflected quiet but utter triumph.

James left without further remark, ready to beat a path to Eaton Square Gardens.

Amidst his rage and anxiety, he could at least find comfort in having one piece of the puzzle in place. Mrs Edwards and Mrs Shaw were in league. Perhaps Mrs Shaw had even conceived this diabolical plan as a route to Mrs Edwards' heart, for there seemed to be an intimacy between them beyond that of platonic friends. Augusta was no more than a sacrificial lamb to her, immolated on the altar of Mrs Edwards.

And she had hired him on the assumption that he would abuse his position and attempt to win Augusta's heart and, thereby, her fortune. The thought gave him pause. Did it make him unnatural, that this had not crossed his mind? Never for a moment had he considered it even possible that Augusta would entertain the idea of marrying him – although, of course, his own situation rendered the possibility void. Had Mrs Shaw known of his unfortunate marital status, would she have hired another man for the job?

She had misread him, and perhaps her attribution of vile motives to everybody might be her downfall. She would not expect him to pursue Augusta now that the money was locked away in the possession of her cousins. She would expect him to fade quietly back into his Holywell Street life, perhaps casting around for a rich widow or another vulnerable and propertied young woman. It conferred a tiny advantage on him, that she laboured under this misapprehension – she would not bother placing obstacles in the way of his search for Augusta, assuming him to have meant his last words to her sincerely.

He was a little early for his meeting with Paulette and he paced around the gardens as if they were a cage rather than a pleasant oasis of flowerbeds and trees, in the statuesque shade of its grand surroundings.

The church clock at nearby St Peter's struck three and still there was no sign of Paulette. He left the gardens and circumambulated them restlessly, too strung up to be aware of the continuing ache and fatigue of his body.

At last she appeared at the corner and he ran across to her, seized her wrist with both hands and dragged her, half-laughing, half-protesting, across to the gardens.

'Rose for your lady love?' asked the flower seller beneath the lamp post by the gate, but he ignored the suggestion and pulled Paulette inside the fences while the vendor chuckled at what she no doubt saw as a lover's impetuosity.

'Mr Stratton!' exclaimed Paulette, once he had sat her and himself down on a bench beneath a spreading London plane tree. 'I'm all a-flutter.'

'I beg your pardon, Paulette. I must express my heartfelt thanks at your coming here. You do me a great favour.'

'It was a little difficult to get away, but once Mrs Shaw was gone out of the house—'

'Yes, she is not at home; I know that. What I do not know – what I must know – is where Augusta is.'

'I hardly know, sir, I wish I could say.'

She was at once frightened and upset at James's intensity of manner and he could see that she genuinely desired to help him. He quelled the urge to dash his fist against the bench and spoke more gently.

'I believe they have taken her to an asylum, Paulette. I need to know which one.'

'I'm not sure how I can—'

'Don't be afraid, I don't mean to shout at you.'

He took her hand and held it affectionately, using its smallness and vulnerability to still the rush of his blood and remind him that none of this was Paulette's fault.

'Just think for me, Paulette, and tell me, if you can, what happened last night. Did Mrs Shaw return to the house with Augusta?'

'Why, yes, sir, they all came back late, after midnight, it

was. I was abed upstairs but I heard the clamour of it, we all did. Her Ladyship was weeping and screaming fit to wake the dead. We all got up and stood about the landing, listening to what was happening.'

'And what *was* happening?' James could barely stand to breathe, so precious was every word Paulette spoke.

'Well, we all got the idea that Miss Augusta was taken bad, while she was out. A doctor was there, saying it was hysteria and nympho-whatnot and he'd find a bed for her in the morning.'

'A bed for her? At an asylum? Think, Paulette, did he mention any names, any places?'

She shook her head, tears glistening in her eyes.

'And when did they take her? Do you recall?'

'It was soon after they came in. I suppose they must have thought of a place to take her after all, but I did not hear. Everything was very confused, very garbled and poor Miss Augusta shrieking over it all . . . It quite froze the blood to hear her . . .'

Paulette shuddered and James felt the vibrations, echoing them in sympathy.

'So she was taken away, in the middle of the night? Did Mrs Shaw go with her?'

'No, she stayed here with the other gentleman, not the doctor. They went into one of the drawing rooms and we didn't hear nothing after that. We saw the cab take Miss Augusta away.'

'A hired cab, no livery or anything?'

'Just a hansom, sir.'

'Where could they go in the middle of the night? To a more general hospital, perhaps, not an asylum? An emergency ward? A prison, even?'

The possibilities jostled each other in his mind, each bigger and meaner than the last.

'I'm sorry,' whispered Paulette. 'You really do care for her, don't you?'

He gave her a weak smile. 'Yes, I do.'

'I wish I could be more help to you. I wish I knew where Dr Tarbuck took her.'

'Wait.' He frowned, squeezing her fingers between his so that she winced a little and tried to unlace them. 'You know the doctor's name? I thought him to be some specialist in diseases of the brain, but he is her regular physician, I suppose? Has he treated you, while you have lived at Eaton Place? Do you know where he might keep his consulting rooms? Harley Street?'

He stood up, unable to keep still while ideas whirled so fast.

'Harley Street,' he repeated. 'It's as good a place to start as any. Tarbuck. Thank you, Paulette. Thank you.'

'No, no,' she said, rising to her feet and taking hold of his arm before he could march off towards Marylebone. 'No, he isn't the family physician, Mr Stratton. I recognised his voice but not from seeing him in Eaton Place.'

'Then where?'

'He is the doctor at the refuge, sir. He treated all us poor girls there. And he weren't none too kind about it either.'

James inhaled so deeply he felt faint and smacked his hand against his forehead.

'Dear God, but I'm a *fool*,' he wailed, causing an alarmed Paulette to take several steps back. 'The refuge, of course, *of course*. And to think that I stood, bare yards from her, only an hour ago . . .' He dashed his forehead again and kicked the bench.

'Please calm down,' said Paulette tremulously. 'You frighten me, sir.'

'There is no time to be lost,' he said, looking at her, but unseeingly. 'They could, even now, be removing her to some remote asylum. Even now. I must gain mastery of my wits and think . . . let me *think*.' Once more he commenced to pace up and down the paths, head clutched in hands, eyes on the paving slabs.

'I must get back,' said Paulette, eyeing the gate.

'Oh – yes – but must you?' He saw her again, and was aware of her, an idea occurring to him. 'No, I'm sorry, you won't do, they'd suspect something at once . . . Yes, run along, dear, if you must.'

'I'm a little worried for you,' she said timidly. 'Are you well?'

'Quite well.' He smiled, with an effort, and took up her hands, kissing her fingertips. 'You may have saved us all, Paulette. Come, I will walk you to the gate.'

This time he bought a spray of roses from the vendor on the pavement and she clucked and smiled her blessing when he gave it to Paulette.

'They will think I slipped out to see a lover,' she protested at the corner, but her cheeks were pink and her eyes dancing as she bade him goodbye and good luck before scampering back off to Eaton Place.

He stood for a while, breathing in the balmy rarefied air enjoyed by the metropolitan rich, before taking a determined path eastwards.

Annie was still in her bed in Holywell Street when he rapped on her door.

'Annie,' he called. 'Annie, it's me. Let me in. I need your help.'

She opened the door after a minute or two, yawning and tousle-haired.

'Been dreaming of you,' she said. 'I thought I'd already earned your undying gratitude. What are you going to give me if I help you now? Guaranteed place in the heavenly choir?'

'I don't have God's ear at present, but if I ever do . . .'

'Sweet talker. Come in then.'

She plumped herself down on the bed and patted the place beside her.

Sitting beside her warm body, clad only in a thin nightdress, James fought to overcome the advance of sensual magnetism radiating from her body in waves. The cotton barely disguised her full, round breasts, even when she pulled a fringed paisley shawl over her shoulders.

'Annie, I am about to ask a great deal of you. I don't have the right to ask it and you have every right to refuse me, but I am going to appeal to your humanity and your . . . sense of sisterhood . . . and ask you all the same.'

'Not sure I like the sound of this,' she said, pulling the shawl tighter. 'Go on.'

'I want you to volunteer to be saved.'

'Saved?'

'I want you to present yourself at the doors of the Society for the Improvement of Fallen Girls and Women on Little Ormond Street and ask to be taken in.'

'That's funny,' she said. 'That's more than funny.'

'Why?'

'I was thinking of going there anyway.'

'Oh God, don't!'

She laughed and stroked his bruised cheek.

'You ain't making sense, sunny Jim. You want me to go there, or you don't want me to go there?'

'Why would you go there of your own accord?'

'I saw some things when I was in the Lock Hospital as I can't unsee, though I wish I could. People mad with the syphilis, their faces half eaten away.'

Her voice faltered and she grew ashy pale and sweaty.

James held her in his arms.

'It was a travesty that you were in that place,' he said.

'No, but perhaps it's as well, lovey. Perhaps it was God's way of showing me I could live a better life, look forward to a better end than those poor souls.'

She was weeping now. James had never seen her cry, never seen her anything other than chirpy and cheery. He was not sure why it affected him so deeply, but it did.

'If you learn to read,' he said, but he couldn't finish the thought, realising with a sickening feeling that he had no plans to remain here and finish his personal tuition of her.

'Well, that's what I thought,' she said, brightening a little and dabbing her eyes with a scrap of lace handkerchief. 'At the refuge, they teaches you all that, don't they? And you don't have to pay no rent – because if I ain't working, I can't keep this room, can I? If nothing else, it'd give me time to think. I've never known nothing but whoring, Jem. I don't know how to live any other way. If I go to the refuge, it might give me some ideas, you see.'

'I don't like their ideas,' said James soberly.

'Why not?'

'I think they oppress the women within their walls. If you must go to a refuge, there are other, kinder ones, I hope. Mrs Edwards' establishment is too much akin to the workhouse for my liking.'

'Oh, I'd never set foot in one of those. My sister Mary went in and never came out.'

Annie shivered, nestling closer to James and resting her head on his shoulder.

'My idea, in asking you to place yourself in the refuge, is to position you as a spy within its walls.'

'A spy?' Annie's eyes were sparkling again, her imagination captured. 'Lor', really? You think I'd make a good one?'

'I do. I would ask you to take your place in Mrs Edwards' establishment and to try to find leisure to look around and find any locked doors, any inaccessible rooms within the building. I have a friend, you see, who is incarcerated there, against her will.'

'Never your fine lady?'

'That is by the by. What you need to know is that a helpless woman – and she is also blind – is held prisoner in that building, and I intend to free her.'

Annie gave him the most sorrowful of looks, the tears threatening, for a moment, to return.

'I wish you'd come to save me, from the Lock Hospital,' she whispered.

'I tried. I came to the front office and ranted and raved.'

'Did you really?'

'I did, really. But they threw me out.'

'Oh.' Her sigh was rapturous, then melancholy. 'Nobody's never cared that much for me,' she said.

He was silent, still filled with that unaccountable emotion her tears had drawn forth.

'Will you help me, Annie?'

'You want me to find the room where they're keeping her? What's her name?'

'Augusta. Lady Heathcote.' He doubted they would be using the Miss Quim moniker in such a stiff-starched moral atmosphere. 'If there is a medical room, or infirm ward, try to have yourself placed there. I imagine they may check you over on arrival anyway. Take careful note of your surroundings. Listen for any cries, any whispered conversations. Anything at all.'

'What if I'm discovered?'

'You won't be discovered. You're a bright young woman, Annie, and you're resourceful.'

'I don't much care for another examination, not after—'

'Tell them about that – they will spare you, perhaps. But complain of a headache or . . . anything. I want you to see the doctor and to keep a watch on him. He will lead you to Augusta.'

'What if I can't find her?'

'You have at least tried. I will keep a watch on the house, while you are there, to see that she is not removed. Tomorrow night, once you have had opportunity to fully reconnoitre the building, I want you let me in, through the back door. We will effect Augusta's liberation together.'

'Jem, far too much could go wrong. Far too much. And if the people are wicked, what might they do to us?'

'Will you place your faith in me, Annie? I wish I did not have to ask it of you, but I give you my word that I will see to it you are unscathed, even if I must suffer as a result. Will you at least try it? If I am caught, I am caught – but I will see that you are safe.'

'Well,' she said, picking up her lace handkerchief again and fidgeting with its scalloped edges. 'You're really smitten with her, ain't you?'

'This is about more than love, Annie. It's about doing right by one's fellow creatures. Nobody else will come to her aid. It falls, therefore, to me.'

'With a little help from good old Annie.'

'Will you?'

She took a deep breath.

'If you'll seal it with a kiss,' she said.

'Of course. As many as you like.'

'Pucker up, then.'

It was not technically infidelity, he told himself, lying in Annie's arms on her disordered bed, if he kissed the woman whose assistance he relied on to rescue his love. It did not cast any shadow on his love for Augusta if he buried his face in Annie's pillowy breasts and breathed in her scent of violet powders and gin-soaked lemon. All the same, he doubted any knight errant about to put on his shining armour and fight dragons for his lady love started his mission with his hand inside another wench's skirts. Reluctantly, he withdrew before he crossed the line into *flagrante delicto* and sat back up.

'Are you ready?' he whispered. 'We mustn't miss a minute. They could, even now, be performing unspeakable horrors on her.'

'Of course,' said Annie, shoulders slumped.

He felt a moment of horrible, piercing guilt, then she picked up her shawl, slid it around her shoulders, hopped off the bed and said, 'I'm ready for my new life, Mr Stratton. Annie the spy is reporting for duty.'

He kissed the top of her head, waited for her to don boots and outdoor clothes and led her down the stairs and through the shop.

'Where do you think you're going?' Uncle Stratton left the customer he was showing leather-bound editions of pornographic texts to and came up close to James, hissing the question.

'I have urgent business,' said James, pushing Annie along towards the door.

'With her? No. You have urgent business with *me*. I mean to keep my eye on you until all this trouble has blown over. Get to your room and get some work done – I refuse to subsidise this nonsense.'

'You won't be subsidising anything,' snapped James. 'I'm not a child and I won't be told what to do and where to go. Good afternoon, uncle.'

He hurried up Holywell Street, ignoring the shout of, 'Let's hope there's still a shop for you to come home to,' that followed him along the cobbles.

'What does he mean by that?' asked Annie, looking back.

'Never mind. I've had my fill of kicking my heels in Holywell Street. I don't intend to spend another day of my life scribbling away at hack work to keep him in business. It's time I spread my wings.'

'What are you going to do?'

'I haven't the slightest idea.'

'You're like me then.'

'Yes, Annie, yes, essentially I am very like you.'

'I suppose she's got money, any rate.'

'She has, by rights, but not in actuality. It has been stolen from her by unscrupulous persons.'

'Deario.'

They emerged from a passage into Little Ormond Street, the Fallen standing like a mixture of cloister and prison on the corner. James scanned it eagerly, as if he might find a way to see through the brick and locate Augusta's place of captivity.

She is in there, somewhere – so close to me and yet so inaccessible.

'Well, then, Annie,' he said, turning to her and seeing that she chewed her lip, trepidation having replaced enthusiasm for her new role. 'You see that there is an inn on the opposite corner of the street. That is where you might find me, in the event of an emergency. I mean to take a room overlooking the refuge.'

'Right you are,' she said, making an effort to portray spirit and pluck. She made to march off across the street, but faltered for a moment, holding on to his coat sleeve. 'Are they very bad people?'

'Only to those who stand against them. They will think nothing of you – you are just another unfortunate girl looking for help in their eyes. Be vigilant and be careful. I will be waiting at the back door tomorrow evening at midnight. If you cannot let me in, leave the refuge that night and come to me at the inn with all the information you possess and we will formulate an alternative plan. Most importantly, do not put yourself at risk. To lose one cherished . . . friend . . . to those people is insupportable enough, but two . . .'

He held her tight for a moment, his eyes damp. When she extricated herself, somewhat violently, and made a run for the refuge, his overwhelming instinct was to run after her and pull her back. But he mastered the rush of blood to the head and stood, his back to the wall, just inside the passage, watching her skip up the steps, crinoline swaying, and knock at the door.

Once she was swallowed up in the grey stone gloom of the refuge, he put his hand over his face and held it there, appalled by what he was doing. How could he have involved that poor girl in this hideous business? How *could* he?

Then he thought of Augusta, having torrents of freezing water poured over her with hosepipes and he forgave himself. Whatever it took to free her, so long as Annie remained unharmed, was what he must do.

He sidled along to the inn, afraid of being seen from the

window of Mrs Edwards' office, and slunk inside, asking to take the first floor front for the night before taking a pint pot of half and half up there with him.

He sat by the window, watching implacably as the shadows of evening began to fall on the refuge. Nobody came out or went in for a very long time. Was Mrs Shaw still there? What if she or the doctor had already taken Augusta away? The ifs and buts and holes and snags of his plan scratched away at his resolve, hour upon hour. It could never work. Even if Annie was able to purloin the back door key and let him in, what if Augusta was triple-bolted in and guarded in shifts? How was he ever to liberate her then? She might be in chains.

She had asked him once, if he could procure chains.

She had wanted him, another time, to play doctor, to diagnose insatiable whoredom and treat her accordingly.

Oh God!

The half and half made him feel sick and he felt he ought to eat, but he couldn't stomach a morsel. The baked potato in Hyde Park was a long time ago now, its effects worried away to nothing.

If this plan failed, it was the French Foreign Legion for him.

Desert dwelling and relentless, gruelling physical effort. Sometimes he thought that was the life he deserved, after all. At least it would not require much thought, other than calculating the bare mechanics of survival.

But thousands lived such a life here in this city, he reflected, looking out at the street with a sigh. A crossing sweeper stood at the corner, a child of nine or so, thin as the railings outside the refuge. The world was such a wicked place – he was hardly the worst.

The pain in his body and head kept him awake all night,

an unexpectedly helpful side-effect. He watched from the window but there was no sign of a carriage or of anybody being taken away. Just after dusk, Mrs Shaw walked down the steps, looking about her briskly as she pulled on her gloves.

Perhaps she is looking for me.

The night drew on, never silent, never holy. From the tavern downstairs, beery singing made the floorboards vibrate beneath James' feet. In the refuge, the upstairs lights went out at nine. Mrs Shaw returned in a hansom and hurried up the steps, her head down.

The little crossing sweeper disappeared about ten o'clock, after handing over some of his hard-earned coppers to an oyster vendor standing on the opposite corner.

Which window, James wondered over and over, was Augusta behind? Who was with her? Was she in pain or was she well tended? And did she curse the day she had ever met him?

Then his thoughts turned to Annie. She would have swapped her frills and flounces for grey serge. Sackcloth and ashes. She would lie in a narrow dormitory bed, forbidden to speak. Was she creeping about the house now, looking for Augusta? What if she were found out? How could he have asked this of her?

'Yes, well done, Stratton,' he muttered to himself. 'Destroy the lives of two women instead of one.' He saw then that he had valued Annie's life at lower worth than Augusta's, and he was disgusted with himself.

But what was done was done, and he could do no other than wait for events to unfold. A chance to redeem himself was still available.

Midnight came and went, the candle burnt out, but still he dared not sleep. The darkest hours of night would be the best to secretly remove a woman, drugged insensible in all probability, to a waiting carriage.

In Mrs Edwards' office, a low light still flickered. The drunks had all been tossed out of the tavern, to wander the streets to their homes or to other places, still open, or with secret basements where the carousing continued till dawn.

The street was as quiet as it was ever likely to be, shouts coming sometimes from the courts behind it, drunken singing from the cobbles as men staggered past. Down in Haymarket, the night would be in full swing, all the girls on the corners, the men sizing them up as they strolled by. In Holywell Street, the cats were out at this time, fighting and yowling, sometimes yelled at or doused with the contents of a chamber pot from the gables overhead.

James wondered that he ever slept at all, recalling the unearthly stillness when he spent the night at Eaton Place with Augusta. He would take her somewhere like that. Somewhere quiet, where the air was sweet.

He thought of it and his fantasies almost sent him nodding off at the window, but he always jolted back to consciousness after a second's blacking out and gave the refuge another urgent scan to ensure he had not missed anything.

The dogs barked and the first cartwheels of morning creaked into action at no later than five. The church bells had rung the quarter hours all night, their chime infiltrating James' brain and settling there so that he heard it constantly, the relentless background music of his watch.

Now he must last the day. How many hours? His mind was almost too tired to count, but at last he came to the answer – thirteen.

How would he stay awake through thirteen hours when his head ached so and his eyelids were coated with grit?

As soon as he heard stirrings downstairs, he went down and requested that the maid be sent to the stationers to buy him paper, pen and ink. He had determined to write his life story, in the hope that it would be lively enough to maintain a state of wakefulness.

It is the custom, when a man sets forth the history of his life, to begin with a portentous paragraph or two, a reflection on the nature of existence itself, perhaps, in stately foreshadowing of the grave and dignified nature of the personage whose exalted description shall form the body of the book, but in my case, I shall forego such intimations of greatness to come, for there will be none. My life is less significant than that of the crossing sweeper I see back at his corner this morning. I am no more than a scoundrel and a hack, but I hope my story might at least amuse, for it will certainly not edify.

Yawning, he dipped his nib into his ink bottle and, always keeping an eye on the building opposite, began his tale.

Trifling with breakfast, he described his gaolbird infancy, his parents and the house of Stratton. By the time he snatched a hurried luncheon, he was running errands for his uncle. He was still working on this wealth of anecdotal material when night began to make its second appearance, the shadows falling on the refuge walls.

At a little after nine, a carriage pulled up and a man, two men, went up the steps together. Men in the refuge? At night? One of them carried a bag. A doctor.

Now he had to put aside his writing in order to pace. A good deal of pacing was required. He almost stumbled on rising, for he was ridiculously tired and his head felt as if somebody had tightened a string around it, but he had made sure to eat well and keep his strength up for the ordeal ahead.

Now all would depend on how well Annie had managed to complete her portion of the task. For all her lack of formal education, she was a bright creature and very good at using her charm and force of personality to get her way. He felt he could rely on her.

The chimes rang out every quarter, and each time James' heart weighed a little heavier and his head hurt a little more.

At a quarter before twelve, the time for action was upon him.

'Cometh the hour,' he muttered, 'cometh the man.' He was out of the side door of the tavern, in the warm summer night air, within a minute.

Nobody was in the street save him. He ran to Southampton Row and called down a hackney cab, asking for it to wait at the corner for him, pressing a sovereign into the cabbie's hand and promising more if he would only do as James asked. The cab secured, he then made a slow approach of the refuge, giving its façade a wide berth in favour of negotiating the warren of side alleys that would take him to the back of the building.

All was in darkness, even Mrs Edwards' office, although there could have been light on the unseen side of the house or in the long sheds that bounded the courtyard.

James flattened his back against the wall and waited.

It would be so easy to shut his eyes. He mustn't shut his eyes . . .

He started and almost cried out at the sudden pinching of his arm.

'Jem.'

'Oh God, I must have—'

'For heaven's sake, don't fall asleep on me!' Her whispers

were urgent and she sounded scared. 'I'm risking my neck for you here.'

She stepped quietly out beside him, twirling the key on one of her fingers.

'So she is there?'

Annie nodded.

'I was so tempted to say that she weren't and just leave here with you now.'

He took her hand and kissed it.

'Thank you. It's not enough, I know, mere thanks, but—'

'*Shh!* No time for speechmaking. Are you coming in or what?'

He followed her inside the back door, in which she turned the key with her breath held, desperate not to disturb a soul.

'You've seen her?'

'No, I ain't, but I know where she is. She's in the sanatorium, in a little private room. I went there to ask for some magnesia for my heartburn, not that I've got any, it was just a ploy, like you suggested.'

'Yes, yes.'

James looked warily towards the hall and staircase, a few yards away from the back kitchen door. Presumably the cook and servants slept in the eaves, or were 'reformed' prostitutes in the dormitory, for no staff members lay on pallets beneath the work surfaces.

'At first I only saw a nurse in there. None of the beds was taken, but I noticed a door to a back room and I asked if that was the morgue for any girls what died in here. "What a morbid creature," she says. "No, that's for girls as might be contagious." I makes out to be shocked and says "There ain't no contagious disease in here now, is there?" She shakes her head, getting the magnesia, measuring it out. And then the door opens and Dr Tarbuck comes out. "You lied!" I shouted, making a big fuss, going all faint and whatnot. "Someone's in there with the cholera or worse. Wait till I tell the other girls! Oh Lord, we're all doomed in here." Well, I had to lay it on a bit, didn't I? Anyway, Tarbuck himself tells me to shut up and that there's no diseased girl behind that door, only a sad unfortunate what's gone mad from the harshness of life on the streets. "Poor thing," I says. "I bet she's seen the worst of it." He smirks at that and says, "Actually, my dear, she hasn't seen a thing."'

James gasped. 'Augusta. It must be.'

'Well, so I reckoned. I took me magnesia, and I did it for you, Jem, for I hates that stuff, and off I went, to try and fiddle the key off the housekeeper. And I succeeded there as well, or you wouldn't be standing here now.'

'Indeed, indeed,' said James, his mind racing with plans. 'Annie, would you go to the infirmary and feign some illness? Say you must have a bed there for the night. I need you to distract the nurse so I can approach the back room.'

'Jem, I don't think—'

'Let us go and see what the situation is there, at least.'

They passed through the kitchen and down some steps to the little door that led out on to the exercise yard.

The outbuildings were in darkness, except at one corner. He recalled Mrs Edwards telling him that the infirmary was there, although she had not shown him inside. At the time, he had presumed it was to protect him from the pall of sickness in the air, but now he was not so sure.

A low light in the only window in that part of the block drew him towards it.

'That's the main part of the infirmary,' whispered Annie. 'The room behind don't seem to have no window.'

James shuddered, wondering what horrors might be taking place in there.

Suddenly, the back door handle of the main building rattled and he dragged Annie swiftly into the darkness of the chapel doorway, hiding there in the helpful shadows while two figures stepped out and crossed the yard.

One was Mrs Edwards; the other, the man with the bag he had seen arriving earlier.

'It's a very new form of surgery,' the man said. 'But we have seen some marked success in the asylums.'

'You have seen women recover from nymphomania as a result?'

'The desire for congress is reduced so far as to be extinguished.'

'That is remarkable. I wonder if it is a procedure we could adopt here for our unfortunates?'

'The clitoridectomy is, as yet, in its infancy. However, I am preparing a paper on it for the professional journals and trust it will be published in the next year or so. My hope is that this will lead to more widespread practice.'

The pair passed on into the infirmary block.

James had stiffened all over and was forced to put a palm flat against the wall for support. Nausea roared in his ears. He could guess what a clitoridectomy was, and he didn't like the sound of it at all.

'What was he saying?' whispered Annie. 'They're going to do something to her?'

'No, they are *not*,' said James. 'Not while I live and breathe.'

He hustled her out of the doorway and strode quickly up to the infirmary.

'Go in,' he said. 'Occupy the nurse. Feign closeness to

death, I don't care how. Keep her facing away from the door if you possibly can.'

'You aren't going to do nothing stupid are you, Jem?'

'I can't promise that, I'm afraid. Stupidity seems to be somewhat natural to me. Now go. I will do what I can to get us all three safely out of here.'

He nudged Annie between the ribs, but before she stepped forward, she turned, hooked her hand behind his neck and kissed him, full and long, on his lips.

'Just so's you know,' she whispered, before hurrying, shoulders hunched and head down, to the door.

He put his hand to his mouth and watched her, guilt lining his heart like lead. She was doing this for him.

He tried to dismiss all thoughts extraneous to effecting a quick and painless exit from the refuge for all of them and stood by the slightly ajar door, watching Annie's antics through the crack.

She clutched at her chest and dry-heaved and staggered on to her knees until the languid posture of the nurse changed to one of briskness. She persuaded Annie on to a bed and bent over her, taking her pulse.

Now was his chance. He made a noiseless entrance into the room and slipped behind the nurse's desk, examining the shelves of bottles over which she held dominion. He had to turn away from Annie and the nurse to do so, his nerves seeming to rattle audibly as he squinted to read each label.

Yes, chloroform, yes, laudanum. He swiped a bottle of each then ducked behind the counter to soak a cloth with the chloroform.

The nurse was still bent over Annie, feeling her forehead for signs of fever.

'If you're having me on, young lady,' she was saying, but she said no more, for James pressed the chloroform-soaked flannel to her face until she fell in a bundle, almost on top of Annie, who had to leap off the bed quite smartly.

'My apologies,' muttered James to her recumbent form. 'I hope you'll understand one day.'

He approached the door at the end of the sick bay with caution, wondering that he had heard no screams or shouts of protest.

It was now that he wished he had something more than a paring knife tucked into his boot. No doubt the doctors would have a bag full of sharp and shiny weapons at their disposal.

He broke the empty chloroform bottle over a bed frame and handed its jagged remains to Annie.

'Your weapon,' he said, then he put his ear to the door and listened.

Low voices could be heard, but there was no way of catching their words. Augusta was silent. She must be drugged. If so, it would be difficult indeed to remove her from here.

'Who's in there?' whispered Annie fearfully.

'I don't know. If we could only make them come out.'

'Leave it with me.'

Annie went to the medicine shelf and commenced picking up the bottles of medicine and pills and hurling them about the room. The first shattering of glass was enough to bring Mrs Edwards and Dr Tarbuck running out of the inner room, neither of them bothering to look sideways, where James stood against the wall.

'Mercy me, another lunatic!' exclaimed Mrs Edwards. 'What has she done to Nurse Ryall? Dr Tarbuck, help me to restrain her.'

But Annie held them off with her broken bottle while James took his opportunity to enter the room behind.

Augusta lay, strapped down on a bed, naked from the waist down but clearly conscious. She was gagged, which accounted for her silence, but her unseeing eyes were wide and fluttering with panic.

Leaning over her, stroking one of her hands and speaking to her in a low tone, was Mrs Shaw. The surgeon was intent on his box of scalpels and knives, so much so that the appearance of another blade at his throat made him splutter with astonishment.

Mrs Shaw looked up immediately.

'You,' she snarled, standing.

He had shut the door behind him, muffling the continuing crash of breaking glass and accompanying screams.

'Yes, Mrs Shaw, me. I must ask you to release Augusta, or risk the neck of this pillar of the medical establishment.' He spoke the words with bitter sarcasm.

Augusta made an inarticulate sound behind her gag and her body convulsed in its bonds.

'Release him immediately, scoundrel.'

She came closer. James uncapped the bottle of laudanum with his teeth and forced it between the lips of the doctor, which were slack with fear. Once a good quarter of the brown liquid had glugged down the surgeon's throat, he let go of him, letting him slump to the floor in an opiated haze.

'No surgery for him tonight,' said James, brandishing his paring knife in Mrs Shaw's face. 'And I have some left over for you. Do you have a taste for laudanum?'

'Get out of here, wretch!' she shouted, loud enough for her voice to carry next door. 'Patricia! Dr Tarbuck! Your assistance, please.'

'I think not.' He jabbed the knife and she flinched. 'Release Augusta from her bonds. Do it or I swear . . .'

She seemed to believe he would hurt her. She knew, after all, that he could hurt a woman, even if it was in pleasure.

'You are a fool,' she muttered, working at the buckles. 'Her fortune is given over to the safekeeping of her cousins. You will never get your hands on a penny of it.'

'I don't think you understand, Mrs Shaw. I don't care about the money. I care about Augusta. You may enjoy the wages of your sin as long as you like. But do remember, Mrs Shaw, what those wages ultimately are.'

She sniffed. 'You will be looking over your shoulder for the rest of your days, mark my words. And saddled with a penniless blind woman. She will be no more than a burden to you, as she was to me.'

'Well, you are free of her now,' said James roughly, pulling the untethered Augusta upright, wishing he could be more gentle in view of her apparent stiffness, but aware of the need to be as hasty as possible. The blade still close up to Mrs Shaw's skin, he had her lie on the bed in Augusta's place, strapping down only her wrists before draping his arm around his love's shoulder and supporting her towards the door.

He had left the laudanum bottle by Mrs Shaw's head.

'You might like a drop,' he suggested, looking back at her. 'A moment's relief from what must be a terrible gnawing at your conscience.'

'Conscience,' she returned derisively, but he stayed to spar no more, snatching up a handful of surgical instruments on his way out.

The infirmary was a wasteland of broken glass. Mrs Edwards had laid herself face down on the bed beside her insensible nurse and was whimpering softly, far from the capable woman he had seen up until now.

As he drew closer, he saw that Annie and Dr Tarbuck were at daggers – or broken bottles – drawn, each circling the other slowly, making feints now and again.

The doctor spoke in a low, authoritative voice designed to bring Annie to her senses, but of course, she was immune to this.

'Now come on, girl, you know this cannot end well for you. Be good and put the bottle down and you will be well taken care of.'

'He lies,' said James laconically.

Dr Tarbuck leapt around, confronted by James' fist, each finger divided by a glinting blade.

'Good God,' he cried. 'And now a madman too.'

'Let us pass and no harm will come to you.' Using his armoured fist, he guided Tarbuck away from Annie and held him against a bed, the points pricking the doctor's throat while James directed Annie to look for the infirmary key.

Once she had found it, he nodded at Dr Tarbuck and wished him a good evening, sweeping swiftly on to the door, Augusta tripping and weeping in his wake.

Annie turned the key in the lock and they stopped for one deep, cleansing breath before heading for the house and door that gave access on to the street.

James scattered the surgical instruments on the doorstep and lifted Augusta, who had been limping, into his arms.

'Southampton Row,' he said to Annie. 'That way. Quickly.'

The sound of a window smashing somewhere nearby led impetus to James' steps. It would not take long for Tarbuck to free Mrs Shaw and have the pair of them try to break their way out of the infirmary. But he felt confident that they would not give too strenuous a chase. Augusta was not important to them, after all, now that the power of attorney was signed.

All the same, while she was at liberty, they could never rest easy in their beds.

Thank heaven, the cab still stood at the corner of Southampton Row, the horse snorting and pulling at the rein.

James climbed in, helped Augusta up beside him and lent his hand again to Annie. The cabman turned around and, seeing Augusta still wearing a gag, stared, then blinked.

'Where to, guv'nor?'

James stared and blinked back, realising somewhere amongst all the adrenalin that he had no idea what to do next.

'Excuse me,' he muttered, unbuckling the gag and removing it from Augusta's mouth. 'I . . .'

Augusta, after coughing fit to strain her ribs, recovered her voice, but it still sounded hoarse when she spoke.

'Eaton Place,' she said.

'We cannot!' said James.

'We can. We need money. I have my mother's diamonds. We can go there – Mrs Shaw will not be there, after all – and get them.'

She was right. They had no money between them, save the small amount in James' bank account, and were unlikely to go far without it.

'Very well,' he said. 'Eaton Place.'

The cab jolted into motion and James wondered what he ought to say. What could one, did one, say at such times?

'Cor, that was a close one,' said Annie cheerfully.

And what to do with Annie? Where would she now go?

'Diamonds,' said James. 'I will go in to get them. I know where you keep them.'

'You will have to break in. I have no key and I cannot dare

let the servants see me. They are so in thrall to Mrs Shaw.'

'What about Paulette? She has helped me. Helped us.'

'She is just a girl. I don't want her placed in Mrs Shaw's line of fire.'

'Neither do I. I rather thought she might come with us – as your maid. But that was when we thought we would have your money.'

Augusta sighed. 'I have been such a dupe.'

'So have I. It cannot now be helped.'

The lovers spent the rest of the journey in sober silence and a tight embrace, reflecting on the close escape Augusta had had from the surgical knife. Annie chirruped away beside them, still apparently as high as a kite after their adventure, but her words fell on ears that, if not quite deaf, were effectively muffled to anything but their private thoughts.

Eaton Place drew nigh too soon. The mews were not yet locked and gated, some of the residents being out in their carriages even at this late hour, so James stepped down from the hansom, bidding the driver wait for him in the hope that he would not be kept long, and walked along the cobbles to Augusta's stableyard.

The small brougham that was her only conveyance – retained more for form than for usage – was out. No doubt it would be found in the environs of the refuge, appropriated for Mrs Shaw's personal employ.

He hastened through the empty stable and out of the back door that led into Augusta's rear yard and garden. The house was in darkness, but that same sash window, a little loose in its frame, through which he had broken in before served his purpose on this second occasion.

He swung one leg over the sill, listening intently for any signs of nocturnal life in the house. There appeared to be

none. Creeping in and tiptoeing across the ballroom floor,
he kept his eyes fixed on the doors at the end. From there,
it was an easy and familiar journey to the hall and up the
stairs.

He paused at the top and breathed in the Eaton Place
air. All the times he had spent here, pleasuring himself with
Augusta – all those times . . .

He should never have accepted the commission.

Too late, now, for such regrets, though, and he moved
with fixity of purpose to Augusta's chambers, conscious of
the need to hurry, lest Mrs Shaw should guess the game and
disturb him at it.

Yes, the diamonds were still here and he paused to catch a
breath. It had been his fear that Augusta's nefarious cousins or
Mrs Shaw might have taken them. Even the servants, caught
up in the whirlwind of events, might have thought the time
propitious to abscond with a handful of choice sparklers.

But the jewels were here, intact, and he filled Augusta's
enamelled and japanned boxes to the brim with the best of
them, sorting rapidly through sapphires, rubies, emeralds,
pearls until no more could be fitted in.

Crossing to her dressing room, he snatched a handful
of gowns off their hangers and draped them over his arm,
congratulating himself on his presence of mind as he did so.

As he emerged back into the chamber, a light fell across
the opposite wall and he saw his erect figure in shadow. He
dropped all that he held and whirled around, whipping the
trusty paring knife from his boot once more, the only other
weapon to hand being a hairbrush he had used, on occasion,
on Augusta's rear. The sight of it had awakened an untimely
throb below his belt, a throb which had not quite abated
when he turned to face his opponent.

'Oh.' He laughed and passed a shaking hand across his brow. 'Paulette.'

'Mr Stratton,' she whispered, shaking no less. 'I thought perhaps you were Mrs Shaw, or even Her Ladyship come back . . .'

'Her Ladyship is never coming back,' said James gravely.

'Have they taken her?'

He shook his head. 'I must say nothing, for it is unfair to burden you with the knowledge. Here.' He picked up a handful of the jewellery he had not been able to fit into the boxes and held it out to Paulette. 'Take my advice, Paulette. Leave London with this. Sell it in some distant city. Buy yourself a life.'

'Oh, sir,' she said, staring at him, unable to accept the strings of necklaces and flashing brilliants. 'I ain't a thief, whatever else I may be.'

'It is not stealing. It is a gift. I am Her Ladyship's intermediary and I give you her blessing.'

'Really? You are sure?'

'Quite sure, Paulette. Take it, please.'

She put trembling fingers on the handful of jewels, then accepted them into her cupped hands. James put his hand over them, briefly patting his approval, then he bent and kissed Paulette's cheek.

'Will you do as I ask, sweet one?' he whispered. 'For me?'

'Oh,' she said, quite overcome, tears gathering in her eyes.

'Put as great a distance between yourself and Mrs Shaw as you can. It is what I intend to do. And now I must go. Farewell and keep yourself safe.'

He squeezed her shoulder and left her to fill the pockets of her dressing gown with unexpected bounty.

He left via the front door, feeling every inch the gentleman thief as he clutched the selection of jewellery boxes and gowns to his chest, almost tripping over the hems of the latter. At the corner, the cab still waited.

'Now then, my man,' he said, climbing back up with Augusta and Annie. 'I wonder if there is an inn with rooms anywhere in the vicinity of London Bridge Station to which you could take us?'

'London Bridge?' said Annie. 'Why would I want to go there?'

'For the boat train,' said James under his breath, not wanting to make the cabman party to more information than he could help.

'I ain't going on no boat train,' said Annie. 'I ain't going on no boat.'

'We have no alternative but to leave the country,' whispered James urgently. 'Augusta and I cannot stay here.'

'Well, that's as maybe, but I ain't going.'

'Annie . . .'

She shook her head.

'Water gives me the horrors,' she said. 'Big open stretches of it, with waves and suchlike. You won't never get me on a boat. Nor on a train for that matter. Ain't that the line where they had that horrible accident last month?'

'At Staplehurst? I suppose it was. Well, what if we go to Portsmouth instead, or Southampton?'

But Annie was resolute.

'I can't go with you anyway,' she said. 'You don't want the likes of me along of you. You want to be together and I . . .'

She broke off, curling her fingers into tense little fists.

'Annie, you have saved us. We owe you everything. You are never, ever unwelcome. I can't cast you into the madness out there, I can't.'

'That madness is my life, Jem,' she said, but her voice was strange and tight. 'It's what I know and what I've always known. And what you've always known too, but now you've got another life to lead, and it's best I leave you to it.'

'Annie, no!'

'Give us one of your toy boxes, then, and I'll leave you be. I'll try and be a good girl and find a good man. I know they exist now, thanks to you, Jem Stratton.'

'I can't let you . . .'

But she had snatched one of the boxes from the seat and already had a foot out of the cab, looking for the pavement.

He made a lunge for her.

'Please don't leave this way.'

She eluded him, jumping lightly down onto the ground.

'Don't touch me, Jem, or I can't . . .' she said in a strangled voice. Her back was to him, her shoulders shaking.

'Annie, for Christ's sake . . .' He was close to jumping out after her, but the sound of wheels rounding the corner of a street beyond made Augusta clutch his wrist and beg to leave Eaton Place.

'All right, all right,' he said, in an agony of spirits. 'London Bridge, and please make haste.'

The cabbie cracked his whip and the conveyance made a jolting start.

'I will write,' shouted James to Annie, who was running now, jewel box hidden somewhere about her skirts. 'Collect your mail at my uncle's shop. But you must learn to read first!'

For the first minutes of the journey he was quite overcome with emotion and even felt like pushing away Augusta's hand when it fell on his thigh and stroked it. She knew nothing of Annie, of that dauntless spirit, so generous and giving. Oh

God, he had used her ill. He sent a silent prayer that she might find happiness and comfort, even at his own expense, for he felt at that moment that he would endure any trouble if it meant she could avoid it.

It was only when he became aware that Augusta wept silently at his side that his attention was deflected to his traumatised lover.

'Oh, my pet,' he said, sliding his arm around her and bringing her wet face down on to his shoulder. 'What a lot of mischief I have brought about. But you are safe now, and you are cared for and loved. Nobody shall treat you ill again.'

'I wish it could be true,' she sobbed. 'I wish it so.'

The inn with rooms was found, and the patrons very put out at being roused from their beds to light their guests upstairs, although it was in the nature of their line of work. The hiss of steam and clank of engines from the railway line outside could scarcely be slept through under normal circumstances, but James felt he could give it a heroic try.

The door shut upon them, and a false name given to the innkeeper along with the money up front for his trouble, Stratton guided Augusta to the bed and fell exhausted beside her.

'It is terribly noisy,' said Augusta. 'I shall never sleep.'

'Did you sleep much at the refuge?'

'I did little else for they drugged me each time I awoke. I know not how long I was there. How long was I there, my love?'

'No more than two days. I was awake for all of it. I'm afraid I will slip away quite soon, my love. Please do not take offence if I cannot keep you company in your wakefulness.'

She reached for his hand, clasping it in hers.

'How could I take offence at anything you do, my love?

After all you have risked for me, all you have done for me?
Did they mean to kill me?'

'They did not tell you their intent?'

'No, for they treated me as a person without wits, even
though Mrs Shaw, at least, knew well that I was as sane as I
have ever been. They told me nothing.'

'I heard the doctor conferring with Mrs Shaw. They
meant to excise a certain portion of your anatomy. But I need
not horrify you with the details, for the danger is passed.'

'Do you think so?'

'They have your fortune. Nothing else is of importance
to those . . . *ugh*.' Unusually for James, his vocabulary failed
him.

'I suppose you are right. All those years I thought Mrs
Shaw—'

'Cared for you?'

'Yes. What a fool I am.' She laughed mirthlessly. 'A blind
fool.'

'You cannot help your blindness. Perhaps, if you could see,
you might have understood her motives. I held a suspicion of
her from the first.'

'Did you really?'

'I have never met such a woman, and I think it likely I
never shall again. Perhaps your life has been too sheltered for
you to realise the true extent of her unusualness.'

'Doubtless it has.'

James yawned fit to crack his jaw. 'Dearest, I simply must
sleep. Let me undress you and put you into bed.'

Poor Augusta, still in the thin cotton shift she wore on
the operating table, was quick and easy to disrobe. For the
first time, James was able to unclothe her skin and handle
her bare flesh without any urge to expend further attentions

on it. He was exhausted and still trembling from the night's exertions and the only siren tempting him tonight was sleep, deep, black-lidded and dreamless.

He placed the covers over Augusta and then undressed himself. Only when he lay down beside his lover did he realise how painfully and profoundly he ached. From his throbbing head to his weary feet, he was a man of sorrows. And he looked as if he had just staggered out of a boxing ring too.

His final thought before sleep was that it might be best to send Augusta into the goldsmiths to have her jewellery valued and sold. Certain conclusions would probably be drawn from his appearance, and he didn't want to alert anybody's attention to him. But, on the other hand, they would certainly try to cheat a blind female customer. No, best he went after all. Perhaps his appearance would serve to intimidate them into honesty. And then the tickets would be bought and the boat boarded and then they would roll upon the waves – the waves, the rolling waves . . .

Chapter Ten

The sun was up when his eyes opened again.

So, it seemed, was Augusta. He felt for her beside him, but found only rumpled sheets. He sat up, blinking out the blur from his eyes, only to see her sitting quietly in a rocking chair in the corner, still as naked as the day she was born.

The smoke-dulled light coming in through the grimy window fell upon her breasts and stomach in rays. Her eyes were shut but she held in her hands one of her necklaces, which she fingered somewhat compulsively.

'Are you not cold, my love?' he said, clearing his throat. 'Come back to bed.'

'We should leave,' she said. 'I tried to dress, but you brought me only gowns. Nothing else.'

'Ah,' he said, realising his mistake. Not the worst mistake, as far as he was concerned. Rather a fortunate one, really.

'It is as well that I never wear crinolines,' she said. 'Nor should I attempt to ascend any ladders or steep stairs.'

'No.' He chuckled, then the consciousness of everything they had endured in the last few days swept over him and he swallowed a strange impulse to sob. 'Did you sleep at all, pet? Please, come back to bed.'

'I did not sleep,' she said, rising carefully and taking slow steps towards the bed, her hands reaching out before her. 'At least, not in any restful sense. I did drift into horrible half-waking nightmares now and again. I thought Mrs Shaw was here.'

'Oh, my darling,' he said, helping her on to the bed before taking her in his arms. 'We need never see her again. Never.'

'That is why we must leave London as soon as we can,' she said, submitting to his stroking of her brow but still stiff in every sinew. 'I will dread every minute we spend here until we can make our escape.'

'Even if those minutes are spent in my arms?' he whispered, feeling that they had at least time to renew their passions before he went out to convert some jewels into gold sovereigns.

She sighed and put her lips up to be kissed, an invitation he accepted with relish.

'I feared I may never see you again,' she said, gathered close now to his chest. She began to cry and he kissed each tear. 'I thought I would live imprisoned in darkness forever.'

'I could never resign you to such a fate,' he said. 'You should have had more faith in me.'

'I wanted to. I wanted to believe you would come. But I didn't dare.'

'I am with you now and will stay with you always.'

'You truly love me. I don't think I understood that before. I do now. I am so blessed, even in all my misfortune.'

James pressed his lips to hers again, giddy with a sense of endless possibility. They could go anywhere and live as they wished. All their ties were undone and they could drift on the wind or find a purpose and pursue it.

But for now, one overwhelming purpose suggested itself to him and it could be achieved in this very bed.

'You know I love you,' he murmured into her ear, loosening his fingers to caress her neck and shoulders. 'You know it. Come to me.'

'Have we the time . . .?'

'We have nothing else, except each other. Let us give ourselves, let us be one.'

'I do feel one with you,' she replied, clasping the back of his neck. 'I do.'

His kiss was deeper this time, his tongue probing her as if to ensure that she realised how very far inside her he intended to go. There was something spiritual about this embrace, something more profound and more serious than he had experienced before. It was a kiss of renewal, the unlocking of a door into the future.

Augusta began to shuffle down, laying herself on her back and pulling him over her. They slipped, entwined, beneath the sheets, tugging them out from beneath the mattress as they rolled and writhed.

James propped himself up on an elbow and held her down with one hand on her stomach.

'Let me look at you,' he whispered. 'Look at what I almost lost.'

'Look at what you shall never lose again,' she said. 'Oh, how I wish I could do the same.'

'You do not miss much,' he said modestly. 'But you . . .' He breathed deeply, drinking in her sensuous contours and the ripe bloom of her skin after their caresses. He put his hand to her breast and allowed it to trace each curve, as slowly as he could, watching her chest rise and fall and her lips part, wet and swollen from kissing.

'Nobody could touch me the way you do,' she said, arching her back to meet his fingertips the sooner. 'The lightest brush of your hand makes my blood rush. It is like some sinful magic trick.'

'I have no idea how I do it, if so,' he said, bending to breathe, as gently as he could, over her fattening nipple. 'But your magic is the stronger, for I am aflame before I even touch you.'

She rubbed her leg along his calf and up his thigh, hooking him into a close embrace. He lay above her, his hard length prodding at her hip, as he kissed her into sweet pliancy. He was bent on ravishment, both knew it, both welcomed it.

With the hand that was not cupping a breast, he reached beneath her and took a firm grasp of one curved buttock.

A little mewl passed from her throat to his mouth.

'Hmm?' he queried, breaking the kiss for a moment.

'It is still bruised,' she said. 'From . . . Do you remember?'

He tried, but everything prior to the traumatic experience at Cremorne seemed to have slipped from his mind.

'Show me.'

He knelt up and turned her on to her stomach. On her bottom, dark bruises traversed both cheeks, in familiar lines. *Dear God, how long ago that seems now – a lifetime distant.* And yet he had applied these fading cane marks only days before.

'I did this,' he said, tracing them with a fingertip.

'You know you did.'

'Sometimes I wonder at my capacity for cruelty.'

'How is it cruel, if it gives me pleasure?'

He nodded – not that she could see it – and felt gratitude

for a world that provided women who enjoyed being whipped, mysterious as he found such inclinations. He had been caned as a boy and never found the experience remotely enjoyable, from first to last. Perhaps if a lover had done it? But no. Even then, he would avoid what he recalled as a near-unbearable pain.

'It gives you pleasure,' he repeated softly. 'Did the doctors see it?'

'They did. They took it as further proof of my madness, that I should wish for a man to do this to me.'

'Would they consider the man who did it mad?'

'No, of course not. They would consider him quite normal. They said as much when they examined me.'

'Really?'

'Yes, one to the other, "Well, one can't blame a man for wanting to stripe this pretty posterior, can one?" And his fellow laughed and agreed with him.'

Egregious deviants, thought James hotly. How did they dare look at Augusta's rear with such lascivious intent? Such rights were reserved for him alone.

He stroked her cheeks with reverence, then leaned over them and kissed each bruise, tonguing the succulent flesh as he did so. Augusta sighed and quivered beneath his attentions. He was conscious of her scent, wafting up from further down, and knew that she would be well prepared when the time came to join with her.

'I wanted to tell them,' she said tremulously. 'That no other man but him I love would be permitted such licence. That it is not madness but love. That I would wrest the cane from the hand of any other and break it across his face. It is for you only, for you, oh my love, oh.'

His lips had ventured into the crease between her bruised

cheeks, which he now held apart, the better to lick and kiss his way downwards towards his eventual goal. She held her legs wide apart for him, showing her eagerness to allow him anything he wanted from her.

Holding her thighs at the top, he had his tongue dance around the little opening he would be filling at his leisure without quite penetrating it. She wriggled and sighed, but he did not grant her what she angled for, moving lower again, for she would be rewarded for her patience when he reached his destination.

The very same place that had been the locus of the doctors' attention.

He sat up quickly, suddenly nauseous at the memory of what they had intended for that sweet, wanton little bud between her lips. He held his forehead for a moment, staring down at his lover's clitoris.

'My love,' she said, a little anxiously. 'Are you well?'

'Do you know,' he asked, 'what operation those doctors intended to perform?'

'Oh, please, don't let's talk about it. Please.'

'Then you did?'

'I can imagine.'

'Dearest love.' He exhaled long and shudderingly. 'It gives me pause to think what might have—'

'Then don't think it,' she urged. 'All is well and they cannot touch me now.'

'But to think that it is done at all. That there are women . . .'

He tried to calm his chaotic breathing.

'They think they are helping those women,' said Augusta. 'God.'

'Try to forget,' she said, and she lifted her bottom a

little and pushed it towards him, which did indeed have the required effect.

He grasped her hips and returned to the feast, establishing himself fully between her lips before licking and sucking and kissing all that lay within them with the relish of a starving man.

The point of his tongue flicked at her clitoris, enjoying its roundness and tenderness and the way it swelled with excitement because of what he did to it. The squirming of her thighs under his hands aroused him even more and he held them firm, keeping Augusta placed where he could achieve the most devastating effect.

Her moans were coming thick and fast, signalling the imminent approach of her melting into ecstasy. He wanted to drink of her, bathe his tongue in her essence, roll it in his mouth like a fine wine.

When she came undone, his name was upon her lips and he crushed his face up against her hot, wet quim and growled. That anyone should have sought to tamper with this, when it belonged to him, was not to be borne. They would have to kill him first before any man laid hands on this delicious morsel.

'I must couple with you,' he muttered, removing his damp cheeks, their whiskers matted with Augusta's juices, from their place of refuge. 'At once.'

'Take me,' she whispered.

He seated himself swiftly, screwing his eyes shut at the exquisite tightness of her and the wet heat that enveloped him.

Her moan of pleasure added to the thrill. He bent and kissed it out of her mouth, lying quite still inside her in an attempt to head off a premature peaking.

Images of the surgeon's blades glinting under the gaslight jets kept his blood down. He contemplated them at leisure, trying to fix them in his mind's eye when he moved into a pattern of slow thrusting.

Steadily, the contours of her body overtook his grim imaginings and he gave into his desires, seeing instead her breasts, glistening with perspiration, and her flushed face, lips parted in rapture.

He was inside her again and it felt like a wedding night as much as a renewal. But he should not think of wedding nights . . .

'Say you are mine,' he urged, speeding his rhythm and moving his fingers to her clitoris. 'Say it. You are mine.'

'I am yours,' she said, pushing herself on to his fingertips and grinding her hips. 'There could be no other . . . none . . . no other . . .'

She clasped her arms around his neck and buried her face in it, her tongue pushing at the malleable flesh beneath his earlobe in a way that drove him half-wild.

'Dear God!' he exclaimed, feeling a chaos of sensation swell his lusts still further, inducing him to speed up to fever pitch.

She fixed her lips to his neck and sucked.

He rubbed at her clit in a frenzy until, yes, there it was, she was there, it was safe, he was ready . . .

He poured into her, his vision whitened and his body overtaken by the force of the pleasure. He had thought to last longer than this, but no power of man could have held off such a surge. She clung to him, her lower muscles milking him dry, while he kissed her face all over, until his breath faltered and his voice ran out.

He lay on top of her, feeling his heart hammer against

hers, fearful of crushing her yet so sapped he wondered if it were even possible for him to raise his head.

'Tell me you love me,' she whispered, her fingers in his hair.

'I love you.'

'I know it.'

'Oh,' he exclaimed, suddenly struck. 'I should not have . . .'

She reached down to where they were still connected at their cores and stroked the inside of his thigh.

'It does not matter,' she said. 'Not at all. It is not the first time, after all.'

'We are not best placed to become parents, my love.'

'Not yet. But we shall be. Once we are across the ocean and have our little house by the sea. Our children will be fisher folk.'

It was a picturesque prospect but James could not prevent misgivings. How easy would it be, truly, to live overseas as man and wife with children to provide for?

Too late to ponder alternatives now, though. The deed was done.

Gathering reserves of strength, despite continuing light-headedness, he withdrew from Augusta's close inner embrace. He saw his essences spill from her, making a whitish pool on the sheet beneath her bottom. The beginnings of life. He shuddered, then lay back down at her side.

'How shall it be between us?' he asked, voicing a question that had nagged at him intermittently since Augusta's recovery from the refuge.

'What do you mean?'

'We came together as master and servant, although it was at your bidding and the power was always yours. Or Mrs Shaw's, I suppose. How do you propose we continue?'

'In the bedroom or in general life?'

'Both.'

She yawned and nestled closer to him, resting her hand on the matted hair of his chest.

'My love, I have said that I am yours. I am at your disposal, in all ways.'

'Then I am to decide?'

'I prefer that you do.'

He thought about this.

'I cannot. Not at present,' he said at length. 'While we travel, I propose that we conduct ourselves as conventionally as possible. We must convince those around us that we are a married couple of some means, perfectly ordinary in every way. It is easier if we do not attract attention by any oddity of demeanour.'

'You are right,' said Augusta. 'But when we are in France . . .'

'When we reach our destination, we will know better how we want to live. There is no necessity to decide such matters now.'

'I agree with you, but I will confess to a hope that you might not retire your rod.'

He laughed and kissed the top of her head.

'Permanent retirement is exceptionally unlikely. Now, we must wash and dress and I must make a visit to Cheapside with one of your bracelets. Money must be raised for our passage.'

They washed each other with tender thoroughness, then dressed individually, Augusta again bemoaning her lack of underwear.

'I will buy you some,' he said. 'While I am out.'

'I wish I could come with you. I will fear for you.'

He strode over and took her in his arms, kissing out the tremor that had seized her.

'There is no need to fear, Augusta. I will make haste.'

'What if you should be seen by—'

'Nobody will seek us. They have their money. They will be content.'

But James could not avoid a little flutter of anxiety on stepping across the threshold of the inn with a diamond bracelet in his inner coat pocket.

If anybody *had* decided to pursue them, they might have a watch on the railway stations and their environs. He put his head down and walked through the steam that enveloped the area until he came to London Bridge and crossed it at a fast pace.

From the opposite embankment, Cheapside was quickly attained through the winding, narrow streets of the old City. He kept his coat wrapped close to his body at all times, wise to all the pickpocketing tricks one could fall prey to. Luckily the day was bright with no trace of fog and such conditions often sent the thieves to their beds where they would lie in wait for dusk.

A likely jewellers was quickly located and the deal done with as much bold face as he could put on it. They probably thought he was a fence or a ponce, but it wasn't to be helped.

Much worse was the necessity of buying ladies' under-garments. For a desperate few moments, he considered buying a bolt of flannel and sewing them himself – but soon rejected the idea as ludicrous. There was nothing for it but to march into the nearest ladies' costumers and request a half dozen chemises and drawers.

'My wife is blind,' he said, in answer to the blinking stares that greeted his request. 'We have no servant.'

All the same, the giggles from the back room as the serving girls went to seek out his order were unmistakable.

It was a great relief to be back in the street and bound for London Bridge once more, with a purse of sovereigns in his pocket and a parcel of wrapped garments beneath his arm.

The traffic was heavy on the bridge and came frequently to a standstill. James passed it all, his eyes fixed on the south bank, ignoring the stamping horses and yelling cabbies. London Bridge station, a brand new building, shone like a beacon in the distance – the symbol of freedom.

He was almost across when the most peculiar sensation crept up the back of his neck. In that instant, he whirled around, suddenly convinced that he was being followed, to see Mrs Shaw a few yards behind him.

She froze when she perceived that she was seen. Not far behind her was a stationary cab with an open door – presumably she had been travelling in it when she had seen him.

Within seconds she had sprung back to life.

'Tell me where she is,' she said, coming up close. 'What have you done with her, you dog?'

'Go back to your cab,' he said. 'Your business with Augusta is finished. You will never see her again.'

'Take me to her. I mean her no harm. I wish only to speak with her.'

'Who is with you in the cab?'

'Nobody. I am quite alone. Look at me, a lone, helpless woman. What threat can I pose a great strapping young man like you?' She turned her palms upwards, supplicating.

'Have you not done enough?'

'Have *you* not? We sought the best of care for Augusta, in the hope that she might recover and be able to live once more as suits her station in life. Now she is ruined. You have ruined her.'

'Oh, you lying witch! You would have put her away forever.'

The altercation, growing heated, attracted the attention of idling cabbies atop their hansom boxes.

'Smack 'im one,' shouted one such helpfully, while the others joined in with catcalls and whistles.

'Come away off the bridge,' said Mrs Shaw levelly. 'We are making a scene.'

'Return to your cab. I have no intention of taking you anywhere near Augusta.'

He turned and walked swiftly on, but he knew that she followed him, and instead of going to the inn, he descended instead some stairs to the wharf below. The area was busy with building work, warehouses under construction, intended to replace those destroyed in the great Tooley Street fire of four years since.

A sense of desolation still prevailed among all the industry and James thought, with a shiver, of the bravery of his namesake, James Braidwood, who had perished in his efforts to douse the flames. He himself had watched the conflagration from the opposite bank.

Here the river was high and fetid with the summer warmth, churning in a brown swirl around the hulls of the boats moored at the quayside. Further into the midstream, the Thames was thick with tugs and steamers going about their daily business.

'What are you doing? Why do you come down here?'

Mrs Shaw's querulous voice drifted down the steps at his back.

'Here I am,' he said, sitting down on a bulwark and placing

his package on his knees. 'And here I shall stay until you go back to your cab. I am in no hurry, Mrs Shaw, and I can wait all day if necessary.' He yawned. 'I like to watch the process of building, don't you?'

'Vile wretch, do not trifle with me. If you do not take me to Augusta, I shall find her. For I surmise that she must be somewhere in this vicinity, on the south bank of the river. At an inn, perhaps? Close to a station, for of course you cannot stay in London now. It will be the work of minutes to find her.'

'Go now, Mrs Shaw. You are very lucky that Augusta and I have decided not to prosecute the criminal acts against her. But we may change our view.'

Mrs Shaw laughed at that, throwing back her head.

Looking at her throat, James thought what a handsome woman she was, or could be, if only she were not so heartless.

'You fool,' she said. 'You know perfectly well that to do any such thing would only embroil you in more trouble than you could imagine. You will rot in jail for the rest of your days, and Augusta will be placed in a nice, quiet asylum.'

'Let us go, Mrs Shaw. We are nothing to you now. You have what you want.'

'Almost,' she said, coming closer. 'Not quite. I miss my little slave girl. I had hoped to have her exactly where I wanted her, to attend to my every wish. Miss Quim needs her mistress's discipline, you see.'

James shook his head, scorn overriding disgust.

'You can find any number of willing girls to perform the same role, I am sure. The streets are rotten with them. Mrs Edwards' refuge is testament to it.'

Mrs Shaw nodded at that, seeming to agree.

'Oh, there is no shortage of little sluts, that's true enough.

Perhaps I might look up your friend. What was her name? Annie, was it?'

He rose at that, as if he would reach out to seize her, but thought better of it and clutched his package to his chest instead.

'Oh, I see that she is dear to you,' goaded Mrs Shaw. 'Your affections are thinly spread. Poor Augusta.'

'Leave her be.'

'Give me my sweet little sightless whore, and I will.'

Mrs Shaw came closer now, hovering within reach of him.

'I have told you. I have nothing more to say on the subject. Go to your friends and your allies. Leave us alone.'

'It seems to me, Mr Stratton,' said Mrs Shaw, moving inexorably nearer, causing James to take another step back, almost to the edge of the quay, 'that you are all that stands between me and everything I ever desired in life. Everything.'

'You have enough,' he said. 'Money, your companion, social position, respectability.'

'Yes, and these are great things to a woman who has fought her way up in the world from nowhere at all. The bastard daughter of a hanged man.'

'If you would like to compare inauspicious starts in life, I should tell you that I was myself born in prison.'

'And you should die there too.'

'No, I should prefer not to.'

'I should never have engaged your services. You are not what I bargained for.'

'Am I not?'

'I thought you might be some louche older man, riddled with pox. I thought it would be easy enough to persuade Augusta that you were young and handsome, for my purposes. But you were. You truly were. I should have hired another instead of continuing with you. Somebody hard-headed and unsentimental. Not a fool like you. For pity's sake – to fall in love with your whipping girl. What idiocy!'

'Better a fool than a witch like you. I should hate you for what you have done but I feel nothing but pity.'

'How dare you pity me!' she screamed.

She launched herself forwards with a substantial shove, but he sidestepped, knowing her purpose too well. He attempted to grasp hold of her as she stumbled on the edge of the quay but it was all done too quickly, and she fell headlong into the brown, sludgy waters below.

James put his hands over his mouth and stared. The clangour of building works meant that the splash went unheard. Nobody on the quay had seen. Nobody on the bridge paid attention. He could . . . He looked up towards the parapet, his gaze tending longingly towards the station hotel, where Augusta waited.

But he couldn't stop himself turning back, down to where Mrs Shaw flailed and splashed, apparently unable to swim.

He put down the package and ran towards some stone steps leading into the water, shedding his coat as he went. He left his boots on the lowest step and waded down, grimacing at the foul odour. A rat swam past as he reached chest-depth and pushed off towards Mrs Shaw, a few yards distant.

She clung and pinched, her weight almost pulling him under the brackish surface, but he managed to keep his head above water and drag her, kicking and gasping, back to the stairs.

He sat her drenched body down, asking his conscience if he ought to try and clear her airways of the rank waters, but his conscience was on his side, for once, and he simply picked up his boots and left her there. On the quayside, he ran across the coachman, whom he had intended to seek out.

'Look to your mistress,' he advised, pointing to the stairway. 'She is on those steps.'

There. He had done more than most men would, and he was free, at last. Free to start anew.

Back at the inn, Augusta ran to him, then screamed on contact with his wet and slimy waistcoat.

'Whatever has passed? You stink like the river!'

He threw the package on the bed.

'Undergarments are hard to come by in this city,' he said. 'But I have got some. And now I fear I must bathe before we can make our onward journey. I have asked downstairs for a tub to be brought up.'

Augusta dressed while James washed in the inn's tin bath, scrubbing all traces of the disgusting river from his skin and hair.

'Did you fall in?' she asked. 'What happened to you?'

'A trivial misfortune,' he said, wielding the bath brush as if it might work on questions as well as dirt. 'Nothing of consequence. You look beautiful, my love, in that dress.'

'Do I? I like to hear you say it, even if I can never know the truth for myself.'

'It is the truth.' He put down the brush and lay back, watching islands of suds settle on his stomach and chest. 'Something you have been ill acquainted with. Henceforth, Augusta, let us swear that we shall be always truthful with one another.'

'Easy for me to do.'

'And for me,' he said. 'You must be honest with me always about what you feel and what you wish for. We live in a world where honesty is rarely valued as it should be. Let us make our own world, from our own hearts.'

'Oh, James. I should like nothing better.'

The platform at London Bridge Station was foggy with steam and the loud hissing and clanking of engines made conversation almost impossible, but James had never felt more tranquil or at peace than he did on handing Augusta into their Folkestone-bound carriage.

They were going away, away from narrow alleys and blackened bricks, the roar and bustle of the crowd, the cab-jammed roads, the calls of painted girls, the smell of stale beer and horse dung, everything he had ever known and called home.

Home was elsewhere now.

Epilogue

Positano, Italy, 17th August 1866

My dear Annie

I have no more than hope to sustain these words; the hope that they will reach you and that you are somewhere in that vast city, contributing to the sum of its gaiety as I trust it contributes to yours. I will continue to send these letters, care of anywhere I knew you to frequent, until I obtain a reply. I regret that I never had the opportunity to complete your education in the skill of literacy, but I sometimes find myself wondering if you found the will within yourself to pursue it without me.

If you did, you might be able to read the occasional dispatches I send to the London Times, as one of its Italian correspondents. Of course, these bulletins are not sufficient to keep me and my small family, so I am a Jem-of-all-trades now, teaching English to the natives and acting as a tour guide to English-speaking visitors. Yes, you will have dwelled on that word 'family', I am sure – for I have one.

*

James put aside his pen, distracted by a familiar plaintive cry from inside the house. He rose from the wrought-iron table beneath the vine-covered arch in the garden and went inside.

'Where is Gianna?'

Augusta leant over the baby's crib. James watched as a small, chubby hand was laid on his lover's cheek. Augusta might not be able to see her child, but she brought every other sense to bear in such full measure that she hardly needed to.

'Augusta?' he prompted her, for she was too absorbed by her communion with the babe to reply.

'Oh, she is fetching a wrap for her. She means to take her for a walk down to the shore. You know how her mother dotes on our little Milly.'

'And how Gianna loves to show her off like an exhibition piece,' said James. 'Yes.'

'She loves the child. This is what one wants of a nursemaid, surely?'

'Yes. It is.'

He stood aside as Gianna swept through, bundled with blankets and scarves. Augusta stepped back and allowed her to pick the baby up and wrap her in her outdoor clothes.

Baby carriages had not yet reached this part of the world and besides, they would be of little use on the rocky paths that led down from the mountains to the sea.

'I bring her back in one hour,' said Gianna, clucking down at the smiling face in her arms. 'When she is hungry, yes?'

'As you please,' said Augusta. 'When she is hungry. I do not need your help while my husband is in the house.'

Gianna nodded and left the house, baby Amelia having forgotten whatever her earlier plaint might have been.

'She will be well,' said James, putting his hands on Augusta's shoulders. 'You must not fret.'

'She is so tiny still. It is hard to be apart from her.'

'In London, in your old life, she would have been given to a wet nurse. You would see her once a day, between teatime and supper.'

'Then I thank God my old life is behind me.' She nestled her head into the crook of James' shoulder. 'I thank God for that every day.'

'As do I.' His face moved down until his lips touched her cheek, skin upon skin. 'My love, do you think . . .?'

She twisted a little to meet him, whispering into his whiskers.

'Yes.'

The word, as simple as it was, acted like magic upon his resolve. In the three months since his daughter's birth, he had waited for Augusta to offer him some sign that she had recovered from her difficult labour. He had been careful not to show any impatience, nor to hasten her into an untimely embrace, but with the return of the roses to her cheeks and the strength to her gait, he found his impulses of desire ever harder to check.

Augusta rubbed her nose against his and then found his lips, inviting him into a kiss of tender intimacy.

He hooked one arm around her waist and pulled her closer, pressing his mouth on hers, then nibbling at her lower lip, signalling all the urgency the rushing of his blood lent him.

Away from the empty crib they stepped in a complicated dance that ended with them falling through the pair of curtains that hid their bed.

He was grateful for the temperate climate of the

region, which made it possible to wear little in the way of undergarments. Within half a minute, Augusta's skirts were about her ears and he engaged in the stroking and caressing of her thighs. The kiss persisted even when his fingers slipped inside her nether lips, finding warmth and slickness there, as of old.

He released her mouth from the tyranny of his tongue and panted, 'You are sure?'

'Do not ask me,' she breathed. 'Take me. I have missed you so . . . missed your way with me.'

His index finger slipped inside her and he felt her muscles tighten against it. No damage had been done. He exhaled with relief and kissed her face all over.

Inside her once more, he felt like a man coming home. He might be in exile from his country, his city, but in his heart he was in no such state. As long as Augusta lay beneath him, her legs wrapped around him, her heart bumping fit to burst from her ribcage, he was where he should be. He kissed at the beads of perspiration on her brow, then quieted her little moans of pleasure with more kissing.

He thought of all the kissing they had done on all those trains last year, from Calais to Paris, from Paris to Lyons, from Lyons to Marseilles, from Marseilles . . . He lost the thread, somewhere in the sticky, fervent memories of a sticky, fervent summer. Content enough to sheath himself in the familiar, heady heat of his lover and kiss her until she spent, he moved his hand down to rub between her lips.

No formality would be needed today, no rituals or roles to play – what they desired was simple, animal reconnection. Perhaps their games would come later, or perhaps they would not – James found, in the exquisite pleasure of this long-awaited coupling, that he didn't much care. If he could look on her face while she melted in bliss, if he could sink into her softness and stay there until he was spent, that was enough.

The sudden sucking-in of her breath was followed by the arching of her back, and then he felt her tighten around him and he knew he could finish, if only he had a mind to. He lingered over it, though, slowing and taking time to stroke her face, mutter broken endearments, slide into that different state of being while all around him ceased to exist.

She put her hands in his hair and kissed his neck, sucking at it until he was driven into his fall, having no choice but to let nature take its course with him, mastering him until the dear life was drained and he collapsed on her breast, gasping for air.

They held each other close, listening to the sounds that broke the stillness – the toll of a church bell, the squawk of sea birds, the distant crash of waves – while their chests rose and fell together.

It was nothing like Holywell Street, thought James. It could be a different world entirely.

Augusta stirred in the rumpled sheets, then found his lips with her fingers. She turned her face to kiss him, long and sweetly.

'You are my life, you know,' she said. 'You and our child. I do not miss that old life at all.'

'You had no life to miss,' he said. 'What you have now – what we both have – is freedom.'

'And love,' she said.

'Yes. Love.' A sea breeze fluttered the curtain at the side of the window, drawing his attention to the slope of multi-coloured rooftops outside and the brilliant blue sea at their foot. 'I wish you could see this view,' he said.

'I have no need of views,' she said. 'I have all I could ever wish for.'

'So do I,' said James. 'But a little more in the way of sleep wouldn't go amiss.'

They laughed in each other's arms and settled in to drowse.

Outside in the garden, the letter he had been writing was picked up and tossed on the warm wind, scudding along the winding track to the seashore, where it was carried out into the foaming waves and lost forever.

Acknowledgements

I'd like to acknowledge Lee Jackson's amazing 'Victorian London' website and a book called *London and Londoners in the 1850s and 1860s* by Alfred Rosling Bennett. Also, every Victorian writer I have ever read (but I couldn't possibly list them!).

Enjoyed *Fallen*?

Read on for an extract from

ON DEMAND

Also by Justine Elyot

No Reservations

(Do you have a reservation? Then this isn't the hotel for you!)

Welcome to the Hotel.
All baggage is to be left at the door.
Please sign in, under whichever name you have chosen, at Reception.
You are now free to explore. Enjoy your stay!

I have always been drawn to hotels.
Call me commitment-phobic, but I love their eternal temporariness, their anonymity, their fluidity and flux. They seduce you without expecting your heart and soul; your home expects time and attention, but your hotel only wants your money, and only for as long as you care to give it. You can walk up the steps as plain Jane Smith and enter the lobby as Lady Furcoat-Noknickers; the hotel does not care what you do, or with whom.

A luxuriously appointed building full of people escaping reality can brew a heady atmosphere – I should know; I've worked here for four years now. Few of the comings and goings here pass me by. Especially the comings.

It all started so innocently.
A delayed train, an hour to kill. I was halfway to the queue for styrofoam-flavour sludge before I stopped myself

and the idea sparked. I could spend my dead minutes on a spit-drenched platform staring at time ticking by on the 'Next Arrival' screen. Or I could spend them in the hotel across the road, drinking half-decent coffee and reading a complimentary magazine.

It was almost one o'clock, so I wouldn't stand out too much amidst the lunchtime rush – if I could find a comfortable chair in a quiet corner, I could pretend to be a bona fide businesswoman meeting a client or something. It would be fun; a tiny masquerade to enliven a dull wait.

This particular hotel was of the swankier variety; a row of international flags flapped above the plate glass, and uniformed doormen stood on sentry duty either side of the revolving entrance. I wondered if they had to remain impassive and still, like Beefeaters, but one of them unbent and smiled at me when I trotted past, intent on getting through the revolving door without a pratfall of some kind.

Sophie Martin, bored office drone and unsuccessful photographer, pushed her hand against the glass.

Sophie Martin, supercharged business bitch, stepped out on the other side.

Not that there was any telephone-box-whirlwind-style action going on in the revolving doors – all it took to turn from drab to diva was exposure to the seductive particles of the hotel lobby air, weighted with possibility and chance and choice and an undertone of wickedness.

My heels click-click-clicked on the marble lobby floor, passing the curved Reception desk, catching a haughty lip-curl from its pointy-nosed custodian. She wouldn't be looking askance at me once she knew exactly who I was, I told myself grandly. I would have her lilac-rinsed head on a platter.

I strutted into the bar, carpeted now so that my heels were muffled, found a corner with an armchair and a copy of some style glossy and sashayed straight over.

Within seconds, a waistcoated waiter was taking my order, hovering and fawning in a manner I could imagine myself getting quite used to. The prices were steep, but when you considered that a morale-boost came with your cappuccino, perhaps they were worth paying.

He was a few years younger than me, maybe twenty or so; the rude whiff of barely post-adolescent testosterone clung to his white shirtsleeves and poorly shaved chin. I wondered what he would do if I flirted with him.

'Do I get anything extra with my cappuccino?' I asked him, dropping the level of my voice a notch or two and hoping it would make me sound like Lauren Bacall. I raised one eyebrow, a forefinger tapping my lower lip to pull it down to a pout.

He coughed slightly. 'A biscotti, Madam,' he said, the tips of his ears reddening. 'And chocolate or cinnamon sprinkles.'

'Oh, cinnamon, I think,' I drawled, striving to keep my voice on the sexy side of forty-fags-a-day. 'I always prefer spicy to sweet, don't you?'

I almost laughed at my own cartoon vampishness, but it seemed to be doing the trick for him. He flushed beautifully and scurried away, leaving me to terrorise him with my eyes over the rim of my magazine until the coffee was ready.

The room was filling up with conference attendees on a lunch break: lots of men in suits talking loudly into mobile phones and gesturing over to whoever was getting the round in at the bar. Mmm, I thought, stretching a leg beneath my table and rotating my ankle slowly. I do like a good suit. Some of these were very well-cut indeed; I wondered what the conference was about. Were they bankers? IT consultants? Estate agents even?

My question was met with a question.

'What did you think of that session? Not enough

statistical evidence, I thought; bit too much reliance on the anecdotal.'

A man slid into the armchair opposite mine, placing a plastic wallet of papers on the table between us. Through the green shade of the cover, I could just make out the words 'Probate Law'. *Ooh, a lawyer*, I thought; *I've never met one of those before. Though if this one is anything to judge by, I should get myself arrested more often.*

Everything about him was top-of-the-range, from the haircut down to the polished Italian leather that peeked from the crossed trouser-leg. The voice was warm and smooth; an asset if he was a barrister. Even as I looked up and smiled back, I tried to picture him in one of those horsehair wigs and a black cloak; it proved to be a surprisingly sexy image.

'Oh, I'm not here for the conference,' I said, flicking the page of my magazine.

'Really? Meeting someone? Am I intruding?'

'No, no.' I waved him back down to his sitting position. 'Just taking a breather,' I told him.

'Right. I thought I hadn't seen you in the meeting room. My attention was wandering a bit from the flipchart, and I'm sure it would have rested on you.'

Wow! He was flirting with me. A man who knows how to wash and earns a wage flirting with me! Unheard-of in the annals of my experience. I had to wonder what all that pure new wool would smell like. Not to mention that subtly tanned skin, from which a hint of expensive aftershave was drifting over, activating my saliva glands.

He had beautiful hands as well; I could picture them gesturing in court. I could also picture them on my hip, my belly, my thigh. All in all, the effect he had on me was instant and acute. I found myself leaning forward, crossing my legs so that my skirt rode a little higher, just to the point where the elasticated part of my hold-up stocking might be a teensy bit visible.

'What's the conference?' I asked. 'Charm school head-masters?'

He laughed, throwing his head back, oh, Adam's apple, oh, deep, rich laugh, oh. I took advantage of his moment's lapse in eye contact to slip open my top button and put aside my magazine. I wanted him in the most sudden and violent way. I wanted to touch the fine cotton of his shirt, open it wide and see if what lay within was as luxurious as its cladding.

'No,' he said eventually, his bright blue eyes damp with mirth and ... something else. 'Solicitors. I specialise in soliciting.'

Now it was my turn to laugh. 'Clearly,' I purred.

Some form of conversation followed, of the kind you might hear between Mae West and Sid James, predicated entirely on smutty innuendo. I don't remember what we said, but I do remember the feeling of being involved in a dirty-minded game of verbal tennis: serve, volley, lob, smash, grunt, new balls please. Just like our more athletic fellows, we were getting sweatier and hotter with each point scored.

Much as we pretended to wit and sophistication, the real gist of what was said was:

Him: Get your kit off.

Me: Work for it.

Him: Look at me like that and I'll have you up against the wall before you can say 'No win no fee'.

Me: Sounds good; prove it.

Before the cinnamon sprinkles of my cappuccino had melted into the froth, he had a proposition for me.

'Listen,' he said, eyes now piercing blue laserbeams of seduction, body wide open in a pose at once relaxed and predatory. 'How long do you have? Do you have to rush back to work?'

I bit my lip and smiled inscrutably.

'Come on, help me out,' he said. 'Do I have to issue a summons?'

This made me laugh again. I can't resist a man with a sense of humour. I also can't resist a man who looks as if he could be in the running for the next James Bond.

'What do you have in mind?' I asked. If he was James Bond, I was pretty close to Pussy Galore at this stage. 'Does it involve handcuffs?'

'Would you like it to?'

My mouth watered.

'You've got me on a technicality,' I told him, standing and taking his proffered pinstriped arm. The warmth and scent of him tripped my switches; I wanted that, just that, just for now.

'What's your room number?' he murmured, sweeping me past the potted plants into the lobby.

Ah.

'Can't we go to yours?'

He stopped smartly, frowning down at me. 'I'm afraid not; the conference finishes today.' He shook his head. 'You aren't staying here?'

I chewed the inside of my cheek, blushing. 'Well, no. Just came in for a coffee.'

'Just a coffee? You aren't another kind of solicitor, are you?'

I breathed in sharply. 'Fuck, no!'

He breathed out for me. 'I'm sorry. I didn't think you ... OK. "Fuck, no," you say, but I'm still thinking, "Fuck? Yes!" If you're with me. Still with me?'

I giggled, a little bit hysterically. It wasn't the first time I'd been taken for a member of the oldest profession, but certainly the least opportune.

'We don't have a room,' I pointed out.

He manoeuvred me behind one of the substantial palms, pulled me against him and patted the seat of my skirt. 'I do have a car,' he growled.

The feel of him, hard chest, taut shoulder, large crotch-bulge, was enough to chase away my doubts. I wanted that, on me, above me, in me.

'Reclining seats?' I asked.

'Of course.'

'Good.'

In the underground car park, he bent me backwards over the bonnet and mashed his lips into mine. That well-cut cloth was covering my feeble manmade fibres, rubbing them up and down, sparking them into static cling. My nylon stockings nudged at his trousers, slinking up beneath his jacket and around his hips, wrapping around his back and clamping that central hardness right into the open maw of my skirt.

I ground my mound around it, enjoying the sensation of the fabrics pressing into me, while his tongue plunged downward and his hand excavated the hidden depths behind my blouse. His fingers plucked and sneaked under the lacy cups; there was pressing and kneading and hot breath and jammed pelvises and mock-thrusting, and all beneath the spotlit concrete ceiling of the public car park.

'Do you want it then?' he asked, holding my wrists pinned to the cool shiny paintwork.

'Maybe *in* the car?' I whispered, moving my head sideways to check for CCTV cameras and irate attendants.

'My command is your wish,' he said, pulling me up as if preparing for an energetic jitterbug and spinning me around to the side of the vehicle. He ducked inside the door, pressed the button to recline the passenger seat and bundled me on to it. I was a little confused when he shut the door, leaving me supine on the chilled leather, but he soon reappeared on the driver's side, kneeling on the seat and looking ravenously down at me.

'Get your knickers off then,' he prompted.

Thrilled at his excellent grasp of the command tone, I wriggled them down my thighs, past my knees, and brought my still-shod feet up in the air to release them from the legholes.

My escort put a steadying hand on one leg, indicating that he wanted them both kept up in that position, and moved his other arm down for a good feel of my newly exposed parts.

'Now that's wet,' he said, impressed. 'A good fuck is what you need.'

I couldn't argue with him. The speed, the suddenness, the rudeness, the wrongness of it all was the turn-on of my life. It was dirty and slutty, but I like dirty and slutty, and so, it seems, did he.

In his haste to mount me, he lost a button from the placket of his trousers, swearing as it pinged into the distance, then he slipped swiftly and efficiently between my knees, levering me up by the bum in order to skewer my dripping centre in one move.

We groaned in chorus as it stole inside so easily, so satisfyingly, filling the hole in perfect proportion.

'Do you do this often?' he asked, beginning to thrust.

'Mmm?' I replied absently, lifting my hips towards his, grabbing his bottom to push him greedily as far in as I could.

'Pick up strange men in hotels for dirty sex? I bet you do it all the time.'

It was on the tip of my tongue to protest, to say no, that I'm not that kind of girl, but before I did, my imagination stepped in front of my indignation and I realised that I liked this idea. I imagined him as one of a string of anonymous men, using my body, day after day, week after week, in the hotel bedrooms, the toilets, the car park. I'm not a whore, but I felt like one, letting this man whose name I didn't even know slam his cock up me within quarter of an hour of meeting.

'Yes,' I said. 'I do.'

'Thought so.'

The windows had steamed up now and I had to spare a thought for the expensive upholstery, which was getting the pounding of all time. I pushed my hands down, clutching at his belt, the buckle end of which slapped lightly against my bottom with each forward motion. These were becoming more frantic now, the jingling urgent, his loosened tie flapping over my face until I sank my teeth into it, irritated by the tickling effect. I could feel the quake, shuddering seconds away, and I accidentally kicked the dashboard quite hard, so that he stopped for a second and turned around to assess any damage. Luckily there was none.

All the same, 'I'll make you pay for that,' he vowed, ratcheting up the force of his thrusts, body-slamming me into a new realm of fierce sensation. The more I pretended to be a hooker, concentrating on servicing my client and avoiding orgasm, the more orgasmic I felt, until the wave crashed and I yelled until I was hoarse.

For a while, it was as if our bodies had melted together; the sweet glue of our exertions filled the air and stuck us to each other. The car seat was slippery now and my thin summer blouse drenched. He unpeeled himself shortly before I had to pass out, crouching between my sore thighs, which were chafed to bits by that pure new wool I had so admired in his trousers. Thank God they hadn't been made of cheap stuff; I would have been skinned alive.

'Nothing like a mid-conference knee-trembler,' he opined, taking a wallet from the glove compartment and stuffing a wad of twenty-pound notes into my cleavage. 'Get yourself something pretty. Off you trot then.'

Eyes on stalks, I removed the money – a hundred pounds – and tried to give it back, but he simply unlocked the car door and opened it, gesturing me away impatiently.

I straightened myself up in the car park, snapped the elastic tops of my hold-ups back in place, pulled my skirt down and re-buttoned my blouse. I would have to sort out my face and hair in the toilets.

Before leaving, I threw the money back inside the car. Much as I could have used a hundred quid, it seemed important that I did not accept it. To do so would have been to concede control of the encounter to him, and I did not want that. If I behave like a trollop, it's because I want to; the pretence is an essential part of the excitement.

Of course, I missed the train.

The memory of my soliciting solicitor sustained me through some long and lonely nights, replaying the scenes on my darkened ceiling while my fingers wandered beneath the sheets.

The hotel was not really on my way anywhere, but sometimes I would take detours just to gaze at its gilded splendour, my eyes moving slowly upwards beyond the striped awning to the windows of the rooms, picturing what might be going on behind those heavy white drapes.

Temptation took a week to lure me back inside.

Another lunch hour, another conference, but this time I was dressed for the occasion in my highest heels, my tightest skirt, my sharpest jacket over a lacy camisole. My eyes cruised the bar while I slunk over to order a drink. Not a coffee this time; they can sour the breath so – this time I would go for a cocktail. Something fruity.

I leant over the counter, wiggling my bum out at the rest of the room. The stuttery waiter was lurking in the background stacking glasses in the washer and he smirked at the barman, a sleazy-looking character, when he swaggered up to ask me if he could help.

'Oh, I'm sure you can,' I said, releasing the inner vixen in full effect. 'What I really fancy just now is a Sloe Comfortable Screw.'

The barman double-took; I had to have a stern word with myself to stifle the unvampish giggle struggling to escape my Bitch Red lips. Then his lip flipped up at an Elvis-like angle, his eyes glazed over slightly and he leant right down.

'I'm sure that can be arranged,' he smarmed. Creepy as he was, there was something primitively attractive about him, though he severely overestimated his own charms. 'Or maybe a Screaming Orgasm?'

Much as I enjoy repetition of this beach-holiday-classic conversation, I was not after shagging the man, so I toned down my performance for his benefit.

'Oh no, I don't think so,' I said primly. 'But I do want an umbrella and a sparkler. The full tarty works, if you can manage that.'

His eyes narrowed and he began shaking ice with venomous purpose. I took advantage of his preoccupation to scope out the room again. Knots of business people in twos and threes were drifting in, beginning to line the counter. Some of them tried to catch my eye; even more so when I took a seat on a high bar stool and sipped at my glass of neon-orange slapper juice. Stocking tops in sight, I unbuttoned and removed my jacket, leaving my shoulders bare and my bra visible beneath the fluttery scrap of camisole. I took a straw from a dispenser on the counter top and began to suck the drink up, pouting my lips.

The barman was barely able to serve the other customers, such was his distraction. I was watching him fumble with a bowl of complimentary olives when a voice behind me caused me to spin around.

'How much for half an hour?'

He was not my type. Shortish, balding, the beginnings of a paunch. But, perversely, the idea of being available to the first bidder was exciting enough to overcome my personal tastes.

I looked him up and down and smiled. 'I don't charge,' I said.

He raised his eyebrows. 'I'm sorry, I got the wrong idea,' he said apologetically, holding up his hands and backing away.

'No, no,' I whispered, beckoning him back. 'I mean, if you can persuade me it will be worth my while, I'll give you a freebie.'

He was motionless for a while, staring at my cleavage consideringly.

'I'm not sure I understand,' he said at last. 'Come and sit with me and tell me what you mean.'

I followed him to an alcove and plonked myself on the cream leather banquette beside him.

'So you aren't a working girl?' he opened, taking a draught of his lager and regarding me enquiringly.

'Oh, I am a working girl,' I contradicted him, deciding to get into character. 'But I'm off-duty at the moment. It was a long night.'

'Oh.' The man chuckled with relief. 'I thought I might have offended you there. So . . . you aren't available then?'

'I'm available to the right client,' I told him. 'Although I had a few earlier on, none of them were up to much. Definitely a case of business rather than pleasure.'

'Really?' The man puffed up his chest a little, clearly preparing to convince me of his Real Man status. 'So you . . . you enjoy your work?'

'Oh, yes, I love it,' I told him, sucking on my straw again. 'Do you? Are you here for the conference?'

'Yes.' He shook his head. 'I like my work, but I hate these dos. Bloody icebreakers, meetings about meetings and all that. I'm dreading this afternoon – role-playing, would you believe?'

'Oh, I like role-playing,' I protested. 'How about we do a little one now, just to get you in the mood?'

'You're quite something, you know,' he said, almost nervously. The power of knowing that this man wanted me, feared rejection from me, would probably go to some lengths to have me, was intoxicating. I felt like Cleopatra.

'Thank you. So are you up for it?'

'Depends what "it" is. What's my brief?'

'You're a wealthy businessman. I'm a prostitute.'

'Well, that's not far from the truth,' he said, brow furrowed.

'Good. It'll be all the more convincing then. Come on, let's play.'

I sat back and waited for him to make the opening gambit, wondering if I would actually go through with it. Sex with a man I didn't really fancy, just for the sake of satisfying my newly discovered kink. It was my fantasy, but would it crumble in the face of reality? I had to know. I decided then and there that I would have one rule in my game, and the rule was that I could not say no. Obviously I *could*, in the face of danger or serious illegality – but up to that point, I would say yes to everything and everyone.

'OK then,' he said, sitting back and determinedly getting into role. 'How much for half an hour?'

'Two hundred,' I said.

'Two hundred? For half an hour? You must be good.'

'I am. Do you want to find out how good?'

'I think I do. Hold on a minute though ... I thought you said this would be a freebie?'

'Yes, yes,' I said impatiently. 'It will be. But in the game, I cost two hundred.' I lowered my voice, looked him straight in the eye. 'In real life, I'm a no-strings free fuck.'

'Christ knows you don't get many of them,' said the man, his voice a little uneven. 'Right then. Let's go to my room, shall we?'

'Yes.'

In the lift on the way up, I stared at the pair of us in the mirror. He looked a little crumpled and slightly sweaty. I looked like a tart. It would have been pretty obvious to all in the bar and lobby what our relationship was.

Now we were out of the public areas of the hotel, he seemed to gain an assertiveness that had been only half-present in the bar.

'So you had a long night,' he said, his tone rather severe.

'Yes.' I blushed. 'I didn't get much sleep.'

'Time for bed then, eh?'

He took my arm as the lift door slid open and escorted me along the corridor, our feet sinking in the deep pile of the carpet as if we were walking through snow.

It was only when he slipped his key card into the slot that I began to have misgivings. The solicitor was one thing – carried along on a wave of lust that knocked doubts for six – but this was another. A strange man's hotel room.

Could I really go through with this?

My escort answered the question for me. He strode straight over to the bed, sat down on the edge and unzipped his fly.

'Right, if I'm paying two hundred for this, I want my money's worth. Let's see you with your clothes off.'

His sudden switch to 'in charge' mode awakened my wilder streak. I straightened my spine, did a little twirl and threw the jacket I was carrying on to a chair. Never having done a striptease before, I was unsure of the ritual, but once I had unbuttoned and shimmied out of my skirt, everything seemed to flow naturally. Down to the lacy camisole, silk French knickers and lace hold-ups, I slowed the action, teasingly pretending to drop something and bending over to pick it up, or standing with one foot on the dresser while I ran my hands up my leg. I could see myself, at a peculiar angle, in the wardrobe mirror and I was impressed by the figure I cut. I momentarily considered a career in burlesque. If only I had a feathery fan and a Venetian mask.

Indeed, I was loving my work so much that I almost forgot my 'client' was waiting until I was forced by his impatient cough to look back at him. His fist was closed around his erect cock, his face quite red and collar loosened.

'We've only got half an hour,' he reminded me brusquely. 'I'm not paying you to dance. Get the rest of your kit off then get down on your knees over here.'

'OK, just one more move,' I promised him, hip-swaying over to the fruit bowl and taking the banana from the top. I peeled it slowly, ran my tongue up the exposed pale yellow flesh and swirled its tip around the top of the fruit.

'On your knees, now!' entreated the client, groaning when I simultaneously put one hand down the front of my knickers and the banana in my mouth, swishing it around in there, sucking on it for all I was worth. 'Sod the banana, wrap your lips around this!'

He leant back, presenting his cock to me in all its fat purple-crowned glory. Giggling, I tossed the banana aside and fell to my knees in mock-worship of his manhood, ogling and caressing it as if it were made of gold. Slowly and deliberately I ran my tongue around my lips, staring boldly up at him, before taking the plunge, closing my mouth over the considerable girth, forming a seal and sucking for all I was worth.

My fingers played with his balls, squeezing gently and sometimes creeping back to push against his perineum, which tightened the sac all the more. Even when my mouth began to ache, I revelled in the effect I was having on him, his helpless little yaps of pleasure spurring me on to greater efforts. He was going to remember this as the blow job of his life; if I was going to play the part of the expensive hooker, I was going to do it properly.

My tongue played lightly against his steely erection, flicking up and down the shaft and around the frenulum. One of my hands closed tightly around his base while I worked at fitting more and more of him into my mouth; the other continued its foray around his testicles. He was shaking now, making strangled utterances, his hands clenching and unclenching in my hair; the end could not be far off.

'Lap it up, slut,' he panted, before roaring and thrusting into my face. A burst of liquid saltiness filled my mouth, pumping in and down my throat for what seemed like a long time. Even when I thought I had swallowed the lot and slid off his cock, an extra jet squirted on to my breasts, staining the lace border of my camisole.

I sat back on my heels and he lay down on the bed, spent.

'You can go now,' he murmured.

'You still have ten minutes,' I pointed out. 'And besides, I want my turn. I'm going to sit in that chair and sort myself out.'

He propped himself up, squinting. 'You aren't a real whore,' he said. 'A real whore would have been off with the money.'

'Like I said, I'm off-duty,' I told him. I sat back in the plush boudoir armchair, slung one leg over an arm, pushed aside the gusset of my knickers and began to delve into the slippery recesses, throwing my head back and shutting my eyes, imagining an audience crowded round me, brandishing twenty-pound notes. I squirmed on the velvet, flicking and plucking and plunging my fingers, pinching and squeezing my tits until I came hard, imagining applause, whistles, a shower of notes.

Then there was real applause; the clapping of my very own audience, now sitting up again with a noticeable erection threatening to poke him in the eye.

I glanced at the clock. Time was up.

'You'd better go down,' I told him, yawning and rising reluctantly from the chair.

'Hang on, though – for two hundred I should get another go, shouldn't I? I haven't even touched your pussy yet.'

'Time's up,' I said briskly, stepping into my skirt. 'And you have a role-play to perform. Not such an interesting one as this, though.'

'But I want to fuck you now,' he moaned.

'Thanks, but no thanks,' I told him, buttoning my jacket. 'You know where to find me if you fancy another go. And you know what it will cost.'

'How can I go downstairs with this?' he beseeched me, staring disconsolately at his treacherous stiffness.

'Good afternoon.' I smiled, opened the door and sailed off down the corridor, surging with wicked glee.

The lift door opened and I crossed the lobby, feeling every eye upon me, X-raying through to the semen stain on my camisole, the wet spot on my silky knickers, the traces of salty spunk on my tongue. *They all know I'm a whore*, I thought, swinging my hips and letting my heels click on the polished floor.

When I got home, I had to bring myself off again.

* * *

After that, the hunger was upon me. It became a game as addictive as any of those online fantasies; truly a second life.

At least once a week I strutted my stuff, maximally tarty and overdone amid the minimalist décor of the bar, lacking only a flashing beacon on my head to proclaim my shamelessness.

The men came in all shapes, sizes, ages, degrees of attractiveness and intelligence; the rule was, I could only say no in the most extreme of situations.

My juices stained dozens of pristine bedsheets; I took it lying down, standing up, on all fours, on chairs and desks and over windowsills; between my tits, in my mouth, cunt, arse; three ways, four ways, six ways till Sunday; with women, with an audience, with a camera, with a blindfold, with a webcam, with a whip, with a will.

There came a time when I could rely on three or four regular 'clients' being in the bar at any one session; sometimes I would only take up the first to offer; on other occasions, I would treat them all, one at a time or as a group. About six weeks into my new 'career', logistics were careering out of hand. The number of men waiting for their free ride every time I entered the bar was becoming unmanageable.

I pitched up one day at a new and unpopular time – half past three in the afternoon – and was relieved to find just me, the waiter and the barman in attendance.

I ordered a strawberry daiquiri and gave my creepy friend a dazzling smile. Perhaps today his luck could be in after all. For once, he smiled back instead of tossing his fringe sulkily.

'Have you heard? We've got a new manager. He wants a word with you.'

My fingers tensed around the stem of my glass. 'Why? How would he know me? What have you said?'

The barman simply shrugged and leered at me. 'His office is behind Reception. Go on and find out what he wants.'

I cannot say no. So I went.

I noticed that the severe-looking middle-aged woman I was used to had been replaced by a young girl with a pierced nose and an antipodean accent; a temp, I guessed. She smiled brightly at me and pointed to the door at the back of the area when I told her the manager wanted to see me.

I had no idea what to expect, but obeyed the terse instruction from the other side of the door to enter, and pushed my way into a huge windowless office. The manager sat behind a massive desk, about half a mile away, or so it seemed.

'Ah,' he said, and crooked a long finger. I made the epic journey across the carpet, my knees already weak, concentrating on keeping atop my heels and avoiding any humiliating wobbling. He did not stand or attempt to shake my hand, but simply looked me up and down through gold-framed spectacles, neither approvingly nor disapprovingly. Eventually he sat back and said, 'I'm new here.'

'So I've heard,' I replied, hoping for a swift cut to the chase.

'But you aren't. Are you?'

'I'm . . . a fairly frequent patron . . . of the bar.'

'You've been inside a few of the bedrooms too, I gather.'

So what? It's not a crime. But I bit my tongue.

'Anyway, that's by the by,' he said, waving a hand. 'I've been studying the books. Bar takings have taken quite a turn for the better in the past six weeks. We have many rebookings for rooms, especially in the traditionally un-popular midweek slots. A little business-minded bird told me you might have something to do with that.'

He really had the gimlet-stare off pat. It was quite

disconcerting, but I faced down the blue-grey gleam and shrugged. 'Not for me to say.'

Finally his lips twisted from rigid to relaxed and a half-chuckle leaked out. 'You needn't be defensive. I'm not about to ban you from the premises. The hooker in the bar is a fact of luxury hotel life; I'm inclined to turn a blind eye.'

'I'm not a hooker,' I blurted.

He frowned. 'It's all right; I've told you where I stand. There's no need to deny it . . .'

'Really. I'm not a hooker. I just . . . it's . . . kind of like . . . a hobby . . .' I broke off, realising that there was nowhere to go with this statement. He would probably prefer a prostitute; somebody with a sharp business mind. A slut, on the other hand . . .

'Now that's very interesting,' he remarked, leaning forward. 'That would explain why these men are spending so much in the bar and on room service, as well as going for the more expensive suites. They aren't paying for . . . anything extra.'

I scowled at him, then looked away.

'Look at me,' he said, and his tone woke me up; a visceral lurch in my stomach. I had never heard anything so commanding. 'I have a proposition for you.'

'Oh?'

He picked up a pen and wrote something with a flourish on some documents ranged on his blotter. He was signing his name, I thought.

'I'm offering you a job, if you're interested. I need a receptionist – somebody like you: smart, sexy, dressed to kill, with a bit of a come-hither behind the professional veneer. Take a look at the details and tell me what you think.'

I skim-read the contract; the terms and conditions seemed fair, the work easy and the money good. I needed good money.

'I . . . think it looks like something I might consider,' I said cautiously.

'And for how long might you consider it?' he asked sternly, his brows creasing at me. He was, I realised in that moment, exceptionally attractive.

Caution scattered into the four winds. 'For a few seconds,' I said, breathing hard and flushing. 'OK. I'll take it. Thanks.'

It was only then that he stood to shake my hand. He had a firm grip, his skin warm and smooth, his hand comfortingly large.

'Good,' he said. 'I'm Christopher Chase; Mr Chase to you. Or Sir.'

'Yes, Sir,' I breathed, feeling funny in a squirmy sort of way at the use of the honorific. 'Oh, yeah, I'm Sophie Martin.'

'I'm very glad to have you on board, Sophie,' he said, and for a millisecond an image of him lying on top of me on the deck of a ship, thrusting manfully, distracted me from the matter at hand.

'You will be friendly but professional behind the desk,' he reminded me. 'What you get up to when you're off-duty, however, is entirely your own . . . affair.'

He perched on the edge of his desk, curling a flirtatious lip at me. Basically, he was encouraging me to carry on my bar-based shaggery for as long as I liked.

I could not say no.

Also available from Black Lace:

Strange Attractions
by Emma Holly

Behind closed doors, the wicked play . . .

Charity Wills is a heartbreaker, and she is determined to
fund her education by any means necessary.

B. G. Grantham is obsessed with the unattainable – the
thrill of being refused the one thing he craves.

Invited to stay with the erotic-minded recluse in his
mansion, Charity provides the challenge he so desires. And
with the arrival of Eric Berne, her sexy 'keeper', she finds
herself tempted by both men . . .

Also available from Black Lace:

Personal Services
by Crystalle Valentino

All's fair in love and war . . .

Rosie Cooper isn't afraid of getting her hands dirty. So when a rival gardening company begins stealing her clients, she doesn't hesitate to confront the man in charge.

But Ben Hunter is a charmer. Having persuaded Rosie's female customers to switch to him, will he also succeed in seducing Rosie into submission?

Black Lace Classics – our best erotic fiction ever from our leading authors.

Also available from Black Lace:

The Seduction of Valentine Day
by Eden Bradley

She lives in a world of silk sheets, champagne, and expensive hotels . . .

She fulfills the deepest fantasies of the most powerful men in the world: Valentine Day is a high-class call girl, pampered and adored by her exclusive clientele.

But Valentine has a secret. Always in control, she's never experienced true pleasure. But now, the woman who spends her life pleasuring others is about to embark on an erotic journey of her own . . .

An irresistible erotic romance, perfect for fans of *Pretty Woman*.